CalFire book 2

Quiet Ember

Sherryl D. Hancock

PRESS

PRESS

Published by Vulpine Press in the United Kingdom in 2021

ISBN: 978-1-83919-176-3

www.vulpine-press.com

To all us plus-sized girls who don't think we deserve love, we deserve everything the world has to offer and then some! Live your life to the fullest, find love, laughter, and joy!

Author's note

The Camp Fire in Butte County started the morning of November 8, 2018, at 5:33 a.m. while it was still dark outside and people were asleep in their homes. Many people were caught unaware, as strong winds moved the fire quickly through populated areas. The fire burned a total of 153,336 acres, destroying 18,804 structures and resulting in 85 civilian fatalities and several firefighter injuries. *The Camp Fire is the deadliest and most destructive fire in California history.* Cal Fire has determined that the Camp Fire was caused by electrical transmission lines owned and operated by Pacific Gas and Electricity (PG&E) located in the Pulga area.

Photograph: Shutterstock

California Firefighters Benevolent Fund

The author will be donating 5% of the profits from the *CalFire* series to the California Firefighters Benevolent Fund.

You can find out more about what they do here: www.cafirefoundation.org/programs/ca-firefighters-benevolent-fund/

Quiet Ember

Prologue

As the fire crew arrived on scene, Dutch could see that the front of the house was almost fully engulfed. She said a quick prayer that there was no one left inside. As she climbed out of the engine, she glanced over at her fire suppression team, giving them the nod to get started.

"Get that hose hooked up and get on it," she barked over the sounds of both engines on the scene, "I'll ascertain if there's any need for search and rescue."

Striding over as she secured her helmet, she headed to the engine that had reached the scene first. She took in the couple that spoke with her counterpart, who was trying to instruct his own people as to where he wanted them. The woman, wrapped in a blanket against the cold, was gesturing wildly at the house, tears streaming down her face.

"My baby is in there!" she yelled as Dutch walked up.

"Ma'am, where is the child in the house?" Dutch asked.

The woman turned her wild gaze up to Dutch and it was easy for her to see the panic there. Dutch reached out and took the woman by the shoulders gently. "I need to know where your child is," she repeated calmly.

"She's in back! Next to the master!"

"And the master is…"

"In the back." The man standing next to his wife said. He could see that Dutch was trying to help, he pointed a finger toward the right side of the house. "Back there."

Dutch looked at the other operator. "TJ, please show me as headed in for search and rescue, Charlie Delta corner of the house."

"Got it." TJ nodded, as he radioed in to dispatch.

At her engine, Dutch ordered her fire suppression team to concentrate on the rear half of the house. Fortunately that section of the home didn't look as bad, although the roof was definitely smoldering.

At the back of the home, one of her crew, Phil Slattery, used his claw tool to pry open the rear slider of the house. Dutch went inside, she realized she was in the master bedroom. Smoke filled the room, and she worried that if the baby's room was filled with smoke too…She immediately shut down that thinking and headed to her left. Stepping into the hallway, she could see that the fire was raging and very nearly to her. The door to the baby's room was closed, so Dutch yanked off a glove to check the door with her hand, noting it was cool, she quickly kicked it open and moved inside, putting her glove back on a she did. The room was smokey, making Dutch wince. Moving to the crib, she noticed that the baby wasn't moving. Taking off her glove, she checked for a pulse and felt a faint thud of a heartbeat. She knew the baby would need oxygen, so she quickly picked the child up, noting that the baby girl stirred slightly–a good sign–and immediately headed back toward the door. Only to discover and the door was now engulfed in flames. Dutch looked around the room again, and noted the only window in the room was behind the crib. She carefully placed the baby back in the crib and moved it to the far side of the room, away from the flames.

She quickly yanked down the blinds and, pulling out her axe, she moved to the window, smashing it outward. Phil was there immediately, having seen the flames starting to shoot through the slider, and assuming correctly they'd made their way to where Dutch was working. Dutch grabbed the baby out of the crib. Noting no movement now, she handed the child to Phil and yelled, "She barely has a pulse! Go!"

Phil ran off taking the baby to the EMTs to get lifesaving measures going. Meanwhile, Dutch had the realization that the small window wouldn't be easy for her to get out of, especially with her airpack on her back. Above her she could hear creaking, meaning the room was about to go, so she had no choice but to dump her airpack and try to scramble out the window.

Sliding it off her shoulders, she took one last deep breath, trying to get as much oxygen in her lungs as she could, then she tossed it out the window. She braced her hands on either side of the window, and pulled herself up, shoving her upper body through the window. Just then there was a loud crash; s she felt something slam into the back of her legs, and an immediate weight pressing down on her back. The pain shot through her light a lightning bolt. She gave a loud yell, just before her vision went dark and she passed out.

Kori Stanton was in her office in San Francisco when she got the call.

"Is she okay?" Kori asked, glancing up as Hunter walked into the office.

"They said they think she'll recover, but she really messed up her back."

"Okay," Kori said nodding, "well, keep me up to date on her progress. How's the baby?"

"The baby made it," Mike Saragosa, Dutch's counterpart at the San Diego Cal Fire office, said.

Kori nodded. "Good! Well, let me know how Chief Lapp is later this week. I'll come up with a light duty assignment for her."

"Sounds good, Director," Mike replied, relieved that someone who understood firefighters had replaced their retiring director.

"Mike, we've known each other for years. You can still call me Kori."

"Yes ma'am," Mike said, his grin widening at his end.

"Thanks for the call."

As Kori hung up, Hunter sat down in the chair across from her.

"What's happening?" Hunter asked, before raising her travel mug of coffee up to her lips.

"One of the chiefs is down in San Diego, she got hurt this morning."

"Who?"

"Rebecca Lapp—Dutch," Kori clarified when Hunter looked mystified.

"Oh, yeah." Hunter nodded, having met the San Diego Fire Chief a few times. "Is she okay?"

"Sounds like she will be, but she apparently hurt her back, so she's going to need a light duty assignment when she's up to it." Kori was already tapping away on the keyboard to her computer.

"What are you thinking?" Hunter queried.

Kori chewed on her lower lip as she scanned the areas of operation in San Diego.

"Maybe a fire camp?" Kori said as she read the list.

"The Rainbow Camp could use a…refresh." Hunter gave her a pointed look, she'd recently received reports of the current Fire

Captain at the camp being overtly misogynistic with the female correctional staff on site.

Kori canted her head. "Explain."

"Andy Kanelos, the current fire captain, has been making comments to the female staff that are, well, let's just say, not right."

"Comments like what..." Kori's voice trailed off ominously, the one thing she couldn't stand was the way some male firefighters treated women. She'd dealt with the chauvinism enough in her career, and felt it was high time it stopped.

Hunter sat back, steepling her fingers in front of her, glancing at the ceiling, "Oh, you know, stuff like, 'women were put on this earth to serve men, that's what you're here for.'"

"Are you kidding me?" Kori deadpanned.

Hunter made a puckering sound, her silver eyes narrowing, as she shook her head. "Wish I was."

"Oh he needs to go," Kori said.

"Well, we'll work on that." Hunter sat forward, putting her hands on Kori's desk. "In the meantime, you could put Dutch there."

Kori thought about it, the Fire Camp was definitely an easy duty, and she figured someone like Dutch Lapp would do well there.

"I like it." Kori nodded.

"There you go." Hunter smiled.

Chapter 1

Inmate Violet Hastings did her best to be quiet as she checked the charts of the two patients that were in the small camp infirmary. She was surprised when she saw the Fire Captain laying in one of the beds. She was laying on her back, her legs were draped over a bolster pillow, covered by her dark blue uniform pants.

Violet had watched the new Fire Captain, "Dutch," in absolute fascination since her arrival at the Cal Fire Rainbow Conservation Camp three weeks before. The woman just had an amazing presence that was hard to ignore. From her long, fade haircut, to her strong, fit physique, to her ice blue eyes, or that whiff of cologne she sometimes got when the captain walked by her, to the timber of her voice when she gave orders to the inmates. Dutch Lapp was definitely one seriously attractive woman.

Walking over to the hospital bed, Violet noted that the Fire Captain's eyes were open, and found them turned toward her as she stepped forward.

"I didn't hear about you getting hurt, Captain, are you okay?" Violet asked, her warm brown eyes reflecting her concern.

"Oh, I'm alright," Dutch replied, a self-effacing grin on her lips, "just a reoccurring injury from having a house fall on me a few of months ago."

"A…seriously, a house?" Violet stammered, looking shocked.

Dutch chuckled warmly, her blue eyes crinkling at the corners. "Yeah, it wasn't really part of my grand plan, but it happens."

"So your back is hurting?" Violet asked, as she reached over to pick up Dutch's chart, only to find that she didn't have one. "Does the camp doc know you're here?"

Dutch nodded. "She does, she gave me some muscle relaxers and just wants me to stick around here to make sure they don't make me see pink elephants or anything."

Violet's eyes widened at that statement. "Is that possible?"

Dutch quirked her lips. "I'm kind of a lightweight when it comes to medication."

"Oh," Violet said nodding, knowing she was probably bugging the captain. With that thought in mind, she withdrew with a quiet, "Let me know if you need anything." After checking on the other patient in the infirmary, she went back to her desk, and did her best to ignore the desire to go back and check on the captain.

A year in jail and I'm a complete lesbo now! she thought to herself. It was ironic, considering she was married to a man on the outside, and her first lesbian encounter hadn't exactly been tender and warm. Not that by far. Regardless, she now tended to notice other women mostly the more butch ones, and often thought they were attractive. She wasn't sure if it was the fact that these women were comfortable being who they felt like, or if she still liked the masculine aspect in partners. She also wondered if her new preference for butch women had more to do with the valiant butch who'd more or less ordered her abuser to stop. It had meant she was under the protection of that particular butch, and kind of a servant to her, but it had also stopped the nightly abuses too. She ended up being a "girlfriend" to another really quiet inmate, and while there had been a great deal of tenderness between them, the intimacy still hadn't been great. Regardless, she'd noticed the captain of the fire team right away and had been fascinated with her ever since.

Rainbow Fire Camp was a Cal Fire/Corrections inmate camp made up of only women. There were a couple of male Corrections staff, but the remaining nineteen staff were women, and they were there to manage a hundred female inmates. The camp was meant to be another line of defense in an ever-growing fire danger in California. Inmates were there to help slow the fires down, by cutting lines in the underbrush and creating fire breaks. It was hot, heavy work, but it was a great way for non-violent inmates to not only get out of the prison setting, but also teach them a trade for possible use on the outside.

The camp allowed inmates a chance to do something for their community of San Diego County, and also to build up their self-esteem and give them a purpose again. The camp had been all female since 1983. It was an opportunity many women tried for, very few managed to pass the physical requirements, and all the testing of knowledge levels they needed. It wasn't an easy job.

Violet was ruminating over her own place there in the camp, when there was a flurry of activity at the door to the infirmary. A woman, dressed in pink and white, very out of place for a dusty, dirty fire camp, came striding into the room, pink high heels clicking on the cement floor. She was wearing a visitor's badge, and it was obvious she was looking for someone. Before Violet could offer to help her, the woman zeroed in on the captain and headed for her. Violet caught the captain's look surprise at seeing the woman, and, since the room wasn't very big, could hear the ensuing conversation from her place at the desk.

"What are you doing here?" Dutch asked with a flat tone. Her eyes surveyed Nancy's outfit, thinking the woman never did know how to tone it down.

"I called your room, and you weren't there, so I called the front office, they said you were in the infirmary! I came right up."

"You shouldn't have come here," Dutch said in a stern tone, her look backing it up.

"Well, I wanted to make sure you're okay!" Nancy blurted out sharply.

Violet could see the captain's lips twitch; it was the only sign of how irritated she was at that moment.

"This is where I work, you don't belong here," Dutch informed the other woman simply.

"I belong where I'm needed," Nancy sniffed.

"You aren't needed here," Dutch said her voice remaining even, "you need to go."

"But I came all the way here! An hour's drive, Dutch!"

"And I'm sorry you did that, it wasn't necessary," Dutch replied calmly.

"I think it was!" Nancy snapped.

Dutch's eyes widened slightly, as her nostrils flared at Nancy's raised tone.

9

"I just don't understand why you do this job," Nancy ranted, "it's just going to kill you one day. You could come work for my father, you'd make lots of money and you wouldn't smell like smoke all the time."

A vague smile crossed Dutch's lips, she knew Nancy would never understand, and that didn't bother her at all.

"I like the work I do," she replied simply.

"It's insane! And so dangerous!" Nancy exclaimed dramatically. "Those people don't even appreciate you!"

"I don't do it for appreciation."

"Well you certainly don't do it for the money!"

"Lower your voice, you will not cause a scene here."

Nancy stared back at Dutch, her stance tense, her lips pursed in anger, she wanted to say something more, and she wanted to cause a scene just because Dutch had just told her not to. She didn't like being told what to do, not by anyone.

One look at the other woman's eyes though, told Nancy not to dare try it. She knew that she wanted to be with Dutch way more than Dutch cared if she was with her, so this wasn't the time or place to test that.

Finally, Nancy gave a long-suffering sigh, shaking her head like she'd never understand the other woman.

"Fine, then I'll go." She leaned in to kiss Dutch.

Dutch immediately held up a hand, looking somewhat alarmed. "Not…here…" she practically hissed.

Nancy huffed, then turned on her heel and marched out of the infirmary.

Violet glanced over at Dutch to see her staring up at the ceiling, her look speculative.

10

Getting up from her desk, Violet walked over where Dutch lay.

"Are you okay? Do you need anything?" she asked gently, her eyes surveying the Fire Captain.

Blue eyes were turned on her then, the captain smiled softly, shaking her head. "I'm fine, thank you."

"She's wrong you know," Violet blurted out suddenly.

"About?"

"About your job, we do appreciate you, I mean, I do, I think what you do is amazing."

A slow grin spread across Dutch's lips, making her eyes crinkle at the corners again, "Thank you, that's very nice of you to say."

"It's true," Violet said, "you guys are the whole reason I wanted to come here."

"To work in the infirmary?" Dutch asked questioning.

"No," Violet said, dropping her eyes from Dutch's, her teeth worrying the inside of her cheek, "I wanted to be one of you."

She looked up quickly to see what Dutch's reaction to that would be. She expected Dutch to snicker or outright laugh at that possibility. She was surprised to note that Dutch did neither, she merely blinked a couple of times.

"So what happened?" Dutch asked.

"You guys don't want people like me," Violet said, shrugging, lowering her eyes once again.

"Like…you…" Dutch repeated. "What does that mean?"

Violet shrugged again, not looking up. She wasn't sure why she'd said anything, but she knew that she didn't like what Nancy had said and had felt like she needed to remind the Fire Captain how great the firefighters were.

"Inmate Hastings?" Dutch queried. Violet looked back up at Dutch, shocked that the fire captain knew her name. "What does that mean?"

Violet drew in a deep breath, willing herself not to cry when she said, "Fat people."

"Did you test to be part of the program?" Dutch asked.

"Yes."

"Did you pass the written tests?"

"Yes."

"Did you pass the initial physical exam?"

"Barely."

"But they sent you here," Dutch clarified.

"Yes."

Dutch nodded slowly, her look considering. "Come see me in my office tomorrow afternoon after lunch."

Violet looked at the Fire Captain, her eyes wide, "I…Yes, ma'am."

The following day, Violet arrived at the Fire Captain's door. She read the lettering that said Captain Rebecca "Dutch" Lapp. She hadn't known the captain's first name before—everyone always called her Dutch. She wondered why, but was pretty sure she'd never be brave enough to ask. Reaching up she knocked lightly on the door, already feeling nervous. She heard Dutch call "come" from the office.

Stepping into the office, Violet looked around her. The room had a very simple look to it, gone were all the posters and wild personal objects that had adorned the previous Fire Captain's office. Dutch had bare walls, a simple metal desk and wooden office chair, with two brown chairs in front and a small couch in the corner. There were no decorations at all.

"Come in, Inmate Hastings," Dutch said from her desk. She finished making notes in the book she had open as Violet moved to stand in front of her. When Dutch looked up, she gestured for her to have a seat.

"So, you want to be a firefighter."

"I…yes, ma'am," Violet stammered.

Dutch nodded, reaching over to pick up and open a file that lay on the desk.

"This says that you tested in the ninety-eighth percentile in the knowledge domains." Blue eyes trained on Violet again. "That's a great score." Looking at the file again she flipped to another page. "This says you requested to leave the program."

Violet blinked a couple of times while the Fire Captain trained her gaze on her again.

"Is that true?" Dutch asked, when Violet didn't say anything.

"I…well, yes ma'am."

Dutch nodded, narrowing her eyes slightly. "Do you want to tell me why?"

Violet pressed her lips together, willing herself not to cry. Even so, tears glazed her eyes as she dropped them from the captain's gaze.

Looking at herself in the mirror was never fun. Some people said they saw her pretty eyes, or her great hair. What she saw was her fat thigh, or her stomach that refused to be tamed into any pair of jeans without hanging over the top. She was fat. That was it, she wasn't "pleasingly plump," she wasn't "chunky" or any of the other damned euphemisms

13

used to state the obvious. She was "pushing maximum density," "the Goodyear blimp," "a beached whale." Those were the words she used to identify herself. There were those who would tell her that she shouldn't say that about herself, or that she just needed "more self-esteem," she would snicker at them and roll her eyes, shaking her head. Yeah, right, says the skinny bitch who's never had a weight problem in her life! She'd think sarcastically to herself. She'd tried every diet, she'd starved herself, she'd eaten nothing but vegetables for what seemed like forever, but then she'd slip and have McDonald's french fries and they were so good! Next thing she knew she'd slingshot right back into her "fat pants" and just keep right on eating. It was hopeless. It had only gotten worse when she'd had Michael, her son. She'd eaten "for two" since the day she found out she was pregnant. Unfortunately, the eating hadn't stopped with is birth, nor had it really abated for the next six years.

"Hastings?" Dutch finally queried when a full five minutes had passed. She had patience, many said that of a saint, but she wasn't Mother Teresa.

"I…I was too fat," Violet blurted out.

"According to…"

Violet shrugged, not wanting to speak out of turn.

"According to who?" Dutch asked.

There was a long pause, silence in the room was pervasive. Finally Violet gave up.

"According to the last captain."

Dutch gave a loud sniff, causing Violet to look up at her. Dutch's lips curled in derision, wondering if the previous Fire

Captain had ever actually looked in a mirror. The man was, by far, no light weight and certainly not the fittest bull in the herd.

Making a quick decision, Dutch stood up.

"Let's go," she said, moving from around the desk, even as Violet rushed to stand and follow Dutch out the door.

Stopping at the front desk, Dutch checked a couple of lists, and then signed herself and Inmate Hastings out of the camp. She led Violet out to her work truck, and older Cal Fire vehicle. Walking to the passenger door, she opened it for Violet and gestured for her to get in. Once Violet got in, Dutch closed the door and went around to get into the driver's seat. She started the vehicle and drove out of the camp.

Dutch drove in silence for almost a half an hour. Violet wasn't sure what was happening, but she stayed silent, not wanting to ask too many questions. She looked out the window, seeing that the captain was headed north towards the mountains. Violet did everything she could to not wring her hands with nervous energy. There was no music on in the vehicle, and Violet found herself wishing there was—at least then she could focus on that. Instead, she watched the brush and shrubbery give way to a rockier terrain.

They drove for a half an hour and by the time Dutch stopped the truck, Violet had no idea where they were. When she looked around, however, she saw a couple of Cal Fire trucks as well as an inmate vehicle. Dutch made no move to get out of the truck but pointed at the twelve men working on the ridge just above where they sat.

"You see those guys?" Dutch asked.

Violet nodded, seeing the men in the orange jumpsuits working at clearing the brush from the ridge.

Dutch looked over at Violet. "What do you notice about them?"

Violet swallowed nervously, thinking this was some kind of test. She looked over at the men again.

"Well, they're inmates, like me..." Her voice trailed off, failing to understand what the Fire Captain was looking for her to say.

Dutch nodded. "Any of them look extremely fit to you?"

"I...Well, no..." Violet said. In fact, many of them were overweight. "But, I—"

"No," Dutch cut in, shaking her head.

Violet stared back at the captain, blinking a couple of times in surprise.

"They aren't fit, but do you know what they are?" Dutch queried.

Violet chewed at the inside of her lip, not sure how to answer.

"What they are is determined," Dutch finally filled in.

Violet's eyes widened at the statement and she nodded, still not sure how this related to her.

"My question for you is whether or not you're actually determined to become a firefighter," Dutch asked, her tone intense. "Because if you're not, that's fine, you can go back to the infirmary and that'll be that." Dutch turned in her seat, looking at Violet, her blue eyes shining brightly. "Now if you want to be a firefighter, I can help you, but it's going to mean work. Are you willing to do the work?"

Again, Violet had to swallow a few times before she could answer. The desire to rise to the challenge fought with the desire to stick with what was safe and easy. What if she failed? What if it turned out she couldn't do it? What if she got hurt? What if everyone looked at her like she was stupid for even trying?

"Inmate!" Dutch's bark brought her quickly out of her deliberations.

"I, ye-yes, ma'am!" Violet snapped, immediately obedient.

"Yes, you want to do this?" Dutch asked, gesturing to the men again.

"Yes," Violet answered, no hesitation in her voice this time.

A smile tugged at Dutch's lips as she nodded. "Good."

With that, she put the truck in gear, honking at the crew working on the ridge and flipping a casual salute to the Cal Fire leader monitoring the inmates, before she backed down the narrow road.

On the road back to the camp, Dutch looked over at Violet—she could see the other woman was nervous. She wondered at that. The woman certainly scared easily; Dutch hoped she wasn't making a mistake. Undaunted, Dutch began to lay out her plan.

"Starting tomorrow, you and I will train. We'll start after breakfast. Eat light, or you might regret it—try to stick to protein. We'll train for two hours in the morning, and then another hour at night after dinner. You have eight weeks until the next qualifications but if you work hard, you can make it."

Violet drew in her breath noisily, then blew it out slowly through her mouth. Finally, she nodded. "So how much weight do I need to lose?"

Dutch grimaced, then shook her head. "You don't need to lose weight, Hastings, you need to gain endurance. I don't give a damn what any scale says, didn't you see those guys out today? You think even half of them tip the scales at less than two hundred? Trust me," she continued when she saw the skeptical look on Violet's face, "they are overweight, but they want to be there, and that's what it takes. Okay?"

"Okay," Violet replied, trying to quell the tiny little light of hope that was starting in her heart. Maybe she could do this, maybe the captain was right.

Back at the camp, Dutch parked the truck and got out, walking around to open Violet's door before she could. Violet climbed out of the truck and stood looking at the fire captain.

"Thank you for this chance, ma'am."

"Don't let me down, Hastings."

"I'll try not to, ma'am."

***

Lancaster, Pennsylvania, 1982

It was 4 a.m. Dawn hadn't even broken yet. Rebecca yawned as she climbed out of her bed, turning with automatic movements born of years of discipline. She bathed quickly and then set to work on her hair, gathering it into a bun, so she could tuck it up under her black prayer covering. As she donned simple cotton dress and apron, she thought longingly of the time she'd had to borrow her brother's pants for a day. The pant had been so much more comfortable and somehow freeing. Stifling her sigh, she finished up and joined her mother in the kitchen. Her day was spent working on breads with her mother for the barn raising the following day, alongside cleaning their home.

At noon, her father and brother Jacob came in to eat lunch. Her father talked about the calf that had been born recently, and the discussion ensued about the elders' choices for a new church bench.

Rebecca found herself tuning out and thinking of other things, until she heard the word "English" mentioned by her father. Suddenly she was focused again and trying to catch up.

Her father spoke of the English family that had bought the farm adjacent to their land. He said that their daughter had come over to introduce herself, and he said that the girl seemed "los"–their word for a wild girl with loose morals. Rebecca listened as her father said that the girl was her age, but seemed much older than "onze dochter" ('our daughter'), referring to Rebecca. Rebecca did her best to be obedient to their beliefs and not wonder about the English, but when the outside world was all around them, it was nearly impossible not to wish some days that she lived in a different family.

Sighing inwardly, Rebecca listened for any more talk of the English, but her father, Samuel, was not one to gossip much. Before long, her father and brother left the house to return to the fields; it was harvest time and they needed every hand they could get. Rebecca longed to be in the field, wearing pants and picking corn, rather than being stuck in the house that was far too warm and dark. She also dreamed of the day she could go on Rumspringa, the Amish people's rite of passage for adolescence to see what the rest of the world was about, it was an escape, but at the age of fifteen that was a full year away. She sighed again as she continued to clean potatoes for dinner. Realizing she'd done so out loud, she glanced over her shoulder and caught her mother's sharp glance. Her mother liked to pretend that everything was always wonderful, and that their life wasn't hard and tedious. Rebecca redoubled her efforts scrubbing at the potatoes. At least tomorrow at the barn raising, she'd see other people her age. It was something to look forward to.

The following day at the barn raising, she found that she was the object of Ian Beiler's attention. Ian was one of the young men in the community that was of marriageable age and was in search of a wife. He continually came to her to get water, or a snack when it was time for a break. He was all smiles and kind words. Rebecca found that she had no idea how to act. At lunch, Ian waited to get food until she was near his seat at the table and then asked her for a drink. As she handed him the glass she'd just filled, he made a point of touching her hand for a long moment. Afterwards as the women cleaned up, the other girls commented on how he was "verliefd" with her, or "sweet" on her and amorous and in love…Rebecca felt her face get hot being embarrassed by such comments.

That evening after chores were done, Rebecca went off to her favorite spot that she'd found one day when walking. It was near a little stream that she could dip her feet in to cool off. It was especially warm that night and she found that her prayer covering was making her head far too hot. Looking around surreptitiously and seeing no one around—there rarely was anyone in the area—she threw caution to the wind and took off the offending garment. She then took off her apron and, pulling up her skirt, removed her shoes and waded into the cool water. It felt so good, she tucked her skirt up under itself as best she could and leaned down to put water on her arms. She felt cool for the first time in days! It was an amazing feeling. She found herself feeling downright giddy.

Moving to try and get to a slightly deeper spot in the stream, she slipped on a rock and fell on her backside. She let out a yelp of surprise, but then grinned at herself feeling both foolish and yet happy at the same time. Getting up she waded back to the area of grass near the stream and sat down near her covering and apron. Sitting there, her knees up to her chest, arms wrapped around her knees, she rested her chin on her knees. Her hair had come loose when she'd fallen and fell in wet waves down to the ground. Amish women never cut their hair, so it was a sight to behold.

Rowena Dillon beheld the sigh with a slight sense of awe. Rowena had located the little stream about a half a mile from her parents' new home the first week they'd moved in. She'd never encountered anyone else at the tiny clearing until that day. As she'd walked through the trees and bushes that obscured the clearing, she'd heard someone cry out. Staying behind a bush, she'd peered through to see the Amish girl wading out of the stream with her dark skirt of her dress pulled up to avoid soaking up more water. She'd watched her sit down and saw the tumble of dirty blonde hair and immediately felt of twist of envy.

Rowena's family had moved from bustling California where everything was hyped and open. Her father's company had been downsizing and he'd lost his corner office, so he'd transferred to the company's main headquarters. They'd moved from a big city, San Francisco, California, to this rural county and so far it had been very strange and a major adjustment. Her father had thought it would be good for her and her little brother to live the "simple country life." Rowena had figured she'd be stuck for a year or two, and then she'd go off to New York or something and leave Pennsylvania far behind.

The country was boring as far as Rowena was concerned, but some of the people were fascinating to her. The Amish people had been a big source of interest for her since they'd moved. Seeing them in buggies instead of cars and hearing that they didn't have electricity or phones or listen to music was just insane to her. She hadn't learned anything about them, because they never talked to anyone in town.

21

She'd met the man that lived in the farm next to them, but only because she'd gotten turned around when leaving the location at the stream and stumbled onto their land. He'd been gruff and generally unfriendly, and had practically glowered at her when she'd asked if he had any kids. It was like he was afraid if she met them, she'd infect them with her big city ways! She'd gotten a good chuckle out of the thought.

Now here she was staring at one of the Amish girls, and she was just bursting with questions for her, but she knew she needed to be a little bit cautious. She didn't want to freak the other girl out. Taking a deep breath, Rowena stepped out of the bushes.

The rustling behind her told Rebecca that she wasn't alone. She turned her head so quickly that her hair flowed around her shoulders.

"Wow," Rowena said, her eyes widening at the sight of the other girl's hair.

"What?" Rebecca asked, shocked by the other girl, and also suddenly feeling strangely self-conscious, her blue eyes darting around her seemingly looking for an escape route.

"It's okay," Rowena said, putting her hands out in a staying gesture, "I'm cool, really."

"Cool?" Rebecca repeated. "It is very hot today."

Rowena laughed, shaking her head. "Oh, sorry, you weren't kidding were you?"

"Kidding?" Rebecca asked, still feeling trapped and for some reason guilty. She started combing her fingers through her hair to start pulling it back together to put back up as it should be.

"Please don't," Rowena said hastily, stepping forward in her urgency. "I, well, your hair is so beautiful."

Rebecca's hand stilled, as she stared back at Rowena in a mix of shock and confusion.

"I'm Rowena, what's your name?"

Again, Rebecca stared back at the stranger, sensing that she was harmless but also knowing that she was breaking all kinds of rules allowing this other girl to see her with her hair down.

"Rebecca," she offered simply.

"Becky, cool," Rowena said, nodding.

"Rebecca," Rebecca repeated, enunciating carefully.

Rowena widened her eyes. "Okay…Rebecca it is." She moved to sit down near the other girl and noticed Rebecca's alarmed look. "Don't worry, I'm not going to rat you out or anything."

"Rat…?" Rebecca queried, looking completely lost now.

Rowena laughed out loud at that comment, shaking her head. "Well, this is going great…" When Rebecca didn't even crack a smile, Rowena sighed in exasperation. "It's a saying, if you 'rat someone out' you are telling on them, like if they did something bad."

Rebecca blinked a couple of times, then finally nodded. Both girls were silent for a few moments, Rebecca fiddled with a loose thread on her dress. Rowena waited, not sure what else to say. She still had questions but wasn't sure how to start asking without sounding completely stupid.

"So…you're…um…Amish?" Rowena asked, making the a, long, like aim.

"We are Amish," Rebecca said, correcting the pronunciation.

"Right, right, Amish," Rowena repeated emphatically.

"Correct," Rebecca said.

"How come you wear those outfits?" Rowena asked, it was one of the most burning questions she'd had since she'd first seen them.

23

Rebecca glanced down at her dress, smoothing her hand over it automatically when she saw that it was somewhat rumpled. "It is our clothing."

"Okay, but how come you all dress the same?"

"We do not dress the same," Rebecca said, furrowing her brow as she did.

"I mean, like a lot alike."

"Our clothing is simple, not ostentatious."

"And you use really big words," Rowena said, eyes widening. "But why simple?"

"We are all equal, what need have we of different?"

"But everyone isn't equal, that's crazy!" Rowena said, flabbergasted.

"In Amish society everyone is," Rebecca informed her.

"Not possible," Rowena countered.

Rebecca didn't answer, she merely looked back at Rowena. She didn't need to convince the other girl of anything. It was one of the Amish doctrines, that they were not to conform to the world, that they were to live simply in faith.

"How do you get your hair so long?" Rowena asked, then rolled her eyes. "Mine won't grow for shit. I mean, I'm sorry, it won't grow, not like that."

"Amish women do not cut their hair," Rebecca said.

"Why?" Rowena asked instantly.

"We are to live simply and as God made us."

"Wow," Rowena said.

Rebecca looked back at the other girl, noting the short spikey hair. As she looked back at the other girl, her eyes trained on the shirt she wore. It depicted a handsome young black man dressed in a white suit with a black shirt.

"You wear faces on your clothing," Rebecca observed.

Rowena looked down at her shirt, then squelching her quick grin, "Oh, this is Michael Jackson, he is our god."

Rebecca blinked rapidly. "You wear your God on a shirt?" she asked in shock. "That is very disrespectful."

Rowena began laughing, shaking her head. "I'm sorry, I was just kidding, he's a singer. I guess you've never heard of him, huh? He's really huge right now."

When Rebecca didn't answer, Rowena bit her lip in consternation. "I'm sorry, it was a joke, and a bad one, apparently, I'm really sorry."

Rebecca didn't answer.

Rowena sighed, knowing that she wasn't getting anywhere. That was further confirmed when Rebecca moved to stand, reaching up to put her hair back into its bun at the nape of her neck.

"Please don't leave," Rowena begged. "I'm sorry, I won't tease you anymore I promise."

"I must get back," Rebecca said.

"Okay, but I really am, sorry, okay?"

"It is alright," Rebecca said, inclining her head, she put her apron back on, and slipped into her shoes. "I must go home and cut my hair, since you have seen it."

"What! No!" Rowena exclaimed, alarmed. "I won't tell anyone that I saw it, I promise, please don't cut your hair!"

Rebecca started to smile. "I was just kidding," she said, mimicking Rowena's words earlier.

Rowena's mouth dropped open in shock, then she started grinning. "Nice one…"

Rebecca pressed her lips together, even though her blue eyes still sparkled with humor.

"Good evening," Rebecca said, then turned and left the clearing.

***

The morning after their trip to the upper ridge, Violet showed up at Dutch's office. Violet was surprised that the captain actually wore shorts and a T-shirt as well as tennis shoes. She'd expected the captain to stand by and tell her what to do, not to actually work out with her. They walked outside and Dutch instructed her on warming up and stretching.

"We're just going to do a hike today, but it's going to be a long one. I want you to take it at a pace you can handle, the course will challenge you enough, okay?"

"Yes, ma'am," Violet said, nodding.

They started out then, and Violet found that at first it was an easy hike, but slowly but surely they started to go up smaller hills. In one place, her foot slipped and she started to go down, but the captain was right there, grabbing her arm and keeping her from landing on her knees. It astounded her how quickly the captain had moved, and how strong her hands were.

"Gotta watch your footing, Hastings," Dutch said, smiling encouragingly, "don't want to get hurt your first day out."

"No, ma'am, God knows the Hindenburg will go down eventually," Violet said, making a joke about her weight as a habit.

Dutch narrowed her eyes at Violet. "Even the fittest of people lose their footing, Hastings."

Violet drew a breath in through her nose, and nodded, appreciating the captain's attempt to be nice. "I know ma'am, sorry."

Dutch nodded and they continued.

Two hours later they made it back to camp. They were both sweating, and Violet was sure she was going to die, but she was proud of herself. Once again, Dutch told her to stretch and showed her the best ways to do that.

"Now," Dutch said, as they finished stretching, "I want to you to go take a really hot shower, to loosen up your muscles. Then take some Ibuprofen to help alleviate some of the soreness you're bound to have. Drink a lot of water today and get a good night's sleep tonight. We'll skip the evening workout tonight but be ready in the morning after breakfast."

"Yes, ma'am, thank you, ma'am," Violet said, somewhat disappointed they weren't going to work out that evening as well.

Later, she was exceedingly grateful for that fact. Her body felt like one big angry muscle. She had no idea how much they'd actually worked out the day before, but her body surely did. She fell into a deep sleep early that night and slept right up until the morning bell rang for breakfast.

At breakfast she found that she was still sore and wondered if she was even going to be able to work out that morning. She ate lightly, finding that she didn't have much of an appetite, but stuck to one egg, and a piece of wheat toast.

When Violet got to the captain's office, Dutch handed her a sheet of paper. The paper listed how many steps she'd taken the day before, the amount of calories she'd burned, how many miles they'd gone, and how long they'd walked.

"Is this…" Violet began, unable to believe the numbers she was looking at.

Dutch smiled, nodding. "That's how far we went yesterday."

Violet blinked rapidly a few times, shaking her head. "I've never walked that far in my life!"

"Well, you did yesterday."

Violet opened her mouth to speak and found she couldn't. A lump formed in her throat, and she was instantly embarrassed that something as simple as having walked ten miles the day before made her want to cry. She squeezed her eyes shut, trying to stop herself, but the tears slid down her cheeks. She felt the captain draw closer and opened her eyes to see that Dutch was holding out a Kleenex to her.

"You should be very proud of yourself," Dutch told her.

"I…I am…I just…" Her voice trailed off as she shook her head again. "This is amazing!"

Very white teeth flashed as Dutch smiled again. "So you ready to go again today?"

Violet drew a deep breath, drawing her resolve around her. "Yes, I am."

"Then let's go," Dutch said, her tone holding her pride.

They hiked again that morning, taking much the same trail they had the day before—not too hilly, but enough to get Violet huffing and puffing. When they got back to camp, Dutch repeated her instructions about taking a hot shower and Ibuprofen.

"We'll meet up after dinner tonight, say six thirty, and we'll do some strength work, okay?"

Violet bit her lip, nodding. "Thanks, Captain."

***

*Why was just walking through the grocery store making her tired?
Violet wondered as she glanced at a large woman riding one of the
electric carts and thought that would make her life easier. As she
reached for a bag of her favorite cookies, she considered the idea. But
wouldn't that make her that fat lady that doesn't even try to lose
weight? One of those fat people from that movie* Wall-E, *that trun-
dled around on air chairs? She didn't want to be a comical version of
herself. Sighing internally, she continued her shopping trip.*

*On the way home, she stopped at McDonald's ostensibly to get her
son, Mikey, a Happy Meal—he loved those. Of course she looked at
the menu to order herself something as well, she had to eat, right? As
the intercom buzzed annoyingly, and the McDonald's staff person
waited for her order, Violet considered her options. She wanted two
Big Mac's with cheese and a ton of fries! But something pricked her
conscience again reminding her that fat people shouldn't eat so much,
she should order something healthy. She looked at the menu again
and focused on the calorie content of each item. Holy crap, one Big
Mac was 540 calories! Large fries were another whopping 510 calories! She didn't even want to look at the super-size fry calorie count.
And she always got a large sweet tea, that's like having water, right?
So if she got her usual, it would be upwards of 1700 calories! Why
did everything that tasted really good, also have a ton of calories?
What had they said she should try to eat each day? Just 1200 calories?
Right, sure, no problem! If she ate lettuce all day every day!*

*Frustration brought tears to her eyes, why did this have to be so
hard? Finally, when the impatient teenager asked her again if she was
ready to order, and she could sense people behind her in the drive thru
getting annoyed, she ordered her usual and a Happy Meal for Mikey*

and drove forward to pick up her order. By the time she got home that day she'd already eaten all of the french fries, doing her best not to think about all the calories. She promised herself she wouldn't eat anything else the rest of the day. In the end, of course she ate, because Jason got home from his two-day stint with a landscaper, who was, by Jason's description "an asshole." Jason, of course, wanted to order a pizza, extra-large with everything. So she ended up eating four pieces, because she couldn't let it go to waste. She also ate most of the large pizza-sized chocolate cookie that was on sale. She went to bed with that usual guilty feeling, knowing she'd overeaten again. Telling herself, Tomorrow I'll eat better.

***

As Hunter and Kori entered the apartment they were sharing, Hunter tossed her keys onto the hall table, glancing around at the empty boxes stacked in various places.

"We really need to get to packing this weekend," Hunter commented.

Kori nodded, the corners of her mouth turning down.

"Don't do that." Hunter moved in, touching Kori's cheek.

"This just sucks." Kori sighed. "I just wish was helping more with the down payment."

They had finally found a house to buy together, they were hoping to close on the house in a few weeks. Things were still a bit unsettled with Kori's divorce from her husband, however, and that was causing complications.

"Tom, we need to talk," Kori had told him when she'd finally come home from helping Hunter move from Fort Bragg into her apartment.

Tom looked up from the paper he was reading in his comfy chair, she could see a look of suspicion cross his face, but then he nodded and smiled, gesturing to the chair across from him.

Kori took a seat, glancing around her, the small house they'd found in San Pablo was nice enough, and only about twenty miles from San Francisco. It had cost them a little more than their house in Los Angeles, and Kori felt like it was too big for the just the two of them, with three bedrooms and three bathrooms, but it worked for them at the time. Now she was wondering how much they could resell it for.

Suddenly Kori realized that Tom was looking at her expectantly, and she focused back on the task at hand. Chewing on her lip, she had no idea how to even start this conversation.

"I think you know," she began hesitantly, wishing there was another way to handle this, "that I haven't been happy for a while..."

Tom looked taken aback, his face reflecting shock. "I can't say that I have known that, no," he said gravely.

Kori stifled the anger that flared instantly, she wanted to say that if he didn't know that, it was because he hadn't cared to see it, but she knew that wouldn't get her anywhere.

Clasping her hands together, her brows snapping together in frustration. Tom was usually so easy going, why did he have to choose now to be difficult?

"Well, I'm sorry this seems to be a surprise, but the fact is we've grown apart in the last few years. Since the kids are out of the house now, I feel like I need to do something for myself now."

Tom looked back at her for a long moment, it was obvious he was trying to process what she'd just said. She was hoping that he'd say that he understood and leave it at that, but that hope was dashed a moment later as tears actually welled in his eyes and he shook his head.

"I don't understand..." he said. "I love you...I love the kids..."

"I'm not saying you don't," Kori said, trying to keep her voice calm, "but I need to do this for me right now."

"And what are you doing?" Tom's voice held a hint of accusation now, and Kori wondered if he really did realize what she was doing and with whom.

"I'm going to go stay with a friend," Kori said, knowing it sounded like a lie, even as she said it.

Tom pressed his lips together in a frown, nodding his head, tears sliding down his cheeks.

"That friend you just moved?"

Kori was sure she could hear him accusing her, but she simply nodded her head—not willing to get into a fight at that point.

Kori had packed a few things and left the house that night, going back to Hunter's apartment.

"I feel like he knows," she'd told Hunter as they lay in bed that night.

"If he's got any kind of sense at all, he suspects at the very least," Hunter told her.

The next day Kori had received a blistering phone call from her daughter.

"What the hell did you do to dad?!" Desolé practically screamed.

"Desa, calm down," Kori said, getting up to close her office door as she did.

"He's devastated, Mom, what did you do?" The accusation rang clearly in Desolé's voice.

"I actually did something for me for a change," Kori replied, feeling vexed. "Thank you for your support."

Desolé was quiet for a moment, then she sighed loudly. "You need to fix this."

Kori's mouth dropped open on her end. "And why's that?" she asked curtly.

"Because you're going to lose the best man you're ever going to find," was the prim reply, and then Desolé hung up.

Things had only spiraled from there, and Tom had contested the divorce, saying he wanted to go to counseling and that Kori needed to give him "a chance." Desolé wouldn't even speak to Kori until she "fixed it."

***

"You can't help that Tom won't accept the divorce," Hunter told her as they walked into the bedroom and got changed for bed. It had been six months, and Tom was still arguing, begging and pleading.

"I know, but I started all of this." Kori said.

Hunter dropped her boot on the floor, looking up at Kori. "You started all of this…" she repeated, "all of what?"

"This," Kori said, gesturing to the apartment, and between them, "us, leaving Tom, making him sad."

Hunter gave Kori a pointed look. "Oh boo hoo, the man is sad," she said. "He's also an adult, Kori, and you have a right to be happy."

"But my daughter," Kori began.

"Is a frigging adult too," Hunter told her, "and needs to learn to grow the fuck up and realize that everything isn't about her."

Kori stared back at Hunter, surprised by her statements, but then realized she shouldn't be. Hunter had always been direct and honest about how she felt, Kori didn't know why she suddenly thought Hunter would be more easy going.

Kori grinned. "Wow, babe, tell me how you really feel."

"I just don't like this emotional blackmail shit they're pulling, and it needs to stop." Hunter made a cutting gesture with her hand.

Kori took a deep breath, blowing it out slowly as she nodded. In her heart she knew that Hunter was right, but it didn't make her feel less like the "asshole" that had destroyed her family.

Chapter 2

Five days into working out with Dutch, Violet thought about every french fry she'd ever eaten and started hating them one by one. They were on one of their usual hikes, but she noticed that Dutch was starting to take her over higher hills. She didn't realize she was muttering until Dutch made a comment.

"What was that?" Dutch asked, glancing back over her shoulder.

"I, oh, did I say something out loud?"

Dutch chuckled, nodding her head as she dropped back to walk next to Violet.

"I was cursing McDonald's silently, I thought."

"Oh, yeah, the evil McDonald's," Dutch said, nodding agreement.

"I guess you don't eat stuff like that, huh?"

"I do, occasionally, I just pay for it later."

"You mean, like killing yourself in the gym?"

"I mean, my stomach killing me, it doesn't like all the grease," Dutch said, grimacing. "I didn't grow up eating that way, and my body frequently reminds me of that."

"Wow, lucky you. I grew up on fast food, which is probably why I'm the size of a house," Violet exclaimed, rolling her eyes.

"Hastings," Dutch began, her tone stern, "you are far too hard on yourself."

Violet shrugged, having heard that kind of sentiment her entire life. "Unfortunately, there are mirrors, even in camp."

"And you hate the reflection you see that much?" Dutch's tone was almost pained in her dismay.

Violet pressed her lips together, knowing it bugged the captain when she was down on herself, but frankly she was tired of having people say nice things they didn't mean to her.

"Wouldn't you?" she practically snapped. "If you had to contend with all of this," she said, running her hand up her fat thighs and belly with utter disdain, "and knowing you were the dumbass that caused it by being Porky the Pig her whole life?"

Dutch stopped walked, standing staring at Violet, her mouth open in shock, and her eyes reflecting that astonishment. It took Violet a minute to realize Dutch had stopped, when she noticed, she turned around looking at the Fire Captain.

"What?" she asked simply.

"Who taught you to talk about yourself this way?" Dutch asked, her tone dumbfounded and obviously thinking very little of whoever had taught Violet to be so self-denigrating.

Violet thought about it for a long moment, then shrugged. "Life, TV, my mom, you name it."

Dutch shook her head, trying to deny what Violet was saying. "Well, it's wrong."

Violet blew air out her nose, in a shocked guffaw. "I don't know where you come from, but it's not wrong where I come from. In fact, it's expected. If you're fat, you're a target."

Dutch looked further dismayed. "It's not right, Hastings."

Shrugging, Violet shook her head. "Right or wrong, it's a fact. In this world if you aren't naturally beautiful, or naturally thin, you are regarded as a grotesque thing to be made fun of."

"But you are the one making fun of yourself," Dutch stated, her voice reflecting the irony of that fact.

"Yeah, 'cause if I say it first, no one else gets the chance," Violet replied defensively.

"And you think that's what I would say to you?"

Violet swallowed, pressing her lips together, blinking a couple of times as she considered what the captain had just said. Finally she shrugged, unable to come up with a suitable answer. She looked away, uncomfortable now with the direction of the conversation. Blowing her breath out, she walked through the brush to an overlook and looked down at the valley below, doing her best not to cry. Here the captain was trying to help her, and she was being a bitch.

Dutch followed Violet after a couple of minutes, stepping closer and reaching out to touch Violet's arm.

"I don't think—" Dutch began, just as a rattling sound began as well. "Zoon van een!" she yelled, as she grabbed Violet's arm, yanking the other woman toward her as she stepped forward, slamming her foot down on the snake that was about to strike.

Violet yelped as she stumbled into the captain and was held fast with a strong arm around her midriff.

Dutch assured that the snake was dead, and then turned to look down at Violet, who was shaking against her. Whereas Dutch assumed she was afraid due to what had just happened, in truth Violet was experiencing her very first major sexual attraction to another woman. Being held against the long, lean, but strong five-foot-eight-inch frame of the Fire Captain was a very definite experience. Violet did everything she could to avert her thoughts, which were quickly jumbled when the captain looked down at her with those bright ice blue eyes.

"Are you okay?" Dutch asked, setting Violet back from her to look her over.

"I'm fine, really," Violet said. "Thank you, I'm fine."

"You're shaking," Dutch pointed out.

Violet made a point of stepping back from the captain and that's when she realized she'd apparently twisted her ankle as pain shot up her leg.

"Ow, ow, ow!" she exclaimed, hopping around trying to keep from putting weight on her ankle.

"Will you hold on a second?" Dutch said, grabbing at Violet's arms to still her. "Come here…"

When Violet calmed momentarily, Dutch drew her over to a large rock.

"Sit down. Where does it hurt?" she asked, even as she ran both of her hands from Violet's bare knee down to her ankle, Violet had to suppress a shudder. "Are you sure you're okay?"

Violet nodded again, mute from the riot of sensations running through her at that moment. She really wanted to look away from the very handsome Captain kneeling on one knee in front of her, all muscle and tanned skin gleaming with a fine sheen of sweat. Good god this woman was insanely gorgeous! *And the Fire Captain, idiot!* her mind screamed at her.

"Hastings?" Dutch repeated, not for the first time. "Are you with me here?"

"I, oh God, Captain, what?"

Dutch shook her head slowly. "It's either the shock or the heat," she muttered. "I asked if you can put any weight on it."

"On what?" Violet asked, her brain still in a haze.

Dutch gave her a glowering look. "Your ankle?"

"Oh, duh, sorry, I, yes, I can do it," she said, moving to stand, and putting her weight on the hurt ankle, immediately crying out and sitting back down. "Okay, maybe not...So, hey, what was that you said a little while ago?"

"When?" Dutch asked, eyebrows furrowing.

"When you stomped on the snake, you said something, and I didn't understand it."

"Oh," Dutch said, doing her best not to grimace, "I said 'son of a.'"

Violet looked back at her blinking a couple of times, "In what language?"

Dutch's lips twitched as she bit down on her bottom lip, annoyed with herself that she'd slipped "Pennsylvania Dutch."

"Huh?" Violet queried dumbly.

"So, it looks like I'll have to carry you back."

Oh like hell! Violet's brain yelled, instantly distracted from the previous conversation. "Captain, you can't do that, you just go back and maybe send someone out with a vehicle or something."

"I'm not leaving you out here," Dutch said, her tone no-nonsense.

"Well, you're not carrying me, that's for damned sure...ma'am," Violet added the last when she saw the captain's blue eyes widen at her tone.

Dutch stood up and bent down to pick Violet up.

"No!" Violet exclaimed loudly, holding up her hands to block Dutch's effort. "You are not picking me up, that's final! I'll just stay out here."

Dutch suppressed a sigh. "Just stay out here?"

"Yep," Violet said, crossing her arms in front of her chest, "if that's what it takes to get you to go back and send someone back for me."

"Are you forgetting that you're an inmate?"

Violet swallowed convulsively. "I, well, yeah…I did kind of forget that in the moment here. Well, it isn't like I'm going to escape, I can't even walk."

Dutch shrugged. "How do I know you're not faking it?"

"What! I am not! Oh my God, do you think I'd really do that? I'm not–" Violet realized suddenly that the captain was grinning. "Okay, now I don't like you very much," she said, her face taking on a pout.

Dutch laughed out loud at that one. It was the first time Violet had heard her laugh and it did nothing to diminish the crush she was having on the captain at that moment. The sound was rich and happy.

"Hastings, you've got to get back to camp to get that looked at, and I can't leave you out here. There are mountain lions in the area, do you want to become dinner?"

"Well, no…"

"So we need to get you back to camp, right?"

Violet sighed. "Right, but you are not carrying me. That's out of the question."

"What if I ordered you?" Dutch asked.

Violet's mouth dropped open, looking horrified by the idea. "You wouldn't...please, ma'am, I...please..." she pleaded, clasping her hands together. The last damn thing she wanted was for the poor captain to put her back out trying to heft her bulk. It would be mortifying to say the very least. She was also fairly certain there was no way the captain could lift her. She weighed 220 pounds; she figured the captain weighed about half that, so there was no way could she pick her up.

Dutch shook her head, knowing this had everything to do with the other woman's weight issues, but knowing that pushing her would only make her freak out more.

"Okay, fine, then we'll walk back together, but you will lean on me, and let me help you, do you understand?"

"Yes, ma'am," Violet said, relieved beyond belief.

Dutch took Violet's hand and helped her up. She put Violet's arm around her neck. "Now hold on to me, okay? Put as little weight on that foot as you can."

"Okay," Violet said unsteadily. She was once again having to concentrate on the task at hand, and not the hand sliding around her waist to support her weight. *Oh good God, I'm like a teenage boy in heat!*

With some effort and a couple of stops and starts, they made their way toward the camp.

"You know what I really miss?" Violet said after a while, wanting to distract herself from both her thoughts and also from the pain in her ankle that was now throbbing steadily.

"What?"

"Music!" Violet exclaimed. "I miss music so much. Not that rap garbage some of the girls play, but good old eighties hair bands, and pop music!"

Dutch chuckled, "You like eighties music?"

"Oh yeah, love it!"

"You aren't old enough to know much about eighties music. When were you born?"

"Are you asking me how old I am, Captain?"

"Yes, yes I am," Dutch said, smiling.

"I'm twenty-seven, and no, I wasn't like a teenager during the eighties, but I've always loved the music. Why? How old are you?"

"Thirty-six," Dutch replied.

"Wow, seriously?" Violet asked, shock coloring her voice.

"Why do I feel like I just got some kind of geriatric label?" Dutch asked, sounding far from offended.

"No, no," Violet assured, laughing. "I just meant, you just don't seem that old, I mean, you seem younger...I mean, ugh!" Reaching up she slapped herself in the forehead. "I'm just going to shut up now."

Once again Dutch laughed. "You are definitely a one woman show," she said, endlessly amused by Violet's animated actions. It was quite different from the impression Dutch had had of the girl previously.

"Thank you, thank you," Violet said, holding up her hand comically. "I'll be here all week, try the veal and tip your waitresses."

Dutch chuckled. "You should consider comedy as a profession."

"Oh sure, I can be the next Roseanne Barr."

"Or someone actually funny, like Ellen DeGeneres," Dutch added, not liking that Violet had immediately gone toward a denigrating comedian who was famously overweight.

"Well, since my gay seems to be kicking in these days..." Violet said before she stopped and thought about what she was saying. "Oh, sorry, that was probably inappropriate."

"Why?" Dutch asked as they moved around a particularly large branch in the path.

"I just...well...It's just probably not appropriate to talk about that..." Violet stammered, trying to think of a way out of the conversation.

"What? Being gay?" Dutch asked.

Violet bit her lips, then shrugged. "I guess, maybe the part of how I figured it out?"

"That you're gay?"

"Yeah," Violet said, still thinking she'd screwed up. "I mean, it kind of...well, it happened in my last facility, but..." Violet grimaced, thinking she was just digging herself in deeper.

"Hastings, I'm not a correctional officer, I'm Cal Fire, it's not my job to bust people for fraternization."

"Oh," Violet said, relief clear in her voice. "I didn't think about that. I guess I forget that you don't work for the prison."

"Not sure if I should take that as a compliment or not," Dutch said, a grin on her lips.

"It's nothing against you at all, Cap, you've been so awesome, please don't think that!"

Dutch chuckled. "Hastings relax, I was kidding."

Violet blew her breath out noisily. "Well, stop it, it's freaking me out."

43

They got within a half a mile of the camp, and Violet's ankle was aching wildly so they found a rock to sit her down on. They rested for a couple of minutes, then Dutch checked her ankle again, shaking her head.

"It's getting more swollen," she said, then moved so swiftly to scoop Violet up in her arms, Violet didn't have time to protest.

"Oh!" Violet let out in a yelp. "I, oh, God, Captain…" she said, stunned that not only had the captain just picked her up, but had done so with little to no effort. "There's no way, you weigh like half…" she began.

"Half?" Dutch repeated, grinning even as she continued to walk toward the camp. "Of what you weigh? Are you crazy?"

"What? Well how much do you weigh? Like what, 110?"

"Try 160," Dutch said.

"No way," Violet said, shaking her head.

"I think I should know."

"Well, your scale must be broken," Violet mumbled, aghast that the captain was actually carrying her. Without thinking, she put her face against the captain's shoulder, so embarrassed. She actually felt the captain chuckle this time.

"It's not, I assure you, muscle weighs a lot."

"Uh-huh, like ten times what fat does…" Violet mumbled, thinking that having her face against the captain's shoulder was way too heavenly. She could smell the faint scent of a woodsy cologne, and the musky but not unpleasant scent of sweat and the outdoors and just a touch of smoke, like it was part of the captain's being.

"So what bands did you like from the eighties?" Dutch asked after a long silence. She could sense that Violet was embarrassed and wanted to distract her; she was truly worried about Violet's ankle and wanted to get her back to camp so the doctor could take a look.

"I, um, like Def Leppard, Poison, Bon Jovi, Mötely Crüe…" Violet said.

"Aww, Bon Jovi, that was the first rock and roll I was ever introduced to," Dutch said.

"Wow, good one to be your first!" Violet enthused. "I loved them!"

"Well, see, that's something we have in common."

"Well there you go," Violet said, "we're just like twins." She rolled her eyes comically.

Dutch chuckled again. It was definitely an interesting day.

***

San Francisco

The silence in the darkened bedroom was broken by the sound of ringing. Hunter groaned, turning over and looking over at her night stand. She nudged Kori.

"It's yours," she told her.

Kori made a whining sound, as she reached blindly for her cell phone.

Hunter turned her head to watch Kori on the phone, it was obvious she was surprised by whoever was calling.

"I, oh…" Kori was saying, her eyes widening as she looked over at Hunter. "Okay, when? Wow, okay. We'll see you then."

After Kori hung up, Hunter raised an eyebrow. "Who will we see, when?"

Kori pressed her lips together, wincing. "Hunter is coming home, and he wants to meet you."

"Great..." Hunter replied, looking like she thought anything but that it was great. "When?"

"Tomorrow night," Kori said, "we need to pick him up at SFO."

"Spectacular."

The following evening, Hunter found herself waiting for her namesake out in front of the San Francisco International Airport. Kori had been called into a last-minute meeting with OES and the Governor, so it had fallen to Hunter to pick up Kori's son at the airport. She was listening to the local classic rock station, sitting in her classic El Camino. Her phone was ringing just as she saw a young man in Army fatigues walk out of the airport. Getting out of her car to wave at him, recognizing Hunter Stanton easily from his pictures, Hunter also answered her phone.

"Briggs," she answered, as Hunter Stanton walked toward her. She could see the young man assessing her, even as she walked around to open the hard cover of the El Camino so he could put his bags in. "What are you wanting to spin up?" she asked the person on the phone as both she and Kori's son got into the vehicle. She threw an apologetic look at her passenger, to which he only grinned, shaking his head. "Jesus fucking Christ, you need the Chinook for that?" Hunter exclaimed into the phone, rolling her eyes, "No, I'm not authorizing retardant for that, you'll put us in the red. Water is sufficient. Spin her up."

After she disconnected, she started the El Camino with a satisfying rumble and glanced over at her passenger. "Sorry about that."

"Duty calls." The young man with Kori's blue eyes chuckled.

"All the damned time!" Hunter exclaimed with a laugh, as she pulled away from the curb.

After a few minutes, the young man looked over at his namesake.

"So, you and my mom are a thing, huh?"

Hunter pursed her lips, regarding her hands on the steering wheel for a long moment, but then nodded, glancing over at him. "Yeah, Hunter, we are."

The younger Hunter nodded, not looking upset by this information. "You can call me Stanton, that's what everyone on base calls me. And my mom was never really happy with my dad."

That surprised her. Glancing over, she could see that Kori's son was watching her for a reaction. He shrugged. "I'm sure my sister thinks differently, because she always sees things the way she wants to see them, but I could always tell that mom wasn't completely in love."

Hunter nodded her head, grinning. "Calling you Stanton will be easier than saying my own name over and over again," Hunter told him, rubbing the bridge of her nose, "and yeah, your sister has been giving your mom a pretty rough time about it."

Stanton frowned. "I knew she wasn't happy about the split, but I thought that maybe she'd keep her mouth shut for once."

"Doesn't seem to be her strong suit," Hunter said, her tone circumspect.

The young man laughed. "There's a reason she's a political science major," he said, curling his lips in a sardonic grin, "she loves to argue!"

Hunter laughed too, thinking she definitely liked Kori's son.

"This is nice," Stanton told her, as he looked around the interior of the El Camino, "What year?"

"Seventy." Hunter beamed.

As the young man ran a hand over the black dash, she could see the reverence he felt. She smiled, nodding her head. "My daughter hates driving in this car, because it doesn't have an iPod jack."

"You have a daughter?" he asked.

"Yeah, Sam, she's eighteen, just starting at Berkley this year."

"That's where Desa goes," he pointed out.

"I know," Hunter told him, "I don't expect them to cross paths much, Sam's an Art major."

He looked surprised. "Wow."

"Yeah, she takes after my wife...well, her mother..." Hunter grimaced, realizing she still referred to Heather as her "wife" even though it had been a year and a half since Heather had passed away.

Blue eyes narrowed slightly. "My mom said something about your wife, that she'd passed..."

Hunter nodded, feeling the usual knot in her throat, whenever Heather came up.

"I'm sorry," he said, his tone kind.

Taking a deep breath through her nose, Hunter blew it out slowly, as she nodded. "Thank you."

Once again silence ensued, and Hunter was desparate to move the topic along. "So your mom says you're a pilot."

"Yup," he replied, smiling widely.

"What do you fly?"

"Apache, Huey, even the occasional Chinook." He raised an eyebrow on the last.

Hunter laughed. "Ever thought about flying after the Army?"

"As a matter of fact…" he replied, his voice trailing off as he smiled blithely.

"Oh ho… Getting ready to hit your mom up for a job?"

Kori's son chuckled, his eyes sparkling with mischief. "Hey, gotta do what ya gotta do to keep flying."

"Oorah," Hunter elicited.

"Damn, I forgot you were Army. You fly too, right?"

"Oh yeah, although not for Cal Fire anymore, but yeah, I have a helicopter."

"Mom said you have an OH-8."

"I do."

"Nice!"

The rest of the ride was spent discussing various helicopters and which ones Cal Fire had in their air force. It went much better than Hunter had expected.

***

It turned out that Violet's ankle was sprained, but fortunately not too badly. The camp doctor wanted her to stay off of it for a couple of days, but Violet was determined not to lose momentum. Dutch ended up giving her some upper body workouts she could do while sitting and after the two days, Violet went back to hiking with Dutch, using a brace. Dutch was very proud of Violet's determination. As such, she decided to surprise her one morning as they drove offsite for a different set of training.

"I have a little surprise for you," Dutch told her as they drove through the gates of the camp.

"Uh-oh…" Violet said, grinning.

Dutch chuckled, then gestured for the power button to the truck's stereo. "Push it."

Violet did and suddenly the opening lines to 'You Give Love a Bad Name' by Bon Jovi filled the truck.

"Oh my God!" Violet yelled, laughing and smiling brightly.

***

"Shot through the heart…" The words sang into the headphones, shocking Rebecca as she hastily removed the headphones and handed them back to Rowena.

"What?" Rowena queried, perplexed.

Rebecca shook her head, her ear still ringing a bit.

"Too loud?"

"What is that?" Rebecca asked, her eyes still widened slightly.

"That is Bon Jovi." Rowena smiled, her eyes sparkling with delight. "It's rock and roll, Becca, sheesh, it won't hurt you."

Rebecca shook her head. "It was loud."

"If it's too loud, you're too old!" Rowena crowed, laughing as she did.

"I am fifteen," Rebecca replied, looking confused.

The two sat in the clearing, where they often met up to "chill," as Rowena put it. They had formed a friendship. Rebecca would explain about Amish beliefs and Rowena would tell Rebecca wild stories about life in the big city and expose Rebecca to some things, like music.

"Okay, I turned it down, try it again." Rowena handed back the headphones, wanting Rebecca to listen to the song.

Rebecca took the headphones hesitantly, and carefully placed them over her ears again, blinking a few times as she listened. The song talked of Heaven and Hell, and an "angel's smile." It was a jumble of words that Rebecca found both interesting and confusing at the same time.

Rowena handed her the cassette cover, and Rebecca took it as if accepting a hymnal, she examined it closely, looking at the picture on the back.

"Who is this?" she asked Rowena, pointing to the picture.

"That's the band."

"They are girls?"

"No silly! They're all guys, hot guys!" Rowena sighed dramatically.

Rebecca blinked a couple of times. "Are you sure?"

Rowena laughed again. "They're long hairs!"

"Long hairs?"

"Men with long hair, in the old days they called then hippies, now they call them long hairs."

Rebecca nodded, still examining the cassette cover. Still trying to grasp the concept.

Rowena rolled her eyes, thinking she'd really blow the other girls mind if she showed her Mötley Crüe's cover.

***

Dutch thoroughly enjoyed Violet's delight. Violet belted out the lyrics enthusiastically, and it was apparent she was overjoyed.

When the first song ended, another began and Violet was thrilled. After a while, she reached over, turning down the stereo a bit.

"Thank you for this," she said to Dutch, gesturing at the stereo, "this was an awesome surprise."

Dutch smiled. "I'm glad you like it. You've been doing so good, I thought you deserved a little reward, and McDonald's fries were out of the question."

Violet laughed, nodding her head emphatically. "Yeah, those would be really, really bad."

After a minute or two Violet looked over at Dutch. "Can I ask you a question?"

"Sure," Dutch replied, nodding.

"So, Pennsylvania Dutch..." Violet began.

Dutch quirked her lips in a grin even as she rolled her eyes, knowing what was coming. "Uh-huh."

"Are you from Pennsylvania originally?"

"Yes," Dutch answered, like a witness on the stand.

"And who speaks Pennsylvania Dutch?"

Dutch hesitated, pressing her lips together, then finally answered. "My family."

"And...they are..."

"Amish," Dutch said simply.

Violet blinked a couple of times, her face reflecting surprise, but she nodded. "That's what I was thinking, but I have to say, I really thought I was wrong. Is that where your nickname came from?"

Dutch chuckled, nodding. "Picked that up in the Navy, when I used one too many Dutch sayings and the guys questioned me about it. When I told them what language it was, they started calling me Dutch. I liked it, so I stuck with it."

Violet nodded, understanding that. "So do a lot of people know? I mean like at the camp? You being Amish I mean."

"I was Amish," Dutch qualified, "but, no."

"But you told me because…"

"Because you asked." Dutch shook her head. "I don't lie about who I was, I just don't talk about it to everyone."

"Who you were…When did you leave?"

"When I was seventeen. Went out on Rumspringa and never went back."

"Wow," Violet said, still surprised, "that must have been really hard."

"It was necessary."

Violet hesitated for a long moment, not sure if she should ask, but her curiosity got the better of her. "Why?"

Dutch shrugged. "I knew I was never going to fit in there, so I knew I needed to leave."

"But leaving your whole family, that must have been difficult."

Dutch considered the statement and then shrugged. "Not as hard as you'd think, being different and hiding it was harder."

Violet pressed her lips together; she was trying to imagine what it would be like to be out on her own at the age of seventeen. No one to depend on but yourself. The idea was scary.

"Is it true that once you leave you can never go back?"

"If you decide to leave the faith, yes basically you're out, shunned."

"But you knew you were leaving when you left?"

"Oh yes," Dutch said seriously, "it did give me the opportunity to say my goodbyes though."

"Wow, that's a lot at the young age of seventeen."

Dutch made a gruff sound in the back of her throat. "Most go on Rumspringa when they're only sixteen. I delayed a year because my mother was sick, and my family needed me."

"Wow," Violet repeated, unable to think of something else to say. She had gained another level of respect for the Fire Captain. As it was, she thought the captain was amazing for all the time she was spending with her to get her ready for qualifications, when it was something she really didn't have to do. Now to hear that things hadn't really been easy for her in her youth, it made Violet feel more awed.

That day Dutch had Violet learn and put into practice the art of cutting a fire line. She taught her use of the tools, including the chain saw. They went over terms and the purpose behind each job. Dutch was impressed with how much Violet knew and remembered. It was easier to teach her without having to explain everything in depth. Violet kept saying, "Oh yeah, I read about this one!" They worked for three hours, then took a break.

They sat on the tailgate of the truck and ate the lunch that Dutch had brought them from the cafeteria. Violet kicked her booted feet back and forth as she chewed.

"Do you really think I can do this?" she asked Dutch, after a swallow of water.

"Yeah, I think you can do this."

Violet nodded, drawing in her breath and blowing it out slowly. "How come you're doing this for me?" she asked, hoping she didn't sound ungrateful.

Dutch looked over at her, seeing the sincere look on Violet's face, she shrugged, "Because that's my job, Hastings, even if the previous Fire Captain didn't get that part. It's my job to help women improve their situation."

"But you don't have to go this far normally, do you?" Violet asked, knowing it was true. She'd never heard of anyone going this far out of their way for an inmate.

Dutch shrugged again. "No, I don't, but you said you wanted this, so I felt like I needed to help."

"And I really, really appreciate it, you have no idea," Violet said, feeling the tears coming on again. Dutch saw it and started to shake her head.

"I know, I know, I'm always crying these days," Violet said, swallowing a few times to try and get her emotions under control. "But you don't know how many people just dismiss people like me....And don't make that face, you know it's true that people see me as fat and therefore useless."

"I don't know that," Dutch said truthfully, "what I do know is that you frequently put yourself in that category and it's wrong. You are not useless. You have a job now where you help people who are sick or have been hurt and you are doing your damnedest to get a job where you can help many more people." Dutch put her hands out plaintively. "Why can't you give yourself some credit? Just because you don't fit some ridiculous ideal of the perfect size? Most women don't, Hastings, and most women never go at something as hard as you've gone at this to try and get what they want. What you need to do is to give yourself a break."

It was the most the captain had ever said to her in a single statement, and the words had Violet's heart turning to mush. Here was this amazing, strong, handsome, accomplished woman telling her that she was worthy. It was a first in Violet's life. The captain wasn't mouthing platitudes that she'd heard a million times, she was talking about things that Violet had done and was doing that proved that she was a good person. It was a miraculous moment and Violet just wanted to savor it.

Dutch watched Violet's face—she could see that she was finally getting through to the other woman. It drove her endlessly crazy to hear the way Violet talked about herself. She knew that it was years of conditioning by the world at large that had created Violet's low self-esteem. The world was not kind to people that weren't their idea of perfect. Dutch knew firsthand how people treated someone that wasn't "normal" in their eyes and people could be really cruel to those who were overweight, something that everyone seemed to believe was easily controllable with "will power". It was a crock and Dutch hated the way society treated its citizens. She hoped that she was finally getting through to Violet, there wasn't going to be a way to change society and its views, but if Violet could at least embrace what was great in her, that would be enough.

***

"What's the story?" Angela asked, flipping long blonde hair behind her back as she held Violet's phone to her ear, her fingers playing with the cord as she did.

Violet sat next to her best friend on her bed in her bedroom, her teeth worrying her bottom lip as she watched her friend talk. Angela looked very serious, her blue eyes sparkling angrily as her lips flattened out in annoyance. Seeing that, Violet's heart sank. They were trying to find out if the boy Violet liked at school was interested in her. Angela had a web of spies that seemed to know everything about everyone.

"Okay, thanks," Angela said flatly into the phone, "I'll see you tomorrow." With that she hung up and looked over at Violet, her look belying what she was about to tell her.

"He doesn't like me," Violet said, knowing it was true.

"He's a jerk anyway," Angela said, not willing to tell Violet what James had said about her being too much of a "wide load" for him.

"I'm too fat, right?" Violet guessed accurately.

"He's just a stupid guy," Angela said, "you can do so much better than him."

Violet nodded, trying to hold back the tears that were choking her throat. She'd hoped that James was different, because he'd been nice to her when they worked on their business project together. He'd told her how smart she was, and how she was so good on the new school computer. She'd wondered if he was just trying to get her to do most of the project, he was a jock after all, not known for smarts, but she'd hoped...Now that hope was dashed yet again. It sucked being fat, people never saw past the big waist and thick thighs. Sure, all her friends told her she was pretty, and that any guy would be lucky to have her. Right, she could see that, they were just lining up! Ha! For Angela—with her long legs and blonde hair and perfect body—they lined up. For her, they snickered behind their hands and laughed *randomly when she walked by. She hated her life, she hated her body, and she knew nothing would ever get better.*

***

"Just pick up your end, higher!" Hunter said to Gun.

"Shit!" Gunn exclaimed as she smashed her finger on the corner of the fence. "Wait, I gotta put it down."

"I told you we should let the movers handle this…" Kori said, eyeing the large pot that contained the tree. It was Heather's burial plot, and it meant everything to Hunter. Kori completely understood why, but she was worried that either Hunter or Gun would hurt themselves, or they'd actually manage to drop the huge pot and break it, thus breaking Hunter's heart.

"The movers scratched it last time," Hunter insisted.

"I know babe, but we were able to fix it. It's just really heavy." Kori bit her lip, her tone as gentle as she could make it.

Hunter turned her head, looking over her shoulder at Kori, she could easily see that Kori was doing her best to be supportive. Heather's burial tree was definitely important, and Hunter realized that Kori would have every right to be hesitant to even have the tree in their new house, but Kori understood what it meant and she was always cognizant of Hunter's feelings when it came to Heather. It said a lot about the kind of person Kori was, and Hunter loved her all the more for it.

Blowing out her breath, Hunter nodded, turning to lean against the fence that surrounded their new yard. "Let's take a break for a minute," Hunter told Gun.

"Works for me." Gun grinned, reaching for a cigarette.

As both Gun and Hunter smoked, Kori went inside to get them both a beer. She was greeted by Sable, Mia and Shiloh. She was still flabbergasted that Gun was married to international super rock star Sable Sands. Mia and Shiloh were the girlfriends of Sydney and Harley who were joining them later that day. Sydney and Harley were the Information Officers for the Office of Emergency Services, and were busy trying to problem solve a network issue in the OES offices in Northern California.

"The bois need beers," Kori told them.

"Well, the salads are made, and the potatoes are roasting," Mia told her.

"I'll text Harley to see when she and Syd will be done and over here," Shiloh put in.

"Will Harley even notice your text?" Mia asked, her eyes sparkling with humor.

"Oh, she has her iWatch now, so it'll buzz her wrist. I made sure I turned the notifications back on this morning before she left for the office." Shiloh laughed as she tapped out a message to her girl.

Harley Marie Davidson had ADHD in spades and was forever shifting her attention to any number of things, but when she was hyper-focused on a project she could forget everything going on around her. She often forgot to eat, or sleep. Shiloh, as not only her assistant, but long-time girlfriend, made sure Harley did those things.

"Syd's getting almost as bad." Mia sighed, shaking out her long rainbow-colored hair.

"Did you just get your color redone?" Sable asked. "It looks so vibrant today! I just love it!"

Mia smiled brightly, being complimented by Sable Sands made her day. "Yeah, I found a new place here in the Castro, my girl Missy is wonderful!"

"I'll get her number from you, maybe it's time I did something to shake Joss up." Sable grinned evilly.

Sable was the only one, besides Gage McGinnis, Gun's long-time partner in the military, that was allowed to call Gun by her given name of Jocelynn.

"Oh my God, she'd die!" Mia said

"I might need that number too." Kori smiled. "I could use some change up."

"Harley says they'll be here in an hour," Shiloh announced.

"I'll tell Hunter to fire up the grill once they get Heather in place," Kori said.

"That's really cool," Mia said. "That her wife's remains are part of the tree."

"Yeah." Kori nodded. "I think it really helps Hunter stay connected to her."

"Is that a good thing though?" Sable asked, raising an eyebrow.

Kori blew her breath out, smiling softly as she did. "In this case, I really think it is. I know Heather approves of our relationship, and it comforts Hunter to know that."

"I'm sorry?" Shiloh put in, looking confused.

Kori opened her mouth, even as a grin tugged at her lips. "Let me take these out and I'll come back and explain."

"I think I need to hear this one too," Sable said.

Kori ran the beers out to Gun and Hunter, telling Hunter about her deadline for grilling, and then went back into the house.

"Okay, explain," Sable said, never one to mince words.

"Well, I need to know whether or not you believe in spirits," Kori began.

Sable looked considering and then finally nodded. "Yeah, I believe that people's essences don't ever truly leave."

"Well, then you'll believe me when I tell you that Heather, Hunter's deceased wife, is still around. She comes to Hunter usually by way of a butterfly, but she also shows up in music on Hunter's stereo in the car, or making things break when Hunter is being difficult."

"Like what breaking?" Mia asked, looking completely fascinated.

"Well, one night before Hunter and I got back together, we were having dinner with Sam, Hunter and Heather's daughter, and Sam was being a little pushy, and Heather sent a tray of dishes crashing to the ground. She did much more than that to Hunter, when she was trying to get Hunter to sell their house in Fort Bragg."

"Wow!" Shiloh put in, her eyes wide, as she listened.

"But how do you know she approves of you?" Sable asked.

"Well, I was staying at their house one weekend, and the pot that your boi and mine are killing themselves to move, was in the foyer of the house. I walked by it and said something to Heather. I can't remember exactly what, but it had to do with Hunter, and wishing this hadn't happened to them. But all of a sudden I could feel a presence next to me, I literally felt her hug me and touch my heart."

"Holy crap!" Mia exclaimed.

"That's incredible," Shiloh agreed. Sable nodded too.

"The funny thing was, I do remember telling Heather that I was willing to try and talk Hunter into selling the house, but if that wasn't what she, Heather, really wanted, that she needed to give me a sign." Kori shook her head, still amazed by the feeling of communicating with Heather.

"What happened?" Sable prompted.

"I actually felt her head on my shoulder…and she touched my heart again," Kori said, unable to keep the tears out of her eyes.

She hadn't heard the slider opened behind her, but she saw Shiloh, Mia and Sable looking behind her. Kori turned around and saw Hunter standing there.

"Say what?" Hunter asked.

"We were talking about Heather," Kori told her.

"She put her head on your shoulder?" Hunter asked, looking a bit dumbfounded.

Kori's eyes softened, she knew any conversation about Heather was hard, she nodded slowly.

"When?" Hunter asked, there was no accusation in her look or tone, just curiosity.

"That night in Fort Bragg, after Piaci's…You know I talked to her…but I said that I'd try to help you through selling the house if that's what she wanted."

"And it was what she wanted." Hunter nodded, understanding now.

"Yep," Kori agreed.

Hunter swallowed convulsively, feeling a lump in her throat, as she always did when talking about Heather. "We just had a butterfly in the back yard. She landed on her tree. I told her she wasn't helping us move it by landing on it. I got pushed." She said the last with a chuckle.

"She's so pushy…" Kori smiled brightly as the others looked on. "You were really tempting fate telling her she was too fat though."

"I know, I'm lucky we already kind of had her in place, otherwise I'm betting there'd have been a pot on my foot."

"Could still happen…" Kori winked.

"Crap," Hunter said, rolling her eyes Heavenward. "Don't do it!" she called to her deceased wife.

Upstairs in the house, a door slammed shut, making everyone jump.

"Was that her answer?" Sable queried with wide eyes.

Hunter huffed out a breath, even as she smiled and nodded. "Probably."

***

Dutch drove the Jupiter Red, Mercedes AMG GT C Roadster down the winding road from Nancy's house in the La Jolla Hills. It was Nancy's car, but she liked Dutch driving her places. Nancy was dressed to the nines in her dark green Valentino dress with matching purse and studded heels. Her long blonde tresses were on full display and her makeup was perfect as always.

Dutch was, as usual, dressed casually in dark jeans and a denim work shirt with the sleeves rolled up to expose her brown leather banded Fossil watch. They were headed to dinner down in La Jolla.

"Why don't you wear the watch I bought you?" Nancy asked.

Dutch sighed, already hearing the tone in Nancy's voice, it was her "Nothing is going to be good enough for me" tone.

"I didn't need a new watch," Dutch said simply.

"Well that doesn't mean you can't wear a different one, you can have more than one, you know…" Nancy's tone was condescending.

"I do have more than one, one for work and one for occasions such as this."

Nancy gave a snide laugh.

"Okay," she said, rolling her eyes, "that was a Rolex, Dutch, I paid a lot of money for it."

"Would you like it back?" Dutch asked mildly.

"No, I would like you to wear it," Nancy snapped.

Dutch narrowed her eyes slightly, but didn't say anything else. She knew better than to attempt to reason with Nancy when she was in this kind of mood. No matter what she said, it would just be another comment, another dig, another complaint. Dutch was anxious to just get the evening over with, she was tired after an exhausting week of drills with the camp firefighters and working with Violet on her days off. Plus, they had an inspection coming and she needed to make sure everything was in order. It was all piling up and she just needed to catch up on some sleep and some downtime. Nancy had insisted that she come "home" that weekend to spend time with her, it had been three weeks. The first thing Nancy demanded was that Dutch take her to dinner. Of course, Dutch's simple truck wasn't good enough, so Nancy insisted that Dutch drive over and they use her car.

The fire captain often wondered why Nancy even dated her, it was obvious to her that Nancy thought she was beneath her.

Then again, Dutch was certain that Nancy was simply dating a very obvious butch woman to shock her friends and her parents. In the beginning it hadn't been so obvious that was what she was doing, but eventually Dutch had begun to feel like cheap arm candy. It became tiresome and Dutch knew that she needed to end things, she just rarely had the energy for all the drama that came with breaking up with women like Nancy.

They drove in silence for a few minutes. Nancy was on her phone, texting her friends. Dutch enjoyed the peace for the moment, it didn't last, and it rarely did.

"Sam says there's a party we just have to go to!" Nancy announced as if she'd finally found something for them to fill their boring evening.

"A party?" Dutch asked, a sigh in her voice.

"Yes, a party," Nancy replied, an edge already in her tone.

"I'm really not up for that tonight," Dutch said, "maybe you can just meet Sam there."

"Sam isn't my date, you are," Nancy's tone grew sharper, "you know this is ridiculous! I don't see you for three frigging weeks, and now you don't want to do anything?"

"We're going to dinner," Dutch said simply, gesturing to the city below them.

"And I want a night out," Nancy said succinctly.

"And I want a good night's sleep," Dutch replied.

"Oh, right, 'cause you're killing yourself with helping that inmate…" Nancy said her voice trailing off ominously. Dutch began to regret even telling Nancy about Violet. It had been unavoidable, since she'd stayed at the camp on the weekends for the last couple of weeks. For some insane reason she'd hoped that

65

Nancy would understand, she should have known better. Nancy had no patience for people who weren't perfect, or for people who interfered with what she wanted.

"I am working with an inmate, but I am also doing drills and preparing for an inspection."

"Uh-huh," Nancy murmured, "well if you weren't working with that inmate all the frigging time, you'd have more of it, wouldn't you?" she snapped angrily. "I still don't get why you're wasting your time."

Dutch's eyes iced over even as she continued to stare straight ahead, "I am not wasting my time, I am doing my job."

"It's your job to whip every fat chick into shape so she can fight fires?" Nancy replied snidely.

Dutch's jaw twitched as she ground her teeth together. Nancy had no idea what women like Violet went through on a daily basis. Nancy would have been lost in a correctional environment, not that she'd ever end up there. Her daddy was a very powerful lawyer who could get his daughter out of a murder charge if he needed to do so. Nancy had lived a very privileged life and had never known any kind of hardship, and in her complete lack of humanity had no empathy for people less fortunate than her.

"I'm doing my job, whether you understand that or not," Dutch finally said.

Nancy was silent for a long minute, seething. "Are you fucking her, Dutch?" she snapped.

Dutch looked over at her, actually shocked by the allegation and unable to formulate a reply for a few long moments. Nancy took that to mean that she didn't know how to tell her.

"Oh my fucking God are you serious!" Nancy screeched grabbing Dutch's forearm, her long nails digging into Dutch's skin as she did.

Dutch looked down at Nancy's blood rail nails on her arm, then looked up at Nancy. Her ice blue eyes were deadly points of fire—fortunately they were at a red light at this point. Nancy took in the look, realized what she was doing and hastily removed her hand from Dutch's arm.

As the light changed, Dutch gunned the engine and turned her attention back to the road. When she was able to get a handle on her fury, she finally answered Nancy.

"Violet is an inmate, it's illegal for me to have a sexual relationship with her."

"Right, 'cause that never happens!" Nancy sneered.

"It doesn't happen with me." Dutch's voice was calm, refusing to be baited into this argument. She knew that protesting vehemently would only make Nancy think she was guilty of something. Nancy was just looking for a reason to fight and was hoping that Dutch would assuage her by going to the party she wanted to go to.

Nancy sat back in her seat. She'd been sure she was going to get where she wanted to go with that line of questioning. She didn't believe for a second that Dutch didn't have sex with any of those inmates she dealt with regularly. She was sure that the little sluts who were "gay for the stay" would be all over Dutch every chance they got. In truth she didn't care, as long as Dutch had what she needed whenever she needed it, she liked that Dutch was such a hot commodity. Every lesbian in their circle coveted

Dutch as a lover, but Nancy had her and she loved lording it over all of them.

"Swear to me that you're not sleeping with her," Nancy said doggedly.

Dutch looked over at her, her look impassive, but said nothing.

"So you won't swear to it?" Nancy concluded.

"I already answered your question," Dutch said calmly.

"But you won't swear to it."

"I don't need to swear to it, I answered you."

"But you could be lying."

"I don't lie."

"That's what liars always say!"

"Don't liars also swear things that are not true?" Dutch replied, her lips curling in derision.

Nancy clamped her mouth shut, knowing she wasn't going to win this argument.

They had their dinner, and in the end, Dutch drove back to Nancy's place, refusing to consider going to the party. Dutch intended to leave, but Nancy begged her to come into the house with her. There she made a point of having Dutch sit down in the living room. Nancy reappeared wearing nothing at all, except for the strappy studded heels she'd been wearing that night.

Dutch's eyes moved over her body, she had to admit Nancy certainly had a body that a lot of men and women would kill for, and she certainly knew how to use it to get what she wanted. She was the classic California blonde Barbie doll type of woman, with an enhanced bustline and a dark tan. She preferred bright pink lipstick and wore contacts that made her brown eyes light green.

She was fake in all the proper places, and aesthetically she was very attractive. Unfortunately, Dutch had seen enough of her inside to know she was a fairly ugly human being. Also unfortunate was that, regardless of what she knew about the woman, Dutch's body also responded to the sexually alluring picture Nancy made standing in front of her naked, tanned and toned.

Reaching up, Dutch pulled Nancy down to her. Nancy obliged by straddling her lap, leaning down to capture Dutch's lips with hers. They kissed for a while, but then, as she always did, Dutch took over, pushing Nancy back on the couch and taking her time to excite the other woman. Within minutes Nancy was breathless and dragging at Dutch in her need, but Dutch refused to be rushed. After what seemed like hours, she allowed Nancy her release. After which, Dutch stood, still fully clothed, and leaning down to kiss the panting Nancy on the lips. She then turned and left the house. Nancy lay on the sofa, staring up at the ceiling as her breathing became normal again. She shook her head, Dutch never did stick around. She wondered at that, but had never bothered to ask. What mattered to her was that she got off, and Dutch was amazing at that, she didn't care why she was the way she was about sex.

Driving home that night, Dutch kicked herself for even bothering with going into Nancy's house. The relationship was lousy and she knew it, but relationships were always odd and difficult for Dutch. At least with Nancy she didn't have to pretend she was something she wasn't, she could simply be. Nancy never asked for explanations, and Dutch didn't offer. It worked for them.

Chapter 3

"What's the point of this anyway?" Officer Burger asked two days later in the camp office.

"The point of what?" Dutch asked, glancing up from her desk and seeing the older woman standing in her doorway.

"This special testing you're doing for Hastings. What's the point? She washed out before, what makes this time any different?" Burger asked, placing her hands on ample hips imperiously.

Dutch looked back at the woman for a long moment, then set down her pen and folded her hands over each other in front of her on the desk canting her head slightly. "Is there a problem?"

"I don't like wasting my time," Burger snapped.

Pursing her lips, Dutch nodded slowly. "What exactly do you consider your job here, Officer Burger?"

Burger hesitated, she had a feeling this was a kind of test by the fire captain, the woman was just too unreadable! Burger adjusted her stance, leaning casually on the door frame to the captain's office. "I'm here to make sure the crews ready and able to do the job."

Dutch nodded, a slight smile tugging at her lips. "And that means testing them, right?"

"Right…" Burger said, curling her lips, "but not every random chick that wants to get out of Corrections."

"Inmate Hastings is not random, she qualified for the program she was encouraged to quit by the previous captain."

"Because she couldn't hack it," Burger put in triumphantly.

"Because no one helped her 'hack' it," Dutch replied, using Burger's word with obvious distaste.

Burger curled her lips in derision, even as she shook her head, rolling her eyes. "Fine, Captain, but I'm not just waving her through because she's your pet project."

"I don't believe I asked you to," Dutch replied mildly.

"Good," Burger snapped, then walked away.

"What's up her ass?" another officer asked as she walked in, handing Dutch a report.

Dutch just shrugged and shook her head.

Violet heard about the exchange later that morning. One of the girls in her bunk house told her about it.

"So the cap's doin' somethin' special for you, huh?" Celia asked, her brown eyes sparkling mischievously.

"She's helping me train so I can qualify, that's all," Violet said, trying to focus on her folding and tidying up her bunk.

"Uh-huh, and there ain't a little somethin' somethin' goin' on on your little hikes?"

"No!" Violet exclaimed, shocked by the question.

"Uh-huh…" the girl intoned. "Right, she does that kind of thing for everyone."

Violet didn't know what to say, she was never sure why the captain was being so nice to her, but she knew there was nothing sordid going on. Women just liked to gossip, Violet knew that.

"There's nothing going on with her, Celia, sheesh!" Violet said, trying to end the conversation.

"It's okay, fornido," Celia said, calling Violet "chunky" in Spanish, it was something many of the Mexican girls liked to call her. "I won't tell no one."

Violet sighed, shaking her head as she continued to fold her laundry.

Later that evening, Violet and Dutch were out on an evening hike. Violet had debated all day about telling Dutch what people were saying. More of the girls from the camp had asked her what was going on with the hot Fire Captain, some of them had been rather nasty about it. There were a lot of women that were interested in Dutch, and the thought of someone like Violet, who was far from what they felt was "attractive" getting the Fire Captain's attention irked them. Violet was sporting a few new bruises to prove their ire.

"Captain?" Violet queried as they walked downhill.

"Yes?"

"I, um, I need to tell you something." Violet's voice held the note of worry that Dutch had knew well.

"Okay, so tell me," Dutch said, thinking that she was going to admit to eating something "bad"—she was still so focused on the ideal that she needed to lose weight, no matter what Dutch said.

"Well, um…" Violet rubbed her hands on her thighs, not sure why she was so nervous, it wasn't like she'd done anything wrong, but she was worried all the same.

Dutch stopped walking. "Just spit it out Hastings," she said, feeling impatient with Violet at the moment, never sure if she'd ever get it through the girl's head that there was nothing wrong with her size.

"I, well, it's something that someone heard, and…well, I just didn't want you thinking that I was saying it."

"Saying what?" Dutch asked.

"That they think there's something…um…going on…here…" Violet gestured to the space between them.

Dutch couldn't help the quick grin that started on her lips, or the snicker that followed it, then she nodded.

"You're not the only one hearing that, Vi," Dutch said, forgetting herself for a moment and referring to Violet the way she thought of her in her head. Violet heard the name and couldn't stop the involuntary skitter of joy her heart did.

Reaching out, Dutch touched Violet on the shoulder. "Women are babbelaars…babblers," she corrected when Violet gave her a strange look. "There's nothing you'll ever be able to do or say to change that."

Violet sighed. "I just didn't want you to think I was telling people that."

Dutch shook her head. "I know better than that."

Violet bit her lip, smiling glad that the captain trusted her that much.

They continued to walk, and as they topped the next big hill, Dutch signaled for them to stop for a rest. Violet sat on a large rock and rubbed her aching calves. She was surprised to note some muscle starting there. They'd been working out for almost a month at this point, and Violet was starting to feel really proud of herself that she'd stuck with it. She knew part of it was because of the captain and not wanting to let her down, but she also found that she liked that her body seemed to be slimming down and that she felt healthier lately.

"So babbelaars is Pennsylvania Dutch, right?" Violet asked as she continued to massage her calf.

"Yes," Dutch replied, sitting on the ground, her knees up to her chest.

"Do you do that a lot? Use Pennsylvania Dutch when you mean to use English?"

Dutch chuckled, wrapping her arms around her legs, and pulling them into her chest. "When I'm comfortable around people it seems to come out more often."

"And you're comfortable around me?" Violet almost squeezed with joy.

Dutch laughed outright at Violet's look. "Yes, as a matter of fact I am."

"Wow…" Violet's voice trailed off shocked.

"Why does that surprise you?" Dutch asked. "You seem to be a very social person. See there it goes again." She'd said the word social with an extended "a" sound.

Violet laughed softly, nodding. "I was, I mean, I used to be, but not really here."

Dutch nodded. "You don't seem like you belong here, in this setting." She gestured toward the camp and at the inmate clothing Violet wore.

Violet bit her lip, grimacing. "You break the law you go to jail, that's how it works, right?"

***

Jeff had lost his job again! Now that he'd dragged them out to the middle of nowhere, he'd lost the job that had brought them there. Violet had promptly gone out and applied for assistance again, food stamps, welfare, whatever they could get. But how was she supposed to pay the space rental on the trailer? How was she supposed to get Michael's medicine? Did Jeff ever think of any of that when he got mouthy with his boss and managed to get fired? No, no he thought only of his pride, of his manhood! "I wasn't going to let him talk to me that way!" "He's a stupid kid, what fuck does he know?" "I'm not going to let anyone fuck me like that!"

So once again things would get tight and she'd have to figure things out. Jeff would brood and drink and watch TV. Then he'd bitch when the cable got turned off, like it all got paid for magically.

She texted Angela, her best friend from high school, telling her about what had happened.

A: What is wrong with that guy?! You need to leave him, Violet!

V: You know I can't do that, Michael needs his father.

A: His worthless father!

V: I know, I know, but what am I going to do? I can't work and take care of Michael too.

A: At least you'd keep your job!

V: If my fat ass could even get one!

A: Oh shut up Violet, you are twice as smart as Jeff!

V: That isn't saying much! LOL!

A: I know, right?

V: What am I going to do? I'm really freaked right now. We're in the middle of nowhere!!

A: You know, I have a friend that can get you some numbers…

V: No Angela! I can't do that!

A: You always say that, but these are people that don't pay any attention to their credit card bills! They're stupid rich!

V: Angela, be real, I can't do that!

A: You need to do something!

V: Yeah, but not that!

***

Dutch looked over at Violet and could see that the girl was getting down on herself again. "People make mistakes, Hastings."

"Yeah, that's true," Violet sighed, moving to stand, "but not everyone's dumb enough to get caught."

Dutch shook her head, the girl just couldn't get away from herself for a minute. "Come on, we need to start heading back before it gets dark."

Violet nodded, following Dutch back the way they'd come. She knew she was annoying the captain with her comments, but she didn't know any other way.

"You know I totally get that what I did was wrong," Violet said after a few long minutes.

"That's good," Dutch said, nodding, "what exactly did you do?"

Violet was silent for a minute, staring at Dutch's back as she walked, "You don't know?"

"Why would I know?"

"Well, you have my file…" Violet said, her tone leading.

"And I read what I needed to know from it, which was your fire camp experience. The rest is none of my business."

Violet blinked in shock a couple of times, concentrating on putting one foot in front of the other, even as she puzzled over the way the captain thought.

"I, uh…" Violet finally began after thinking about it for a long time, "committed fraud, by stealing people's credit card numbers…" Dutch only nodded, waiting for more. "I mean, technically someone else stole the numbers, I just used them to pay for stuff."

"Like what?" Dutch asked, surprising her.

"Um, like…stuff that I'd get to return to the store for cash."

"To pay for what?"

Again, Violet paused, sure that Dutch thought she was paying for drugs or something. "To pay for our space rent, to pay for my son's medications."

Dutch nodded again. "So necessities."

"Yes," Violet said, "but it wasn't my money, and it wasn't right."

Dutch glanced over her shoulder. "I'm not your judge and jury, Vi."

Violet drew in a sharp breath, grimacing, "I know."

They were both silent as they walked. The silence stretched and Violet began to worry that she'd said something wrong. She was searching for something to say when Dutch surprised her by saying, "Where was your husband?"

"I'm sorry, what?" Violet stammered.

"Where was your husband, shouldn't he have been helping you?"

Violet hesitated, not sure how to answer that question without sounding bitter and angry. Finally she shrugged. "He'd lost his job for the umpteenth time."

Dutch sniffed, drawing her upper lip up at one corner in obvious disgust. "What about your family, could they not help?"

Violet chuckled at that. "Well, they could have, if I'd told them what was going on, but I wasn't willing to deal with that too."

"Deal with what?"

"With my mother's snide comments and judgement."

"You do not get along with her?"

"Oh sure, as long as I do what she wants and act the way she wants me to act," Violet said, frowning.

Dutch nodded again, she well understood doing what was expected of her.

***

"But we were supposed to go this *summer!" Rowena argued again.*

"I cannot," Rebecca stated, "with my mother ill, I must take care of our home."

"But it's Rumspringa! Everybody's going!" Rowena cried.

"I am sorry," Rebecca said, wanting to remind Rowena that she was free to leave, that she was not bound by Amish beliefs that family came first.

"Damn!" Rowena blew out in a gust, throwing herself back on the new spring grass. She lay there looking up at the leaves of the trees, her mind going a mile a minute. She glanced over at Rebecca, who sat with her knees up to her chest, her skirts cover them. "Will you maybe be able to leave in the Fall?"

Rebecca put her chin to her knees, shaking her head forlornly. "Probably not. The doctor's say that she will need many months of bed rest once the infection has cleared. If it clears..."

Rowena swallowed the sigh that wanted to come, she wanted to ask, "What if your mother dies?" but she knew that it would only hurt Rebecca to ask that, and frankly she didn't want to hear the answer.

This trip to New York had become too important to her, and she didn't want to hear that it was never going to happen. Finally she'd found someone to go with her! She couldn't lose the opportunity now! But another year? Damn it all to Hell anyway!

"Maybe I'll go back to San Francisco for the summer," she said flatly.

Rebecca looked over her shoulder at her, surprised by the statement. "They will let you go?"

Rowena shrugged. "Yeah, they're already tired of me and this is just spring break, they're probably dying to get rid of me for the summer."

"What will you do in San Francisco?" Rebecca asked wistfully, already jealous of the experience.

Rowena said up, her short dark hair rumpled. "Probably see my girlfriend, and my ex, and make them both jealous!" she said, her eyes sparkling mischievously.

"Jealous?" Rebecca asked.

"Yeah, I'll tell then all about the hot Amish chick I'm dating!" Rowena said, laughing as she did.

"What?" Rebecca's eyes were as round as saucers and Rowena couldn't help but laugh.

"Oh, didn't I tell you that I'm bi?"

"Bi?" Rebecca repeated, not understanding at all.

"Bi-sexual," Rowena explained.

Rebecca simply looked back at her with confusion clear on her face.

"It means I like guys and girls," Rowena clarified.

Rebecca processed this information, blinking a few times as if actually computing it. "You like girls? In the way that men and women..." Her voice trailed off as she blushed furiously.

"Yeah, like sex and stuff," Rowena said, knowing she was shocking her friend, but finding that it was kind of exciting her to talk to Rebecca about this kind of thing.

Rebecca drew in her breath deeply, blowing it out through her nose as she canted her head considering. "So you kiss girls?"

"Yes."

"And boys?"

"Yes."

"But how did you know this about yourself?"

Rowena laughed. "Well, I did live in San Francisco..." When Rebecca looked back at her blankly she explained, "San Francisco is kind of like the gay mecca. It's like lots of gay people live there."

"But certainly not everyone is gay..."

Rowena laughed out loud. "No, it's not like it's something in the water or anything. I guess it's just more accepting of gay people. I mean, we had the first gay politician in history. Haven't you ever heard of Harvey Milk?"

Rebecca shook her head and was silent again, her mind still trying to grasp the concept.

"I was just kidding about dating you, you know, we're just friends you and me," Rowena finally said, worried that she was making Rebecca rethink their friendship. She truly liked the Amish girl, finding that once she got past all the formal rhetoric, Rebecca was actually very funny and insightful.

"How did you find out that you liked girls?" Rebecca asked, her tone circumspect.

Rowena shrugged. "There was this guy in school when I was in seventh grade, he was the one everyone wanted to be with, and he was with the coolest girl in the school, Michelle Stanley. Every one of my friends had all these fantasies about him and how he'd break up with Michelle and suddenly be interested in them. We'd all watch them at lunch, and the girls would sigh over how he touched her arm or leaned over to kiss her. He was so cool!" Rowena smiled at the phrase and then sighed. "But I found myself fantasizing about how great it would be if Michelle touched my arm or looked at me the way she looked at him." She shrugged, then. "That's when I knew."

Rebecca looked alarmed suddenly, blinking rapidly and moving to stand up.

"What's wrong?" Rowena asked, thinking she'd grossed the other girl out.

"I...nothing. I need to get back," she said, and rushed out of the clearing.

The conversation sat with Rebecca for the next couple of weeks and she didn't go back to the clearing in that time. Rowena was beside herself. In the other girl's absence she realized that she thought of Rebecca as her best friend now, and she was terribly worried that she'd scared the girl off for good. She knew she'd been trying to scandalize Rebecca, but she really hadn't meant to completely freak her out.

It was two full weeks until Rebecca reappeared in the clearing. Rowena was sitting listening to her Walkman, her feet in the cool

81

water of the stream. Rebecca walked over, kicking off her shoes and sat down next to her friend.

"There's this boy…" Rebecca began.

Rowena was so thrilled that Rebecca had returned she hugged the girl, then nodded, "Okay, go on."

"His name is Ian and he is interested in me."

"Is he cute?"

"He is handsome, yes. All of the other girls are swooning over him."

"But not you," Rowena deduced.

Rebecca shook her head, looking concerned.

"That doesn't mean you're gay, Becca," Rowena said, knowing exactly where her friend was headed, and understanding now why she'd been so freaked out.

Rebecca nodded, looking like she desperately wanted to believe that.

"Have there been other guys that you thought were cute?" Rowena asked helpfully.

Rebecca considered the answer, then making a face, she shook her head. "I have never noticed them the way the other girls do."

"Maybe you're just a late bloomer," Rowena said, grinning.

"I like to wear men's trousers," Rebecca whispered her tone scandalized.

"Don't we all!" Rowena crowed, putting her arm around Rebecca's shoulders. "That doesn't make you gay either, it just means you hate dresses! You could be a tomboy, that's not gay either."

"Okay," Rebecca said, willing to believe anything Rowena said at this point.

"Stick with me," Rowena said winking at her conspiratorially, "we'll get you straightened out." She laughed then, getting a kick out of the double entendre. Rebecca just shook her head at the girl. Rebecca shook her head, but couldn't help but laugh too, Rowena's laugh was infectious.

***

"So you made a mistake," Dutch summed up, "and you're paying the price for that mistake."

Violet nodded. "Yep, that's it, exactly."

"But you're doing more than that," Dutch added, "you're learning a trade, so that you won't have to rely on anyone but yourself when you're done here."

Violet considered that statement, taking a deep breath in as she realized that the Fire Captain was right. If she could pass the physical agility test and get on the fire crew she would get invaluable experience that she could take anywhere. It made her even more determined to accomplish this task.

Dutch could see Violet's resolve strengthen, and she was happy to see that finally the girl was gaining some confidence in herself.

The last month before the CPAT (Candidate Physical Agility Test), Dutch started training her on the specific tasks. They'd hike in the morning, going up steeper and steeper terrain.

"This is to get you ready for the stair climb," Dutch told her. She'd also started adding a weight vest on the hikes. All candidates had to wear a fifty-pound weighted vest for the length of the CPAT.

In the evenings after dinner, Dutch would work her on different aspects of the test. There was the hose drag where the candidate had to drag and gather fifty feet of fire hose. Then there was the equipment carry—Violet had to carry two thirty-five-pound pieces of equipment a chain saw and another saw for two hundred feet without dropping them. Dutch drilled her on the ladder raise, having her drag to her a twenty-pound weight connected to the style of nylon ropes used to raise ladders. The rope was slippery and it made it hard to work with, but it was something Violet would have to learn to handle. There was a wall break portion of the test where candidates had to simulate breach a wall or door, by hitting a six square inch metal plate until it indicated a break through. Dutch had Violet use a sledgehammer and a large tire to hit over and over to build up her strength.

She also had Violet crawl through an area that simulated a victim search. In the test it was a large closed off area that was darkened, the candidate had to crawl through the entire section. Afterwards there was also a 165-pound dummy drag of one hundred feet. Dutch managed to get ahold of an old dummy they were no longer using to help Violet learn that part of the test. Lastly there was the ceiling breach test, where the candidate had to force a weighted door upwards, and then pull down on a weighted lever. This was done for three sets of five repetitions each. Dutch used weights and a heavy sheet of plywood nailed to four by fours to simulate the upward punch, and a weighted rope to simulate the pulling.

By the night before the test was scheduled, Violet was nervous but confident.

"You can do this, you know," Dutch told her as they were finishing up their work out.

Violet nodded as she wiped her face with a towel breathing heavily. "If you say so."

Dutch gave her a stern look. "You are ready."

Violet blew her breath out, nodding again. "I just hope I don't forget anything."

"We'll be there to remind you of each step. You don't have to remember it all by yourself."

"Will you be there?" Violet asked, not sure if she meant the collective "we."

"I will be there," Dutch told her.

Violet breathed a loud sigh of relief. "I was afraid it was going to just be Officer Burger and I...I don't think she likes me."

"She's not required to like you," Dutch told her mildly, "she's required to do her job."

Violet bit her lip and nodded, she wished that the captain could be the one to test her, not Officer Burger, who'd been giving her dirty looks for a month since her confrontation with Dutch.

"You just go in there and prove to her that you deserve a spot on the team," Dutch said. "Because you do, Vi, okay?"

Violet smiled, happy to have at least one champion in this battle.

As it turned out, she had more than one champion. Not only was Dutch there, but a few of the other officers; the doctor and many of the girls already on the fire team came out to cheer her on too. Dutch stood at the side of the testing area, her Cal Fire dark blue uniform on, her legs braced wide apart and her arms folded in front of her chest. Violet was standing on the camp stair stepper, with the weighted vest on, she had to do the stair climber for three minutes. She knew she had no more than ten minutes and twenty seconds to complete the entire course. Violet looked over at the captain as she got the instructions from Officer Burger. She did her best not to laugh when Dutch actually winked at her with a grin. And then the test was on.

She walked the steps, thinking that it had been a really good thing she'd done all that hiking, it had made her calves strong. Even so, she was feeling tired by the time the first three minutes were up. She did the hose drag fairly well, thankfully the gloves Dutch had provided her helped her keep her grip, that was something the previous Fire Captain hadn't bothered with. The equipment carry was tough, especially after the other two parts of the test done, but she glanced over at Dutch who simply nodded to her, a determined look on her face. It made Violet grip the handles tighter as she walked the distance required. The ladder raise was another challenging part, but Dutch had shown her a couple of things to help keep the rope from slipping out of her grip. The wall break was the part she'd been worried about most, afraid the "wall" would be harder to break than the tire had been. She found that she managed to hit the small square eight times with good force and suddenly it was buzzing which meant she'd passed that portion. The body drag was challenging because it was heavy, she was tired and she had to walk backwards. She did as Dutch had told her and concentrated on holding onto the dummy and putting her feet carefully behind her, one step at a time.

The whole time she kept hearing the captain's words in her head, "You can do this, you can do this." And suddenly she was past the cones and moved on to the last part of the test. She was shocked that the door she had to force upwards was actually easier to move than the weight of the plywood she'd been practicing with, as was the weight of the pull down. Within a minute she was done and everyone was cheering for her. What Violet noticed was Dutch's look of pride as she nodded a smile on her face. Then Violet was caught up in everyone's embrace and accolades. She couldn't believe she'd done it! She'd made it!

Dutch walked over to Officer Burger, glancing down at Violet's time. She'd beat the required time by a full minute.

"Guess she was qualified," Dutch said simply, and then walked over to Violet extending her hand to the girl. Violet took Dutch's hand and was suddenly pulled into a hug by the usually stayed captain. "Great job, Vi, great job." Dutch said into her ear.

"Thank you so much," Violet whispered fervently, tears making her voice gruff, "I could never have done this without you."

"Yes, you could," Dutch said, smiling all the same.

***

"You're doing this on purpose…" Hunter accused with narrowed eyes.

Kori laughed at the irony of the situation. "I swear I'm not!" she exclaimed, her eyes sparkling with humor. She reached up, touching Hunter on the cheek as she grew serious. "I really am sorry, I'll cancel dinner with Desa, we'll just reschedule."

Hunter blew her breath out, shaking her head.

"No twenty-one-year-old woman has intimidated me yet, your daughter will be no exception," she predicted with a wink as she put her Cal Fire hat on. "I'll go get her, and we'll meet you at the restaurant." She gave Kori a pointed look. "Don't make me wait. I don't care if it is the governor!"

"I'll let Midnight know how you feel." Kori winked.

"You do that," Hunter told her, rolling her eyes as she headed out of Kori's office.

The plan had been for them to drive over to Berkley and pick Desolé up together to take her to dinner to discuss things. Kori's daughter hadn't eased up on her barrage of complaints leveled at Kori, and Hunter felt it was high time that they sit the young woman down and get her to see reason. Unfortunately, Midnight's secretary had contacted Kori five minutes before they were set to leave, saying that Midnight would be calling in from the road in ten minutes. It had, naturally, thrown their plans out the window. Midnight Chevalier, the Governor for the State of California, had been the one to appoint Kori to the Directorship, and had been her staunch supporter over the last year. When Midnight called, Kori answered.

Forty-five minutes and a lot of traffic later, Hunter sat in front of very modern looking dormitories of UC Berkley. Leaning back in the driver's seat of her Lexus, Hunter imagined she looked out of place with her Cal Fire hat and the black tank top she wore, having shed her more formal black jacket since it was so warm, even in Berkley that time of year. As usual, she wore her thick, black banded watch and various silver rings, including her Fleur de Lis ring, and her wedding band that she'd moved to her index finger.

88

As she watched the college students walk in and out of the building, she wondered if Kori had remembered to text Desolé that she wasn't going to be there to pick her up. She got the answer to that question quickly enough when she saw the young woman with long blonde hair stride out of the building, look around, pin her eyes on the blue Lexus, and then head toward her. It was obvious the moment Desolé Stanton realized her mother wasn't in the car, since she stopped dead in her tracks and stared open mouthed at Hunter.

Turning her hand palm up, Hunter used two fingers to gesture to Desa to come forward. It took an extra full minute for Desa to do so. Finally, she walked over, hands on her hips, looking very much like her mother. She looked down at Hunter, open hostility read easily on her face.

"Your mother got hung up at work, she's meeting us at the restaurant," Hunter told her, no apology in her tone.

"I'm just supposed to go with you?" Desa asked, anger tinging her voice.

Hunter looked back at the young woman for a long moment, blinking a couple of times as a slight smile curved her lips. "Or you can walk."

Desa's mouth dropped open in shock. It was obvious she was debating her options. Hunter waited calmly, refusing to say anything to try and convince the other woman. Finally, Desa huffed and walked around to get into the passenger seat of the vehicle. Without another word, Hunter started the Lexus and drove back toward the freeway.

A classic radio station played in the silence that stretched in the car. Hunter couldn't help but grin and shake her head when

"You've Got Another Thing Coming" by Judas Priest came on. She wondered mildly if her deceased wife Heather was trying to send her a message.

"What?" Desolé snapped, seeing Hunter's grin.

Hunter raised an eyebrow at Desolé's tone, but didn't reply. The last thing she planned to do was to pander to the woman-child's temperament. Desa was quiet for another five minutes, but then turning in her seat, she looked at Hunter.

"So," she began, her tone snide, "you're what my mom left my dad for."

Hunter pursed her lips, her silver eyes narrowed slightly at the "what," but refused to be baited into defending her existence by the petulant young woman.

"I'm who your mother is with now, yes," she answered calmly.

"Do you want to explain to me why?" Desa asked.

A slight sneer curled Hunter's lips. "Nope."

"What's that supposed to mean?" Desa questioned, shock making her tone sharp.

"It means I don't have to explain anything to you," Hunter replied mildly.

"I think you damned well do!"

Hunter took the opportunity of traffic being at a dead stop to look over at Kori's daughter, her look was assessing, her face gave nothing away, but her lack of reaction to Desa's demand only served to further infuriate the young woman.

"Well?" Desa prompted.

"Let me ask you something," Hunter said, her eyes still on the road ahead of her, "is there anything I can say right now that's going to matter to you?"

"Not a damned thing," Desa proclaimed proudly.

Hunter shrugged. "Then why bother?"

"What's that supposed to mean?" Desa practically screeched.

Hunter chuckled as she shook her head, the girl was far too high strung. "It means, that I don't see the point in trying to explain anything to you."

"But…" Desa began, but her voice trailed off as she realized that she had no idea what to say to that. "I don't understand." She sighed, shaking her head.

Hunter's lips twitched in mild agitation. "I think the problem here is a bit of a misunderstanding."

"What am I misunderstanding?"

"Well, you seem to think that I need something from you."

Desa looked perplexed, in that confusion she forgot for a moment that she was annoyed. "What is that supposed to mean?"

"It means that I don't need anything from you, including your approval," Hunter was succinct.

It was Desa's turn to blink in surprise. "You don't want my approval?" she asked quizzically.

"Don't want, don't need, don't care," Hunter stated.

Desa opened her mouth to reply, but no words came out. She closed her mouth, and it was obvious she was trying to reconcile this information. She'd truly thought that Hunter Briggs was going to do everything in her power to win her over. She'd talked to her twin brother, and he'd told her that Hunter was great and that he liked her. Desa hadn't been swayed in the slightest, her brother had always been an easy sell on people.

"You don't think it might be easier if I approve?"

"On who?" Hunter asked.

Desa hesitated. "What?"

"Easier on who? On me? On your mother?"

"For you and my mother."

Hunter shrugged. "No skin off my nose if you don't approve, I don't live with you."

"What's that supposed to mean?"

"It means I don't expect to have to see you much, so I don't really care if you don't like me," Hunter said, a hint of annoyance showing finally. "What you could do, though is give your mother a break, she's the only mother you have."

"Give her a break, so it's easier for you."

Hunter looked over at Desa, canting her head slightly. "Your mom told me you're smart, so I know you're being purposely obtuse right now, and it's starting to irritate me. What I'm telling you is this, you only have so much time on this earth with your mother, and if you're smart you'll stop wasting it acting like a brat."

Once again Desa was stunned into silence. This wasn't how she'd thought this meeting would go. She sat in the passenger seat, trying to collect herself. Who was this woman? She wasn't sure what she'd been expecting, but this tough looking woman with an attitude definitely wasn't it.

"What did you mean by only having so much time on this earth with my mother?" Desa asked, as she wondered suddenly if her mother was sick and hadn't told them.

Hunter drew in a deep breath, wincing slightly at the sharp stab of memory in her heart. "I just mean that you need to treasure every moment you have, because tomorrow is never guaranteed."

"But she's not…" Desa began, her look fearful.

"No," Hunter assured the young woman. "I'm sorry, I didn't mean to scare you with that. I just have some experience with loss, so I tend to be a bit vehement about it."

Desa nodded, blowing her breath out in relief.

"I just want things to be like they were," Desa said after a couple of minutes.

"What's changed?" Hunter asked.

"My family," Desa said, "my parents, my dad…"

"Your family is still your family, your parents are still your parents," Hunter told her, "and your dad is an adult with the ability to move forward with his life."

"But not with my mom, he's not happy anymore," Desa insisted.

"What about your mom's happiness? What's that worth?" Hunter asked.

Desa looked shocked by the question. "She was happy with my dad."

Hunter looked over at her again. "Are you sure about that?"

"Well she never said anything about being a lesbian."

"That doesn't mean she was happy with your father."

"Well, no, but…all of this…" Desa lifted her hands spreading them wide. "There was never any of this before."

Hunter did her best not to laugh, but still snorted quietly. "If that's true, why are you and your brother named after me?"

Desa's mouth dropped open, as she realized what Hunter was saying. "I know my brother…but…I just thought…but me?" she stammered.

"My middle name is Desolé," Hunter told her.

"Holy…" Desa breathed, then she gave Hunter an accusatory look, "So you and she… before we were born?"

"Yep." Hunter nodded.

"But, I… how?"

"Does it really matter?" Hunter asked. "The point is, she has a right to be happy. She's happy with me."

"But my dad…"

"Isn't the only one that gets to be happy in a marriage," Hunter stated.

Desolé didn't look pleased with that statement, but she really couldn't argue the point. She definitely had some thinking to do.

***

Violet received her certificate a week after meeting the physical qualifications. She was very excited that day, because her mother was bringing her son up to the camp for the presentation. It had been six months since she'd seen her son, Michael. Two hours before the presentation, Violet paced at the front office waiting for them to arrive. When her mother's sleek white sedan pulled into the gates, Violet wanted nothing more than to run out to the car to greet them, but it was one of the times when she had to pull herself up short. There were so many times when she forgot that she was actually an inmate, it was always bracing to remember and it always made her feel ashamed.

"Oh mommy! Police car!" six-year-old Michael exclaimed excitedly, he loved police cars, ambulances and fire trucks.

Violet looked out the window of the trailer, wondering if the couple across the street were fighting again. As she watched, the police officer climbed out of his vehicle and walked toward their trailer. A sudden cold vice clutched at Violet's heart, it couldn't be…

The quick rap on wood had her jumping and trying not to completely panic. She walked to the door, even as Michael got there ahead of her, throwing it open excitedly.

"Hi!" Michael enthused.

The police officer, a stone-faced man in his early twenties, didn't even crack a smile. He looked at Violet as she stepped up behind Michael.

"Can I help you?" she asked politely, fear still constricting her throat. Her voice came out as a croak.

"Are you Violet Marie Hastings?" the officer nearly barked.

"I, um, yes, I am," Violet said, her voice shaking now.

"You need to come with me, ma'am," the officer said, his officious tone sounding even more menacing to Violet.

"But my son, I don't have anyone to watch him," Violet reasoned.

"Can I come?" Michael asked hopefully, his bright eyes shining with excitement.

Violet felt sick. She was about to be arrested and her son would not only have to witness it, but he'd be excited about riding in a police car with her? No, no, this wasn't happening. It was a nightmare and she'd wake up soon. But it was happening, and it was very, very real.

In the end, she had to go next door to ask Mrs. Bings to watch Michael, while she "went downtown" with the officer. She was informed by the stone-faced officer that she would be able to call Jeff from the police station to "make arrangements" for her son.

The next five hours were a blur of people talking to her, and the horrible feeling of metal cuffs put on far too tightly to her wrists; mug shots, fingerprints, and a very cold cell. It only worsened when she had *to explain to Jeff that she'd been arrested for Identity Theft and Credit Card Fraud. He called her a criminal and said that she shouldn't be around his son. She spent that first night in jail crying, thankfully alone in a small impersonal cell.*

In the end she plead guilty and was convicted of a felony for Credit Card Fraud for the possession and use of stolen credit card information to obtain goods, services and cash in excess of $950. Due to the multiple charges she was sentenced to three years in a state prison. Neither Jeff nor her family attended either the hearing or the sentencing. It took a full six months of phone calls and pleas to get her mother to bring Michael to see her. Even then it had been so traumatic that Violet hadn't wanted her son to be subjected to the prison environment again.

***

Violet waited in the anteroom, for her mother and son to come through and sign in. Then it was finally time to see them. To Violet's complete delight, Michael ran straight into her arms and hugged her fiercely.

"Is it true that you're going to be a firefighter, Mom?" Michael's voice squeaked with the excitement his face reflected.

Violet beamed, proud beyond words at the joy she saw in her son's eyes. "Yep," she said, not trusting her voice to say more, since she could feel her throat constricting with tears. She reached over to hug her mother to try and recover her composure. "Thanks for bringing him up, Mom, I know it's a long drive."

"Well, we made a day of it," her mother, Esther, replied, her tone falsely bright for Michael's benefit. Violet could see that her mother still wasn't pleased by the idea. It was her thought that Violet should hide away until her penance was done.

Violet walked them around the camp, showing them the bunk house and the cafeteria. She was happy when many of her fellow firefighters were especially nice to Michael. Many of them had children too, so they understood what it meant for Violet to have her son there.

They ended up at the Fire Captain's door. Violet knocked lightly and heard Dutch call for her to come in. Opening the door, Violet poked her head in the door. "Captain, do you have a moment?" she asked.

Dutch looked up, smiling brightly. "Of course."

Violet opened the door wider and Dutch could see Michael and Esther standing with Violet, so she stood. She was handsome as always in her Cal Fire uniform, but this day she had on her white uniform shirt, her tanned skin setting the shirt off nicely. Violet ushered her mother and son inside.

"Captain, I'd like to introduce you to my mom, Esther, and my son, Michael. Mom, this is the captain that helped me make it through the test. She trained me."

Michael stepped forward, extending his small hand to Dutch. Dutch smiled down at the boy and took his proffered hand shaking in seriously.

"Are you really a firefighter?" Michael asked in a reverent tone.

"I really am," Dutch said, smiling and stepping to the side so she could extend her hand to Esther. "Good to meet you, ma'am," she said politely.

Esther looked surprised by not only the handshake, but by the captain herself. Her eyes darted from the captain and back to

Violet, but she put her hand out, stammering. "It's… good to meet you…too."

"Your daughter has done amazing work to get here, you should be very proud," Dutch pronounced, her eyes touching on Violet who did her best not to cry once again.

Esther nodded dumbly, unable to think of a reply other than to say, "I am, thank you."

"Do you guys drive real fire trucks?" Michael inserted unable to contain his excitement.

"Have you taken Michael over to the garage yet?" Dutch asked Violet.

"No, ma'am," Violet replied, having not wanted to assume it would be okay.

"Well," Dutch said, reaching back into her drawer to grab her keys and pocket them, "let's go."

Dutch led the way out of the room. Michael practically danced in excitement as he took Violet's hand dragging her along. Esther followed less enthusiastically.

At the garage Dutch opened the doors, letting Michael run in ahead gleefully.

"Michael, be careful!" Violet called. "And do not climb onto that truck without me right there."

"Hurry up, Mom!" Michael called back, anxious to see what it was like to be on an actual fire truck.

Dutch showed Michael the various vehicles and told him what each one did. Then she took him into the cab of one of the larger trucks to show him the different instrument panels.

"Oh my God, oh my God, oh my God," Michael chanted as Dutch let him sit in the driver's seat of the truck and pretend to steer. "Mom are you going to get to drive this?" he asked hopefully.

"No, honey, the real firefighters get to drive these," Violet said.

"Violet," Dutch began, using her full first name for the first time, not wanting to refer to her as "inmate" or by her last name in front of her son. "You are a real firefighter," she said, her tone as pointed as her look. "What your mom meant was that usually the Cal Fire people like me drive the trucks. Your mom has a much more important job."

"What's that?" Michael breathed, his eyes wide. More important than driving the fire truck? He couldn't believe that!

"She helps stop the fire," Dutch said, the proper gravity to her voice, "she and her fellow firefighters stops the fire dead in its tracks. She's the real hero here."

Michael blinked a few times, then looked at his mother again, his mouth open in shock.

Violet didn't think she could adore the captain more at that moment. In one statement, Dutch had made her son believe she was a hero. It was too much, Violet smiled, tears gathering in her eyes.

"I'll be right back," she said, holding up a finger and then walking to the back of the truck.

In a moment, Dutch was standing beside her, offering her a handkerchief. "Never have a tissue when you need one, Hastings," she said, a smile in her voice.

Violet pressed her lips together, laughing as she took the handkerchief and wiped at her tears. "Thank you for what you said."

"What I said was the truth, Vi," Dutch told her sincerely.

That only had Violet's tears starting again.

"You get your composure back, I'll entertain," Dutch told her, giving her a wink.

Dutch walked away then, and Violet couldn't get a handle on her emotions. Here was this woman who didn't have to be nice, didn't have to help, and definitely didn't need to build up this inmate that had barely made it through the testing, and yet she was. Violet was so warmed by the captain's words and behavior she knew that she'd do anything to work for this woman. Even if she had to stop the fires that came single-handedly!

In the end, Dutch thrilled Michael immensely by taking him for a ride in one of the fire trucks. He was beyond words. Violet was too, she was happy to see her son so excited, even her mother seemed to have a bit of a good time, not that she'd ever admit it.

Later at the small ceremony, the camp commander gave Violet her certificate naming her as a firefighter, while all the girls from the team cheered and said, "Firefighter, firefighter!" over and over. It was a great day.

The next morning the drills started and went on for another month and a half until the very first fire of the season. It was fortunately a bit of a late start to the season, but nonetheless it was the first fire Violet had gotten to fight.

Driving up to the site where they'd started cutting the fire line, Dutch went over processes and assigned teams. Violet was put on a team with five other girls. They would be acting as buckers, the ones that remove the vegetation as it gets cut by the other parts of the team. It was one of the simple jobs, but Dutch didn't want Violet trying to do too much on her first fire out.

Sweat poured down her back and slicked her face, but Violet worked hard, making a point of resting only when she absolutely needed to. The last thing she wanted was for anyone to second guess why she was on the crew. She wanted to do the captain proud, so she soldiered on, ignoring her aching muscles and the desire to strip down to nothing just to cool off.

"Drink," Dutch, who suddenly stood beside her, said, handing her a canteen of water.

Violet took it gratefully and almost sighed in ecstasy when the water in the canteen was cold.

"You have to make sure you stay hydrated, Hastings," Dutch told her, touching Violet's arm that was wet with sweat, "you have to replace all the moisture your body is losing. Okay?"

"Yes, ma'am," Violet said nodding. "Thank you, ma'am."

Dutch nodded as she Violet handed her the canteen back. Dutch moved on then, giving instruction and encouragement as she moved the through the group.

Two hours into the job, they could see the smoke of the approaching fire—fortunately it was slow moving. Dutch used the opportunity of the slow burn to instruct and give each of the women on the teams a chance to use each tool. There were turns at the two different saws, and various hand tools. By the time Dutch called a halt to the work and pulled the crew back, the fire was a mile away. The crew withdrew and waited to hear where they were needed next. They got lucky, however, and were sent back to camp for the day as the fire was under control.

That night Violet took a long shower and got Ibuprofen from the camp doctor, then crawled gratefully into her bunk and fell into a deep sleep. The next morning she was very sore and already dreading having to go out to work the fire line again, but knowing she'd do whatever she was told needed to be done. Fortunately, there wasn't another fire that day and the previous days fire was in mop up, so it wasn't something that required their team. Violet reflected on the work they'd done and was proud of herself and the crew. It felt good to be part of something important and knowing that she was doing something to make a difference, not just marking time until she received her out date.

Chapter 4

The fire season arrived late, but it arrived with a vengeance and the crews were working almost non-stop. Violet barely had time to take a shower and fall into bed at night. She was finding, however, that the work was getting easier for her to handle.

One morning she was getting ready for heading out again and was looking in the mirror to see how bad her sunburn from the day before was. She had on her orange pants and one of the white tank tops she'd been issued to wear under her orange uniform shirt, but while noticing the sunburn she also noticed that she was very definitely seeing the cut of muscle along her upper arm. Her heart did a slight somersault, she'd never had muscle on her arms! Reaching up she ran a finger along the line of her tricep, feeling slightly giddy. Sure there was still fat there too, but there was definitely muscle! She heard someone coming into the bathroom then, so she quickly pulled on her over-shirt. Even so, she spent the day working thinking that she was definitely getting more and more muscle.

"Why are you so happy?" one of the girls from the crew growled at her later that day.

Violet pressed her lips together to keep from smiling, then shrugged. "Just happy to be here," she said, her tone slightly sarcastic, as any other inmate would expect. Inside she was dying to gush, but she knew better.

Later, on a break, Violet decided took a walk she didn't stray too far, but purposely over a slight rise so no one would see her remove her cover shirt. She was still self-conscious about her weight, and didn't want anyone making fun of her fat.

"And what's going on here?" Dutch asked as she stood behind her a few minutes later.

Violet looked up and back, shading her eyes from the mid-afternoon sun.

"Hi Captain!" she said smiling. "I'm just trying to cool off."

"I see," Dutch said, nodding as she sat down across from Violet. "So, how's it going?"

"Good," Violet said, smiling widely, "great, actually."

Dutch nodded, then tilted her head. "I see you're cutting nicely," she said, her eyes on Violet's arm closest to her.

"I," Violet began, and the beamed, "I know, it's awesome!"

Dutch laughed, nodding her head. "It is really great, Hastings, you're doing really well."

Violet basked in the praise, blushing slightly, although it was impossible to tell in the heat of the day. "I just noticed it this morning when I was trying to check out my sunburn."

"You should be proud. And you're doing good work out here too."

"I'm trying, I don't have a handle on the chainsaw yet, but I hear it's something you have to work up to."

"It definitely is, it takes a lot of strength to hold on to and keep good control," Dutch agreed, nodding.

Violet nodded, looking thoughtful. Dutch noticed that Violet started to say something, but then stopped herself, shaking her head.

"What?" Dutch asked, knowing that Violet frequently second guessed herself.

"I just, I had a thought, but it's probably too much to ask."

"What was the thought?" Dutch prompted gently.

"Would it be too much to ask for you to show me some workouts I can do to improve my strength? I mean, so I can handle the chainsaw," she added hurriedly.

Dutch grinned, delighted that Violet had this level of commitment to the job, she wondered if Violet had any idea how much she had changed in the last few months. She'd become more confident and very capable.

"I work out every morning from seven to nine. You're welcome to join me and we'll see what we can do about getting those arms even tougher," Dutch said with a wink.

"That would be great!" Violet replied excitedly. "Thank you so much, Captain."

They talked for a while longer and then the lunch break was over. Violet found herself feeling really grateful for the captain once again. The fact that she was willing to help her was a constant source of amazement. Violet had no idea that Dutch had missed their workouts as much as she had. To Violet's way of thinking, the captain had enough to do without having to deal with inmates constantly. Dutch's way of looking at it was that if someone wanted to improve their situation, it was her job to help, she also liked Violet and thought the woman deserved every chance.

This thought was further confirmed the next day when they began working out. Dutch showed Violet how to use some of the free weights located in the gym at the camp.

"Now this one will improve your pectoral muscles," Dutch instructed, handing Violet a ten-pound weight, and demonstrating the lift with her own thirty-pound weight.

Violet watched, and nodded, getting her hands in the right position around the ends of the weight and mimicking the lift.

"Good," Dutch said, "just make sure you don't lift your shoulders," she said, reaching out to put her hands on Violet's shoulders pressing them down. "Okay lift again, relax your shoulders… good, right! See the difference?"

"Yes!" Violet said, smiling and nodding as she did.

"Okay, I want you to do three sets of ten reps, resting in between, okay? Don't rush through it, just take your time to make sure you're lifting right."

Violet did as she was told. Dutch could see commitment written all over the other woman's face. They continued their work out, and afterwards sat on the floor stretching and breathing heavily.

"Man, at this rate I'm going to have to join a gym when I get out!" Violet exclaimed.

Dutch smiled. "What else do you want to do when you get out?"

Violet looked pensive, then shrugged. "Just get my life back on track I guess."

"Well, you could definitely do fire fighting for a living."

"You really think so?" Violet asked, her tone shocked.

"Why wouldn't you be able to?"

"You think any of the other fire chiefs would let heifers on their crew?" Violet asked, grinning as she did.

"Will you stop that?" Dutch asked, annoyance in her voice, then pressing her lips together, she nodded. "I'm sorry, but you never give yourself credit and it's a bit crazy making."

"I'm sorry, it's just a habit," Violet admitted. "So do you really think I could be a firefighter in the real world?" she asked doggedly.

"Yes, I do," Dutch said nodding.

"Wow…" Violet's looked dazed by the idea, her eyes taking on a faraway look. "If I could get a good job like that, maybe someday I could actually travel."

"Is that what you want to do?"

"I've always wanted to travel," Violet said, "my parents do it all the time, but they never really take me."

"Well, you should take yourself," Dutch said, her tone encouraging.

"Yeah…visit all those places…" Her tone was wondrous.

"Like where?" Dutch asked, pulling her knees up to her chest.

"Like Europe, Hawaii, New York…" Violet named.

"New York, huh?" Dutch's face took on an amused look.

"Yeah, why? Have you been there?"

"Oh yeah, but certainly not in the tourist capacity…"

***

"I don't think they fit right," Rebecca said as she came out of the bus station bathroom stall, dragging at the denim material of the jeans.

Rowena looked at her friend, then canted her head.

107

"I fucking hate you," she said her tone sour, shocking Rebecca, "they look awesome on you!' She grabbed Rebecca's hands, holding them wide apart as she looked her friend over. "They probably just feel weird 'cause you're used to dresses."

Rebecca nodded, thinking Rowena was probably right. She walked over to the full-length mirror and looked at herself, blinking a few times, unsure if she was just dreaming or if this was really happening.

They were in Lancaster station, waiting for their bus to New York to leave. It was already snowing outside, so who knew when they'd actually get to New York. They'd gotten a lot later start than they'd expected on their trip. Rumspringa had been put on hold for almost a year and a half, and naturally it had been an early winter! Fortunately, her mother had finally recovered and gotten back on her feet. Unfortunately, it had then been time for Rebecca to tell her family that she was leaving and didn't plan to come back.

Her father had been shocked. Apparently he'd always had it in his head that she would never leave them, even for Rumspringa. Her brother was sad, but her mother seemed to understand completely. After the discussion, Hannah Lapp took her daughter's hand and led her to the backroom where Hannah did her sewing at night. She walked over to a bookshelf and reached high up to a shelf picking up a box and bringing it down. She sat down, and gestured for Rebecca to sit with her, she then handed Rebecca the box.

"Voor jou," Hannah said, telling Rebecca the box was for her.

Rebecca opened the hand carved box and was surprised by what lay there. Neatly folded was a small pile of hundred-dollar bills.

"Mama…" Rebecca began, surprised and bereaved in the same moment. Had her mother always known that her daughter was different and not meant for this life? "Maar hoe?" Rebecca asked, her voice soft, she was so moved.

"I have saved for you since you were a small girl. I thought that you would someday use it to marry or as a dowry…" Hannah's voice trailed off as she shrugged. "Or to leave," she added.

Rebecca nodded, knowing it had to be the last reason, since Amish girls were not required to provide a dowry or to pay money to be wed. So she had always known. Rebecca hugged her mother with tears in her eyes that evening. She'd told them that she would leave at first light in the morning. And so she had.

She'd met Rowena at the main road above their houses, and they got a ride to the station with one of Rowena's many boyfriends. She'd presented Rebecca with the jeans and a sweatshirt to go with it along with a pair of beat-up tennis shoes. Looking at herself in the mirror, Rebecca was sure she'd never recognize herself dressed like this.

What should have been a three-hour bus ride turned into a ten-hour one, with miles spent sitting in traffic. They arrived in New York cold, hungry and tired, walking for a half an hour to find a hotel that they felt like they could afford. The room was seedy, smelly, and cold. Regardless, they checked in and then went looking for food. They ended up at a diner that served greasy food that made Rebecca feel ill immediately. She spent the night throwing up and feeling horrible. It was a terrible first night.

It took them a week to find an apartment. The rent was an appalling $350 a month for a one-bedroom, run-down dump in "historic Williamsburg."

"Yeah, if historic is code for crap," Rowena often muttered. The heater never worked properly, and there were cockroaches. The room had a couple of windows that were nailed shut "for safety" the superintendent told them, and they were so dirty it was hard to see out of them. There was a refrigerator that didn't really keep things cold, and a freezer that made things into bricks so hard they were impossible to thaw. The walls were painted a sickly green, and there were brownish spots on the walls that neither of the girls wanted to ask about. Rowena wondered if it was blood from the last tenants, but didn't tell Rebecca her thoughts.

Rebecca was experiencing complete culture shock. She wasn't used to the way people spoke, she wasn't used to the music, she definitely wasn't used to the cat calls and lurid comments coming from many of the male population. The apartment was awful, but she'd discovered that a roof over your head was imperative, especially in the nasty New York winter.

After stripping the one queen sized bed in the room and laying out a quilt that Rebecca had brought from home, they lay down, fully clothed and facing each other.

"This sucks," Rowena said, having her hopes of the exciting New York life dashed soundly.

"We will make it better," Rebecca said, her tone confident.

"Uh-huh," Rowena replied unconvinced. She shivered again, reaching for her other light jacket she'd brought, laying it over her.

"Tomorrow we will get some things to clean with, I can make this place better."

Rowena rolled her eyes. "Good luck with that."

The next day they'd gone "shopping" at the nearest market. There was two feet of snow on the ground and they weren't brave enough to try and traipse much farther.

At the market they were shocked by the prices for things, but bought what they needed for food and cleaning products. Rebecca had *improvised a few things for cleaning to save themselves money. She managed to get the apartment cleaner than Rowena would have ever expected, but nothing was going to make it less shabby.*

Money was a problem. Rowena had brought $2,000 with her, and Rebecca's money from her mother had turned out to be $1,500. With the $35 a night they'd spent at the motel, and money for food, they'd spent well over $300 their first week in New York. The superintendent of the motel had charged them a deposit and first and last month's rent so that was another $1,100. Their money was dwindling quickly and neither of them had a line on a job at all. Rowena had been applying at stores to be a cashier or whatever they needed. Rebecca had no idea what she could do. She'd applied only in a few places needing to gain confidence. Regardless they were all part-time, minimum wage jobs.

With minimum wage set at $3.35 an hour, even full-time jobs would make them stretch their money, but no one seemed to be hiring and the few jobs there were only part time. The recession had finally ended, but no one seemed to want to hire just in case things went downward again. It was a terrible time to be out of work.

***

"So you're saying New York sucked?" Violet queried, noting the regretful look in the captain's eyes.

Dutch chuckled softly. "Let's just say I wasn't in the best neighborhood or under the best circumstances and at a really lousy time in our economic history."

"Wow, all that, huh?" Violet asked, grinning as she did.

Dutch coughed, picking up her water bottle to take a drink, while nodding. "I'll tell you about it sometime."

"Sounds intriguing," Violet smiled widely.

Dutch rolled her eyes then moved to stand. "Okay, so the usual instructions, hot shower, Ibuprofen."

"Yes, ma'am," Violet said, moving to stand, and pleasantly surprised when Dutch held out a hand to help her up.

They both went about their business and met up again the next day at the same time. It became a routine.

Within a month, Violet had worked up enough strength to hold the chainsaw with confidence and became a master at using it. Dutch was once again quite proud of the other woman, ever amazed at Violet's ability to adapt and improve.

Two months into the fire season, the fire camp crews were asked to move into the hills to protect some of the homes. The small crew Violet was part of was sent to line up the hoses to make sure the Cal Fire and visiting firefighters would have plenty of hoses to use to defend the house if the need arose. In the meantime, Dutch and a few others went to the houses to talk to the home-owners that had remained in their homes to "defend" their properties if needed.

Dutch knocked on one door and waited, a man came to the door, accompanied by a yapping dog at his heels who proceeded to bark at Dutch the entire time she talked to the man.

"Sir, are you aware that the homes in this are being evacuated at this time?" she asked politely.

The big man took a long swipe of a meaty hand across his mouth, nodding. "Yeah, but we've had this happen before..." he began.

"I understand it's an inconvenience sir, but it's for your own safety," Dutch stated amicably.

"Bullshit," the man practically spat, "this shit happens every year, and every year one of you come up here and tell me a gotta leave, blah, blah, blah…Not going." He finished he statement pushing out his impressive beer belly and sneering at her.

Dutch frowned slightly, as if considering his statement, then she nodded her head. "I completely understand sir," she said reaching up to pull a pad of paper and a pen out of her shirt pocket. "Can you please give me your dentist's name and contact phone number?" she asked, all amiability and pleasantness.

"My what?" the man asked, very obviously confused by her response.

"It's so we have access to your dental records."

"What the fuck for?" the man snapped.

"Well," Dutch said, crossing her arms over her chest, in an affable manner, gesturing over her shoulder at the other firefighters laying out hoses, and the smoke in the not-too-distant area. "You see, when that fire does come up this ridge and you can't get out in time, we're going to need a way to identify your charred remains, and dental records are the best way, since teeth don't burn." She poised pen to pad once again, and looked at him, as if still waiting for the information to be supplied. She noted to her amusement that he'd paled significantly.

"I well, I…Okay, I'll pack some stuff and leave," he finally said, nodding.

"Thank you for your cooperation, sir!" Dutch said brightly, turning on her heel and walking away.

She walked back out to her truck and made some notes, then headed to the next house. It was another two hours when she got reports that the fire was indeed headed in their direction.

"How're the lines coming, Hastings?" Dutch asked, walking over to Violet.

"I think we're pretty covered," Violet said, nodding. "I'm going to check back over there," she said pointing toward a house higher up on the hill. "I just want to make sure."

Dutch nodded, grinning as she watched Violet hike up the hill. She was pleased to see how well Violet was learning and adjusting. This was a new task for her, yet she was handling it well. It made Dutch know that she'd made the right choice in helping the other woman get ready for qualifications. She'd also come to find that Violet was a natural leader: she was able to cajole and reason with all of the other inmates to get them to do something that may not have wanted to do originally. The Fire Captain was seriously considering Violet for Swamper, a term they used for the inmate supervisor of a crew. Violet had the skills, the patience and she was learning fast, it was a good combination.

Two hours later, the battle was on. Dutch had pushed the girls back up the hill to have them work on clear cutting, but was constantly scanning the ridge to check on where they were in relation to the fire. Dutch was running the fire lines and checking on hoses, when she happened to look up to where Violet was working. As she watched, Violet walked over to the back of the house she was closest to. Dutch watched as Violet peered into the windows of the house, moving around to the other side of the house and out of Dutch's sight. Feeling a cold chill climb up her spine, Dutch started hiking up the hill towards the house, it was a good four hundred yards away. When she got up the hill even with the house, still a couple hundred yards away she was shocked to see that Violet was using her axe to force open the rear slider of the house.

This is not happening! Dutch's mind screamed, even as she moved toward the house. It wasn't possible that Violet Hastings would be using the fire crew as an opportunity to steal from homeowners who'd trusted them! Dutch found that she felt sick at the idea. She'd trusted Violet! A gust of wind blew smoke up into their faces, and Dutch found herself choked with smoke and ash. She reached around grabbing her handkerchief and tied it around her face, seeing that the other inmates were doing the same. She pushed herself, her eyes tearing to get to the house. As she got to the house, she saw Violet emerge with a bulge under her shirt. The fire captain strode over to her, noting that when Violet looked at her, she looked afraid.

"Captain, I…" Violet began, but Dutch shook her head, her eyes blazing in anger.

"Down the hill Hastings and into the bus, now!" Dutch ordered.

Violet jumped at the timber of Dutch's voice and hurried down the hill, stumbling a bit on the way. Dutch marched behind her, ensuring that they were well out of the fire line now. On the bus, Violet turned to the captain.

"Ma'am, I'm sorry—"

"Don't even say it, Violet!" Dutch yelled, and right then there was a yelping sound and the bulge under Violet's shirt moved. Dutch canted her head. "What in the hell?"

Violet bit her lip and untucked her shirt, drawing out a golden lab puppy that didn't look more than a month and a half old. It was smudged with soot.

"I'm sorry, ma'am, I heard him in the house crying and I just couldn't leave him in there…"

Shocked, Dutch started to laugh, shaking her head as she sat down on one of the seats. "You know, I didn't think anyone could surprise me again…"

"What?" Violet asked, not understanding.

"Never mind, so what do you plan to do with your little friend there?"

"I don't know…Can I leave him here in the bus?"

"Not till we're sure this fire is under control… You don't want to smoke him out," Dutch said, grimacing. "Look, I'll take him and put him down in my truck in the bed, he's too small to climb out and I'll give him some water. We should be wrapping up here soon, so that should be okay."

Violet smiled, nodding. "Thank you, Captain."

It was another hour until they were released to go back to camp. Dutch drove with the very grateful (if the tail wags and licks to the face were an indication) puppy back down to the camp behind the bus. At the camp, she got the dog set up in her bunk and found some food for him. Violet came by to check on him.

"He's so cute!" Violet exclaimed as the puppy flopped into her lap. She bit her lip, looking at Dutch who sat on her bunk. "Do we have to give him back? They just left him there to die!"

"Well, maybe they couldn't get back," Dutch reasoned.

116

"Captain, they were there, packing up all their valuables, he kept getting underfoot, they had a mama and other babies too. They didn't take him."

Dutch's lips twitched, looking at the puppy. "He's pretty small, maybe he was the runt and they didn't think they could get anything for him..." She looked thoughtful for a minute, but then nodded. "If they look for him, or post signs anywhere, we'll have to give him back, but if they don't, we can see if any of the officers want a puppy."

"Thank you, Captain!" Violet petted the puppy. She was sitting on the floor, cross legged, with him on her lap. They were both quiet for a long minute. "You thought I was trying to steal something in that house, didn't you?" Violet asked softly, her eyes still on the bundle of fur.

Dutch nodded. "Yeah, I did. It wouldn't be the first time an inmate on a fire crew did that..." she said by way of explanation.

Violet drew a deep breath, nodding as she expelled it. Then she looked up at Dutch, warm brown eyes sincere, "I would never do that, Captain, not to you." Dutch looked perplexed so she went on. "I know you put a lot of trust in us on the crew, and I know you have a lot of faith in me since you've helped me so much, so I would never betray that trust, not for anything in the world."

Dutch smiled, her blue eyes warm. "I think I knew that, but people have shocked me before, I was really hoping this wasn't another occasion."

Violet pressed her lips together, "I'm sorry that happened, but I promise, you can trust me. You have done so much for me, and

I can't imagine anything being more important than repaying that faith with nothing but good things."

Dutch extended her hand to Violet. "That's a deal."

Violet took the captain's hand, shaking it. Dutch gave her hand an extra squeeze. "Now, go get some sleep, we'll probably be back out there tomorrow."

"What should we name him? Temporarily," Violet hastened to add as she picked up the puppy and placed him on the floor and then moved to get up.

"You think of it and let me know," Dutch said, holding out her hand to help Violet up off the floor.

"I'll sleep on it," Violet said, smiling.

"Do that," Dutch replied.

"Soot," Violet said when Dutch opened her door to her office the next morning, and the puppy came bounding toward her. "I think we should name him Soot."

Dutch smiled. "Soot it is."

Three days later the fire was finally contained. By a week after that, no one had claimed the puppy, they'd even gone so far as to list him "found" on a website for fire victims, still no one claimed him. The Camp Commander had deemed Soot the camp mascot and had authorized him to live on-site. Violet was thrilled. Soot spent many nights wandering from bunk house to bunk house checking on the women that were now his family. He also checked on the officers and patrolled the grounds. He was a great addition to the camp.

***

Her first month in prison at best was scary, at worst Violet's biggest nightmare. Some women were alright: nice enough, there to do their time and go home like her. But others were aggressive and angry and got right into your face if you looked at them wrong. Violet quickly learned to keep her head down and not look directly at anyone. She had a few run-ins with a tall black woman named Ingrid, who intimidated the hell out of a lot of women.

The first time she ran into Ingrid it was in the women's room. She was doing her best to stay out of everyone's way but was also trying to brush her teeth before they were called to chow. Finally, a spot at the wall long sinks opened up so she moved in that direction, but suddenly her way was blocked. Violet raised her eyes to the woman who was leaning on the counter facing her. She took in the very dark complexion, large brown eyes, and hair pulled back into a tight, small ponytail that stuck out at an odd angle.

"What?" the woman practically barked at Violet.

"I…" Violet began, but instead shook her head and did her best to shrink back away from the woman.

"The fuck you want?" the woman shouted, making other women around them stop what they were doing and stare.

"N-n-nothing," Violet stuttered, terrified now.

"So why was you coming toward me?" Ingrid sneered.

"I wasn't!" Violet exclaimed her voice trembling with the fear she was feeling, a cold shiver went down her spine. "I just…I was trying to brush my teeth…" she uttered meekly.

"Oh, fine white lady needs to brush her mother fuckin' teeth!" Ingrid mocked, showing off teeth that were yellow, missing or decaying as she did. "Poor little white girl, stuck in here with all us niggas, huh?"

119

Violet blinked rapidly, feeling sick to her stomach. "I never, I wouldn't...I didn't..." she began and suddenly felt the bile rise in her throat. She ran toward the toilet stalls, but another girl blocked her way. "Please!" she cried while praying she wouldn't throw up on front of everyone.

The other girl, a heavy-set Mexican girl with braids and silver teeth that shined when she smiled maliciously crossed her arms and stood firmly.

Violet put her hand to her mouth, trying to physically hold back what wanted to come out so desperately. She could hear people jeering and laughing. It was everything she'd been afraid of in coming to prison. She was so far out of her element she had no idea how to cope. Suddenly she was throwing up and bile was spewing from around the hand she had clamped over her mouth, she dropped to her knees and heard everyone laughing and calling her a "fat pig" and saying "you're gonna have to clean that up!" She heard Ingrid say "yeah lick it up!". She felt a sharp kick to her rear and another to her shoulder. It was too much, it was all too much, she was crying and trying to curl up into a ball on the floor wanting to shut out everything.

Then the correctional officers were there breaking it up and helping her up off the floor. They took her to the infirmary, even though she said she was fine. The doctor in the infirmary checked her out and agreed that she was indeed fine, and gave her a stern words about "fighting" in the bathroom. She stared at the man with disbelief, did he really think she was fighting? Finally, she simply nodded and left the infirmary. Breakfast forgotten, Violet returned to her bunk where she lay and cried for the next hour.

There were more run-ins with other women- one was a Latina who decided to start "visiting" her in the middle of the night. The first time, Violet was fast asleep. She woke to the feeling of someone shoving their hand in her pants. Her assailant was behind her so she couldn't see.

"Be quiet bitch!" the woman hissed in her ear. Violet could smell the bad breath of someone who obviously needed a dental visit or twenty.

Violet froze in fear, not sure what was happening. Suddenly the woman jammed her finger inside of her. Violet squealed in pain and fear, but the woman continued shoving her finger in and dragging it out, scraping and ripping skin as she did. She could feel the woman rubbing up against her backside and breathing heavily. Apparently raping her was exciting the woman. Violet clenched her teeth and just waited for it to be over. She could feel the sticky feeling of blood and knew that she was being viciously violated. Hearing the woman's breath become more jagged, Violet hoped that meant that she was going to be done soon.

"Fucking white bitch cunt..." the woman muttered harshly against Violet's neck, "you like that don't you, fucking cunt..." She jammed her finger in as deeply as it would go and gave a grunt of satisfaction, then was suddenly gone.

Violet lay shaking after the woman left, she once again felt sick and wanted desperately to go clean up, but she also didn't want to chance running into the woman if she was still around. So she lay in her bunk trying not to think about the fact that she'd just been raped. She tried to think of other things and happier times, but all the while she could feel the burning pain between her legs.

The next morning she was still hurting and still bleeding so she decided to go to the infirmary, hoping that there would be least be a female doctor for female issues, but that hope was dashed. She got the *same male doctor who examined her and told her that she needed to take it easier on herself when she "masturbated."*

"No need to be so rough on yourself," he chided with a wink, his dull brown eyes practically dancing with barely leashed glee. It was something new to tell his buddies about.

Violet stared back at the man, once again wondering if he could possibly be that clueless. She knew that technically it was against the rules for inmates to "fraternize," and it was definitely against the law for correctional officers to have sex with inmates, but both happened and with a great deal of frequency, and not all of it consensual. She wondered remotely as she put her clothes back on if the man was saying that so that he wasn't liable for anything if she complained, or if he just wanted to pretend that she'd done that to herself.

Regardless, she knew she couldn't identify her assailant, and it would do no good to start trouble. It happened frequently for a few months. Often times she'd end up at the infirmary, but never requested an examination again. She simply complained of cramps so they'd give her pain meds.

"Again?" Mercy, one of the inmates that worked in the infirmary asked, dismayed.

Violet shrugged, nodding.

Mercy looked her over with kind brown eyes. "Is it those new bitches in D Block?" she asked harshly. Referring to a rival gang of Latinas who had been making a lot of trouble in the cells at night lately.

Violet's eyes widened, she didn't know what to say.

"Just nod, honey, if it's them," Mercy said, handing her two Motrins.

Violet nodded slowly as she took the pills swallowing them with the small cup of water Mercy handed her. Mercy nodded too, looking pensive.

Later that day there was a commotion in the yard and Violet heard that it was between a Latina named Silvie and the new girls' leader, Rosa. That evening at dinner, Violet was told to come to Silvie's bunk at nine. She had no idea what that meant, but was afraid not to show up.

At nine she got to the bunk that was four cells down from her. Silvie was a tough looking Latina with tattoos of tears on her face— two on one side of an eye and three on the other. She also had a visible spider web tattoo on her neck. Silvie sat in a chair looking like a queen. As a very butch looking women, she had a hard, mean look to her, almost aggressive like a man. Her posture was casual, but it was apparent even to Violet that she missed nothing with her dark eyes.

"Bien aqui guera, come in…" Silvie said, beckoning her.

Violet bit her lips, almost stumbling into the cell, looking at the other women gathered around Silvie. They all looked mean and tough with various tattoos and makeup styles all versions of the black liner all the "girls" wore. They were almost like Silvie's harem, was the way that Violet saw it. When Silvie put her hand to her face, Violet could see the letters "SUR" tattooed on her fingers. She vaguely remembered reading something about one of the biggest Mexican gangs in San Diego being the Surenos. Her heart rate tripped and started pounding in her chest, had she just gone from bad to worse?

Silvie was studying her, her index finger rubbing back and forth over her chin.

"So one of the Norteno bitches is hassling you?" Silvie asked.

"Nor...what?" Violet stammered, knowing she sounded stupid, but having no idea what she meant.

"It's their name, stupida," one of the girls told her,

"Oh, um..." Violet stammered, not sure if she should even say anything to these women or not.

"You can tell her," Mercy said, her tone assuring, "she can help."

Violet looked back at Mercy, pressing her hands together and feeling how sweaty her palms were. She was doing her best not to actually wring her hands in dismay. Finally she nodded.

Silvie made a sucking sound through her teeth, nodding as she did, the other girls nodded too. "That shit gonna stop tonight," Silvie pronounced.

Later that night, Violet was in her bunk, trying to do her best to sleep. Suddenly there was a hushed ruckus outside of the cell, grunting and scuffling of feet and then it was quiet again.

The next morning at breakfast, Mercy came to stand by the table Violet was sitting alone at. "You're comin' to our table," Mercy said, picking up Violet's tray and walking away fully expecting Violet to follow her, which Violet did after a few moments of confusion. At the table, Silvie sat at the head, "like the dad" Violet thought to herself. A couple of other white women sat amongst Silvie's girls. They seemed very comfortable and it made Violet relax a little.

"So no visits last night, huh?" Silvie asked, picking her teeth with a fork.

"No visits," Violet said softly.

Silvie nodded, looking confident.

After that no one bothered Violet, but she was then under the protection of Silvie and her girls and essentially property of those girls.

124

Fortunately, it meant a lot less abuse, and a newly gained admiration for the power of fear. She also gained an appreciation for butch women and their more protective ways.

Chapter 4

Things in New York were not going according to plan. It had been hard enough to land part-time jobs but keeping them was even harder. There were far too many "hungry" people out there, that all it took was calling in sick one day to lose a job. Both Rebecca and Rowena were experiencing health issues, between the unimpeded cold of the winter months, and the broiling hot summer months they did their best to avoid sickness. Even so they both landed and lost a number of jobs between them. Worse still, they were racking up unpaid hospital bills when things got dangerous.

One such time was the first transition from winter to spring. Rowena got a cough that would not abate no matter how much cough medicine she drank straight from the bottle. Rebecca finally talked her into trying to go to the free clinic, but they waited there so long that they gave up. When things got decidedly worse, Rebecca hurried her, via a very expensive cab ride, to the emergency room. Rowena was diagnosed with pneumonia and had to stay in the hospital for three days while she was given antibiotics and had her lungs drained of fluid. When Rowena finally came home to the apartment, Rebecca did her best to take care of her friend.

A month later Rowena was finally feeling healthy again, and was on the job search once again. When she came home to a bill from the hospital and it was well over a thousand dollars—not counting the follow up visits that they would eventually billed for as well—she felt sick again. It was one more thing they didn't have money for. They ate next to nothing, didn't drive cars or have nights out, they were lucky to make rent, pay their electric bill and have a phone. Groceries were sparse and never healthy enough. Rebecca insisted on saving money when they could, and ferreted the money away in the bank, which was a Godsend when one (or both) of them were out of work so they didn't starve.

Things just go worse and worse and piled up little by little. By the time they'd lived in New York for a year, things were getting desperate. It was the end of the month and they didn't have the rent money. With both of them out of work, their savings had been completely depleted. They both worried constantly about being out on the street in the middle of winter. Rowena decided it was time to take matters into her own hands.

Rebecca got home after a day of job hunting, she was feeling completely frozen and was starving because she had only had an orange for breakfast and nothing the rest of the day. Rowena met her at the door, wearing an oddly skimpy outfit of short shorts and a camisole top, it was cold in the apartment as always.

"Ro, are you sick?" Rebecca asked, immediately worried that Rowena had a fever again, hence the light dress. She noticed too that Rowena was wearing a lot of makeup, which was strange for her as well.

"No, I'm fine," Rowena said, holding her hands up to stop Rebecca's forward movement. "But I need you to do me a favor."

Rebecca canted her head, noting Rowena's anxious look over her shoulder, only then did Rebecca notice the man standing in the small kitchen portion of the apartment.

"What?" Rebecca asked, confused immediately.

"I need you to go hang out at the coffee shop for about an hour," Rowena said, starting to push Rebecca back through the door.

The man took a step forward then, and Rebecca could see the leer on his face even before he spoke. "Hey I'd pay more for a threesome..."

"What!" Rebecca yelped, even as Rowena managed to get her out the door into the hallway. "Wat is hier aan de hand?" shaking her head, Rebecca translated her own words harshly "What's going on here?" she demanded of Rowena.

Rowena shrugged, her eyes not meeting Rebecca's. "We need the cash."

"Nee," Rebecca said firmly shaking her head, still using Pennsylvania Dutch in her intensity.

"Becca, it's okay, no big deal," Rowena placated.

"No, Rowena, absolutely not," Rebecca repeated vehemently, shaking her head for emphasis.

"I need to," Rowena said. "We need rent, damn it!"

"Not like this," Rebecca said, moving past Rowena and walking into the apartment to look at the man. "You need to leave," she told him.

"No!" Rowena said, putting her hand out to stop the man from moving to do what Rebecca had practically ordered. Then she turned to Rebecca. "This is my choice, this is what I need to do to keep a roof over our heads," she insisted.

"No!" Rebecca snapped. "Not like this! I won't leave." She crossed her arms over her chest and sat down on the battered couch in their living room.

Rowena looked back at her for a long moment, surprised by Rebecca's forcefulness, but also desperate to do what they needed to do to keep the apartment. Trying to find another would be impossible, especially in the dead of winter. Finally she sighed loudly, turning her head to look at the guy, then looking back at Rebecca.

"Fine then we will," she said to Rebecca, then nodded toward the man. "Let's go," she said, reaching over to pick up her coat and shove her feet into her bedraggled second-hand pink snow boots.

Before Rebecca could even form a response they were gone. She paced and worried for the next two hours. When Rowena walked back into the apartment her lips were blue she was so cold. Rebecca immediately dragged the afghan blanket off the back of the couch and threw it around her friend and hugged her close to try and warm her. It took a half an hour for Rowena's teeth to stop chattering and for normal color to return to her lips.

"We cannot live like this," Rebecca stated simply.

Rowena pressed her head into the hollow of Rebecca's shoulder. "We have to live somehow."

"Not like this." Rebecca repeated, her ice blue eyes narrowed in determination.

The next day Rowena was surprised when she returned to the apartment after a frustrating day of interviews and turn downs. She sat down on the couch, feeling dejected and still a bit disgusted with herself for what she'd done the day before, but it had gotten them a hundred dollars closer to rent for that month. Rebecca entered the apartment ten minutes later, removing her coat and hanging it up, kicking off her boots and placing them neatly in the closet by the door. Then she moved to sit down next to Rowena, handing her an envelope as she did.

"What's this?" Rowena asked, humor in her tone, even as she opened the envelope. "You win the lottery or something?"

"I joined the navy," Rebecca said, not one for beating around the bush.

"I see that," Rowena said as she stared down at the check for $5,000 from the United States Navy. She looked over at her friend concerned. "You know you just traded one family that won't accept you for another family that won't, right? In fact this family," she said holding up the check, "will kick you out for being gay."

Rebecca looked unphased by the comment. "We have not established that I am gay," she said simply.

"We haven't established what you are," Rowena corrected, "but if it turns out you're gay, in the navy you're screwed."

Rebecca considered Rowena's words. While they had talked a few times about Rebecca's sexual orientation, they had never managed to come to a conclusion. Rebecca didn't find men attractive, and in her own words, did find women's appearance "more pleasing," but that had been as close to establishing anything as they'd gotten.

"We need money to survive. With this enlistment bonus you can keep up with the payments while you look for work. I will send my checks to you so you can use them to pay for whatever you need."

"You don't think you're going to want money?" Rowena asked, her tone mild.

"The navy will feed me, clothe me and I will have a place to live. What more do I need?"

Rowena looked over at her friend, ever astounded at Rebecca's life philosophy.

"I don't know, maybe you want a cool car, or a nice stereo or something," Rowena finally said, thinking of the things that she'd want if she had money to buy it with.

"I don't drive and I only listen to music if you are playing it."

Rowena shook her head. "I'm never going to totally get you, am I?" she mused.

"Probably not," Rebecca said, smiling softly.

In their time in New York they'd become even better friends than before. Rowena was forever trying to get Rebecca to do things differently, "live!" and in some instances Rebecca would try things, and other times she wouldn't. Her Amish upbringing came to bear often and she just couldn't shake the sense of living simply. She accepted things like electricity and some modern conveniences, but she still didn't watch TV, or listen to music, or take a cab or the subway unless she had to do so. It was a learning experience for Rowena, and it had definitely given her a different perspective on things and life in the big city.

They both sat on the couch for a long time, neither of them talking.

"Well, this is going to suck," Rowena finally said breaking the silence. Rebecca nodded resolutely. Rowena grinned. "At least you already cut your hair, that'll make it easier."

Rebecca had finally cut her extremely long hair during the hot summer, so it now hung just two inches past her shoulders. It had been traumatic for her, but it had seemed necessary and she felt much freer without the weight of it.

Rebecca left four days later for the Great Lakes Naval Training Center.

***

Things in the camp had settled into a routine. There were fires regularly, and the crews spent hours and hours working on and mopping up after them. Violet felt her body getting stronger with her continued work outs as well as the physical activity during the fires. She knew she would never be considered "skinny" by any means, but she was very excited when she got to go down a couple of pants sizes in the camp. She was proud of the hard work she'd been doing.

One morning she found herself alone in the bathroom, which was rare. She'd just gotten out of the shower after her workout with the captain and had a towel wrapped around her. Checking around her, and even bending down to make sure no one was in one of the stalls in the bathroom, Violet slowly opened her towel in front of the full-length mirror. She still saw the tummy that was far too jiggly for her taste, but she did her best to look past that. She saw that if she flexed her legs she could see muscle on her thighs and calves. She dropped the towel and touched her middle.

"Still a slide area..." she muttered unhappily, but as she bent down to pick up her towel, she noticed how much more defined her arms were becoming. "Not so bad there," she said, smiling softly, then lifted her arms and waving them back and forth, fat still hung on the backs of them. "Aw, but I still have my bingo arms..." she said, having always equated fat arms to old ladies at the bingo parlor, holding up their waggly arms and yelling "Bingo!" She wondered remotely if those ever went away, or if she'd have to have some kind of surgery to have the extra fat and skin removed. "Which means I'll never have proper arms," Violet said to no one.

She talked to the captain about it the next morning in their session.

"So will this area always be a slide area?" she asked pointing to her middle.

Dutch looked back at Violet blinking a couple of times trying to comprehend her description, "Slide area?"

"Yeah, you know," Violet replied grinning, her tone facetious, "like a mud slide, takes out all the definition of the terrain? Just kind of a blobby area."

Dutch shook her head, sighing. The woman came up with every possible negative way to talk about herself. "You are wondering when your mid-section will tighten up?"

"Yeah, let's go with that," Violet said, smiling her brown eyes sparkling humorously.

"Het hangt ervan," Dutch said off-handedly, grinning when she saw Violet roll her eyes. Violet had found that when Dutch didn't want to answer a question directly, she tended to use Pennsylvania Dutch, to put off answering.

"Which means…" Violet put in.

Dutch blew her breath out. "It depends."

"On?"

"On how your body responds to exercise, how much core work you do, what you eat, a lot of things."

"So you can't say," Violet clarified.

"Juist," Dutch said, nodding. "Correct."

Violet nodded, knowing she was driving the captain crazy with her way of handling her weight. Usually she tried to be better about not being negative, but she'd been so desperate for some kind of timeline that she hadn't tried hard enough. At least the Captain didn't seem too annoyed with her at that point.

Sitting back, Violet looked at Dutch, taking in her toned, strong arms, her non-existent waistline, and her solidly muscled legs pulled up in front of her chest.

"Have you ever been overweight, Captain?" Violet asked.

Dutch shook her head.

Violet nodded. "It's something that creeps up on you, you know?"

"How so?" Dutch asked, canting her head, wanting to understand.

"Well, when you're a kid you can eat anything, at least I always could. So you go along eating whatever you want. I used to love going down to the local store and buying a box of macaroni and cheese, a one litre bottle of Pepsi and a huge Caramello bar. Oh that was the best lunch ever! Got knows how many calories that was, probably in the four thousand range, but it never mattered, I was always skinny. But then I got older, and suddenly stuff started to stick. At first it was cool, because I finally got boobs, yay me!" There was a flash of a grin and a twinkling of eyes at this point. "But then it started getting harder and harder." She picked at her shirt, her head down as she recalled that time in her life. "Before I knew it, I was a hundred and sixty pounds, and I was only in sixth grade! Every girl in my class was getting prettier, and I was getting zits from all the garbage I ate, but nobody told me that was why. McDonald's French fries were vegetables, right? And so is ketchup, it's made out of tomatoes! But no one said fried food was bad, no one said ketchup had tons of sugar in it! All I knew was that I didn't look like my friends and boys weren't looking at me..." Her voice trailed off as she shook her head, wondering if she was talking too much. Peering up at the captain she could see kind blue eyes looking back at her.

She shrugged. "So I tried stuff, to lose the weight."

Dutch sensed an undertone in what Violet had just said. "What did you try?"

Violet shrugged, her leg starting to bounce unconsciously in her internal agitation. "Well, I tried every diet known to man, Dexatrim, that AYDS stuff, you know it tasted like chocolate but it was supposed to suppress your appetite, liquid diets, only eating bananas for days, and then I found the whole laxative thing and throwing up…"

Dutch grimaced, knowing how dangerous many of those diets would have been. "Were you seeing a medical doctor through any of this?"

Violet laughed ruefully, shaking her head. "Oh Hell no, my mother refused to take me to a doctor for my 'lack of will power'!" She said the last with air quotes.

"None of them worked," Dutch stated, it wasn't a question.

"They all worked for a day or two. I couldn't do the throwing up thing, but the laxative thing landed me in the hospital where they told me I just needed to 'eat right and exercise' to lose my 'baby fat.' Every medical problem I've ever had has been blamed on my weight."

"What do you mean?" Dutch asked, her tone foreboding.

"Oh, I kept passing out for no apparent reason, they claimed it was my weight. I kept having abdominal pain and really bad periods, they said if I just would lose fifty to a hundred pounds it would make all the difference. It turned out I had a huge cyst, but they only discovered that when it burst and almost killed me."

"Heavens Hastings…" Dutch breathed, shaking her head. "I'm sorry that happened."

Violet shrugged. "It's the people that are worse, I've been called every name in the book used for fat people. Whale, cow, pig, heifer, my personal favorite is when they make a mooing sound when I walk by, or say something like 'Call SeaWorld, someone let Shamu escape!'" There were tears in her eyes this time. She hadn't meant to get emotional, she'd only wanted the Captain to understand why she needed to know if she was ever going to be "normal."

Dutch reached out, putting her hand on Violet's hands that rested in her lap. "You do know that what people say isn't personal, right? They aren't talking about you."

"Huh?" Violet asked, looking shocked at the statement, and wondering if the captain was losing her marbles.

"When people say things to other people it's not a reflection of the person they're talking to, it's a reflection of their fears and concerns about themselves."

"How do you figure?"

Dutch cleared her throat. "People react to situations and other people out of their own personal reality." When she could see that Violet was still staring at her like she was insane she continued. "Everyone is a product of their environment and their experiences. Someone who has spent their life being told that being fat is wrong, being ridiculed for everything they put in their mouth, or shamed by every extra pound they carry will reflect that onto you when they deal with you. They will say mean things about you because it's what worries them most, they don't know you, they don't know your struggle, they only see what makes them afraid for themselves. And it may just be a reaction from a moment in time, maybe they don't always care about that, but maybe their mother just told them that they were getting 'chubby' and they took it out on you."

Violet did her best to understand. "But you don't do that…"

"Because I was never raised to believe that outward appearance is that important. That it's what is inside that's beautiful. Being kind of heart, generous of spirit, and strong of beliefs—those are what are important to me."

Violet blew her breath out slowly, nodding as she did. "So you're saying I need to change my thinking."

"I feel you need to change your perspective."

"My perspective?"

"The way that you see the world," Dutch said.

"And how do you see it?" Violet asked, feeling like she was growing closer to grasping how the captain's mind worked, and maybe even a revelation for herself.

"I don't worry about what the world thinks of me, I work on what I want to be. I do my best to understand people and give them what they need to succeed. I try to make a difference in the world around me, without impacting it greatly with my own way of being."

"Wow…" Violet said, suddenly understanding why the captain was the way she was. "How do you do that? How do you avoid all the negativity out there?"

Dutch shrugged. "I don't take it into myself."

Violet shook her head, amazed at this woman. "Okay, so how do you do that?"

Dutch thought for a long moment. "The other day," she began, her tone taking on a storytelling tone, "I was confronted by a woman who had very definite opinions on my appearance. She called me a dyke and said that I should just 'become a man already.'"

"What the hell?" Violet uttered in annoyance.

Dutch smiled, seeing Violet's nostrils flare in her anger. "See? That's taking it into yourself."

"How could you not?" Violet queried shocked.

"Because she wasn't really talking to me, she was talking to herself, and addressing her own fears and misunderstandings about the gay community."

"So what did you do?"

"I smiled at her and told her to have a lovely day and then walked away."

"How'd she react to that?"

"I have no idea, I never looked back. There was no need to, what she said wasn't about me."

Violet shook her head. "I don't think I could ever do that."

"What would I have achieved if I'd addressed her complaints about me?" Dutch asked.

"Maybe woken her stupid, ignorant ass up," Violet snapped, angry for Dutch.

Dutch chuckled. "Do you honestly think she would have seen me any differently if I'd been mean to her?"

Violet considered that question, then shook her head, realizing that people like that woman weren't likely to change their mind about gays ever.

"Probably not."

"But how do you think others would have viewed me if I'd blasted her with some nasty comeback?"

Violet dropped her head, seeing exactly what the captain was saying now, "Negatively, and probably thinking you were being mean to the lady."

"Thus enhancing the stereotype, or making it worse."

"So why give her that satisfaction," Violet added.

"Juist," Dutch nodded with a smile.

"Correct," Violet translated.

"Very good."

"I'm working on it," Violet said smiling.

"And doing well."

Violet looked back at the captain for a very long moment, realizing that Rebecca "Dutch" Lapp was nothing like she'd thought.

***

Rowena was unable to believe the person she was looking at was actually Rebecca. Standing at the door to the apartment they shared was a leaner, tanner and very short haired butch looking woman that only slightly resembled the girl Rebecca had been. It had been almost five months since she'd seen Rebecca, between boot camp and 'A School' where Rebecca had trained to be a Fireman Apprentice.

"Who the Hell are you?" Rowena queried, even though she was already smiling.

"Very funny," Rebecca said, stepping forward to hug her friend.

They walked into the apartment then, Rebecca put her duffel bag down next to the couch.

"What's with this?" Rowena asked, seeing the word "Dutch" on Rebecca's duffle bag.

Rebecca shrugged. "It's a nickname they gave me."

"Seriously?" Rowena asked raising an eyebrow.

"I like it," Rebecca said simply.

"You like it," Rowena said, nodding, still trying to get over the changes in her friend. "Well, I don't know how long it's going to take me to get used to this."

She reached up to ruffle Rebecca's much-shorter hair. She actually had a mullet with the hair on top shorter than the back of the hair, but even the back barely reached her collar.

"You don't like it?" Rebecca asked, reaching up self-consciously and touching her head. "It was so hard to deal with every day, so I thought this would be easier."

Rowena nodded. "It's actually pretty hot," she said, grinning.

"Hot?" Rebecca asked, looking dumbfounded.

"You look like a pretty hot little butchie," Rowena said.

"Explain," Rebecca said as she moved to sit on the couch.

"You seem to be starting to identify with your masculine side," Rowena said, "your inner boy." When Rebecca only looked further befuddled she continued, "You remember how you said you liked to wear pants? And how you've now switched to only wearing pants? It's kind of part of who you're becoming."

"You mean gay?"

"I mean, your identity," Rowena said, "you could totally just be a tomboy that doesn't like dresses and girlie stuff and that's totally cool."

Rebecca pressed her lips together in consternation, looking instantly guilty.

"Okay, you're going to need to explain that look!" Rowena exclaimed excitedly.

"Well, there was this girl at boot camp...she invited me to this place one Friday night..."

"Oh my God you went to a lesbo bar!"

"Yes," Rebecca said, sounding very circumspect, "it was definitely all women there."

"So?" Rowena asked excitedly.

Rebecca shrugged. "I felt out of place, but she did kiss me and...well...it felt pretty good."

"Oh ho! Okay, now we're talking!" Rowena crowed happily. "So are you going to date her, or?"

"They are very against gay people in the navy, so I would not take that chance," Rebecca reasoned.

"Of course not," Rowena said, mentally rolling her eyes, because she knew damned good and well people did it all the time, they just hid it.

"How are you? How is your new job going?"

Rowena knew that Rebecca was avoiding the subject, but also knew better than to give the other woman too much grief. Rebecca talked about what she wanted to when she chose and no amount of pushing would change that.

They talked about Rowena's job, a low paying cashiering gig at a big department store. Later they decided to go out to dinner to celebrate Rebecca's graduation from A school and pending assignment to an aircraft carrier.

To Rebecca's surprise, Rowena drank a few drinks that night and was fairly tipsy when they got back to the apartment. Little did she know that Rowena was actually a bit nervous in Rebecca's presence suddenly.

Entering the apartment, Rowena chattered aimlessly about the latest stupidity from their landlord.

"He actually doesn't think that we need a new faucet, like seriously? 'Cause this one leaks like crazy and half the time you end up taking a shower when you turn it too far to the left! I mean, come on! The guy is so frigging bogus!"

Rebecca nodded, noting Rowena's discomfit, but not understanding it.

"I think I'm gonna take a shower, I'm feeling all buzzy and stuff," Rowena announced, then disappeared into the bathroom closing the door.

Rebecca wandered around the apartment, straightening up out of habit. In the Navy she'd put all her old habits to good use, cleaning up, making things just right. She'd found it easy to adjust to military life. Her experiences with the other recruits had been surprisingly smooth. Her easy-going nature and ability to obey rules no matter how odd or stringent was part of her success. She'd become a model soldier and the higher-ranking officers had loved her. She never boasted about her success, and that had kept the other enlisted soldiers from hating her. All in all, it had been a very easy transition for her.

After a half an hour when Rowena hadn't come out of the bathroom Rebecca knocked on the door lightly, she could hear the shower running.

"Everything alright?" Rebecca asked.

There was a long pause before Rowena answered. "I'll be out in a few!"

Rebecca found that she was getting tired, she'd been up since very early that morning, so she decided to go to bed. She had changed into a tank top undershirt and sweatpants, what she was used to wearing to bed in the barracks. She was laying on her back, just getting comfortable when Rowena finally emerged from the bathroom.

Wrapped in a towel, her hair piled on top of her head in a messy bun, Rowena walked into the bedroom area of the apartment. Her eyes scanned Rebecca and she hesitated.

"Are you okay?" Rebecca felt the need to ask again.

"Yeah," Rowena said, shivering slightly. "I was trying to soak something out..." she said mysteriously.

"Soak something out?"

"Yeah," Rowena said, walking over to the side of the bed that Rebecca lay on, to Rebecca's complete shock, she moved to lay on top of Rebecca, levering herself up on her arms and looking down at the other girl. "Have you ever wanted to kiss me?" she asked, adding to Rebecca's shock.

"I..." Rebecca stammered looking both terrified and confused, but then another look took over in her eyes and Rowena was thrilled to note desire. "Yes, but—"

Whatever Rebecca was about to say was cut off by Rowena's lips on hers. Rebecca's lips parted in shock at first, but with insistent pressure from Rowena's lips, they yielded and accepted the kiss. Rowena's hands grasped the sheets on either side of Rebecca's head as desire flowed through her. They kissed for a long few minutes, and Rowena was surprised when Rebecca moaned softly and her lips became more insistent.

Tugging at the damp towel between them, Rowena pulled the towel out from between them. "Touch me!" she demanded in a ragged gasp.

Rebecca hesitated, but when Rowena's tongue slipped between her lips, she grasped at Rowena's skin involuntarily. Rowena's resulting moan and thrust of her hips had desire grasping at Rebecca's very core. Sliding her hands up Rowena's back, Rebecca felt unsure what to do next. Sensing her friend's hesitation, Rowena broke the kiss, leaning up to look down at Rebecca.

"Remember that movie I made you watch with me? The one with the love scene that made you blush?"

Rebecca nodded, remembering the movie well. It had been Blue Lagoon with Brook Shields and it had caused all kinds of odd feelings for her.

"Touch me like that," Rowena whispered against her lips.

Sliding her hands over Rowena's skin again, Rebecca marveled at the smoothness and heat emanating from the other woman's skin. She moved her hands down to the rise of Rowena's lower back, stopping short of touching her ass, then slid her hands up Rowena's sides. She felt Rowena shudder and tremble under hands. Rowena's lips met hers again, repeatedly, growing in intensity as her hands slid upwards.

Rowena felt like she was going up in flames, she hadn't realized she was attracted to Rebecca until she'd seen her that afternoon with her short hair, healthy glow and emanating a quiet strength that came from a new confidence in herself. Now she was amazed at how her body was reacting to the idea of teaching Rebecca how to make love. She wanted everything at once, but she realized that wasn't going to happen, since her partner was new to all of this.

144

Levering herself up slightly, she looked down at those bright blue eyes, then leaned her head down to whisper in Rebecca's ear, "Touch my breasts…"

Rebecca did as she was told, moving her hands to touch tentatively at first, but Rowena's immediate response, a low deep moan, goaded her to bolder moves. She felt Rowena's nipples grow hard under her fingers and teased them all the more. Before long Rowena was writhing and grinding her pelvis against her, moaning and breathing heavily. Rebecca found herself excited by Rowena's movements and the sounds she was making.

Wanting more, Rowena dragged her lips away from Rebecca's, and moved her body upward, hovering one of her nipples over Rebecca's mouth and pressing it down against Rebecca's lips.

"Lick me," Rowena demanded in an urgent whisper, "grab my ass!"

Rebecca did as she was commanded, her hands grabbing at Rowen's ass, her long fingers meeting in the space between Rowena's thighs, her tongue sliding over an extremely hard nipple. Rowena gave a long low moan which had Rebecca's hands tightening on Rowena's rear, pressing her fingers closer to her core. Rowena's knees pushed Rebecca's legs apart and Rowena settled herself between those strong thighs, pressing closer to Rebecca at the same time. Wanting further contact, Rowena pushed herself down against Rebecca's hands, urging her fingers closer to the wetness between her legs. Rebecca felt the slick heat and pressed her fingers closer, her mouth moving over the nipple now making Rowena moan repeatedly. Rebecca could feel a coiling of desire in her belly, and felt heat between her legs as well, a feeling of something coming, she didn't understand it, but it definitely felt good.

"Move your hands in more, touch my pussy with your fingers," Rowena finally begged, unable to take anymore. As if she'd been waiting for that command, Rebecca slid her hands further between Rowena's legs, and Rowena began to cry out and buck against her at that very moment. Rowena grinded her hips against Rebecca's core and that caused so much friction that Rebecca felt her whole body grow taut and release with the most amazing sensations. Everything was bursting at once and it felt so wonderful, her body just shuddered and tingled everywhere.

Rowena moved to lay next to Rebecca and was pleasantly surprised when Rebecca's arms stayed around her. She lay against Rebecca, her head in the hollow of the other woman's shoulders, and they both fell into a contented sleep.

The next morning dawned and Rebecca woke early as usual. Rowena was still laying against her so she didn't get up as she usually would, knowing she would wake the other woman. Instead, she lay and thought about what had occurred the night before. In the light of day it made sense to her. Rowena had been her closest friend and it had been Rowena who she'd discussed the possibility of being gay with a number of times. They'd never crossed the line into something physical, but now that they had, Rebecca felt that she was indeed gay and that their union had really seemed very natural to her.

An hour later Rowena finally stirred.

"Always awake early…" Rowena said, her tone joking even as she complained. *"And probably completely freaking out…"* she said as she levered herself up on her elbow to look down at Rebecca.

"No, I am fine," Rebecca said, surprising her friend.

"Really?" Rowena asked wide-eyed.

Rebecca nodded. *"You have always been my friend."*

"But not your lover," Rowena added.

"But I do love you," Rebecca said in such a matter-of-fact tone that Rowena knew she meant as a friend.

"Okay," she said cautiously, "but you're okay with what we did last night?"

"Yes," Rebecca said, "it felt good."

"Well, hell yeah it felt good!" Rowena laughed. "But you're okay with that happening between us?"

"Because we are not married?"

"No, dummy, because we're girls!" Rowena said, exasperated at Rebecca's confusion.

"Oh," Rebecca said, blinking a couple of times, "so you are thinking that I am afraid of being gay?"

"Yeah, kinda," Rowena said, befuddled by Rebecca's calm appearance, she truly expected the other woman to freak out.

Rebecca looked considering, then blew her breath out through her nose slowly, "I have always known that I was different, I didn't know what was different until I met you and you told me about being with girls. I didn't know if I liked women that way, but I knew that I did not like men that way. So this," she said gesturing between them, "tells me that I do like women this way, and so I am gay. It's actually a relief of sorts."

"How?" Rowena asked, struggling to understand her friend's thought process.

Rebecca shrugged slightly. "Because now I know what I am, and that leaving the Amish was the right thing to do."

"Ah-huh," Rowena mumbled. "Okay then…" She was shocked that it was that simple for Rebecca. She'd expected a very different reaction, but it wasn't the first time Rebecca surprised her with her

altered way of thinking. Rebecca really didn't think like everyone else did, it was hard to get used to.

***

"Why won't you consider getting sleeves?" Nancy asked, her tone annoyed as usual.

Dutch looked back at Nancy passively, taking in the makeup, the perfectly dyed hair with streaks and extensions, the fake nails, the outrageously expensive outfit in a bright shade of tangerine. It flitted through her mind that she wanted to say she didn't want to look fake like Nancy did, but knew it wouldn't go over well.

"I don't want tattoos," Dutch said, not for the first time.

"But it would look so hot on you!" Nancy exclaimed, as if that alone should change Dutch's mind.

Dutch blinked a couple of times, her lips curling slightly in a sardonic grin, but she refused to answer again. She continued to eat her meal and glanced around the décor of The Marine Room. Outside the window the ocean spread for miles, the sunset cast spectacular hues of orange, red and purple in the few clouds in the sky. It was a beautiful view, but Nancy noticed nothing. She was busy trying to figure out what to say to Dutch to get her to change her mind.

"I don't know why you have to be so obstinate all the time," Nancy argued. "You're way too set in your ways to for your age."

"Age has nothing to do with my ways."

"Right, I know, you're a simple boi, leading a simple life," Nancy commented with a sigh, her tone annoyed still.

Dutch canted her head slightly. "I don't feel the need to decorate my skin with pictures, why is that so bothersome for you?"

"I just think that people in a relationship should do things for the other person, because the other person's opinions should count for something."

Dutch's lips pressed together as she suppressed the desire to laugh outright at Nancy's statement. She wanted to point out that Nancy had never done anything any differently just because Dutch didn't agree with it. She just went about doing as she pleased, and what anyone thought didn't make any difference to her.

"I see," Dutch finally murmured.

"I don't think you do, but whatever," Nancy snapped, as she looked away.

Dutch's lips twitched in amusement, Nancy always thought she'd get her way by being difficult and acting angry. She wasn't sure when the other woman would learn that it never worked with her. Nancy obviously didn't realize that her angry silence was a welcome break for Dutch.

They finished their meal in silence. It took until they were back in Nancy's car with Dutch driving for Nancy to finally break the silence.

"Are you coming back to my place?" Nancy asked, her tone even.

Dutch considered the question, not sure if she wanted to re-inforce Nancy's behavior thinking she got her way by being a snot. Then she thought about the fact that it had been a month and maybe she was being unfair. In her mind, as a butch she was responsible for taking care of her woman, even if that meant just sexually since Nancy pretty much did everything else for herself or had servants who did. Sighing, she finally nodded.

She spent the next two hours dutifully taking care of Nancy's sexual needs, not once did she feel a flicker of desire. When they'd met, Nancy had been hot and heavy with the moans, sighs and words. It was the reactions she got from women that gave Dutch satisfaction, not usually any kind of physical touching by the other woman. Nancy knew that and yet had become more and more stoic during sex, even when Dutch did everything she could to please her, and did in fact bring her to orgasm over and over again. Regardless, Dutch knew that it was her decision not to go to the trouble of breaking things off with Nancy, so to her way of thinking she still needed to do her "duty."

***

"You're going to be into pillow princesses, I just know it," Rowena told her on another occasion when she'd reached a climax and Rebecca hadn't. It happened a lot when Rebecca came home on leave.

"What does that mean? Pillow Princess?" Rebecca asked glancing over at Rowena who was curled up next to her on the bed.

"It's a chick who only wants to receive sex, not actually return the favor." Rebecca blinked a couple of times, trying to reason out that term. Rowena sighed, "You don't let me touch you, and you don't insist on getting off yourself."

"I enjoy what we do," Rebecca said, her tone complacent.

Rowena blew her breath out in a rush, she knew she wasn't going to win this argument, but she also knew she was probably right. Rebecca didn't really like to be touched. On the rare occasion Rowena was brazen enough to try, Rebecca managed to move away enough to keep that from happening and then distracted her with some other sexual move. It wasn't unheard of in the world of butch lesbians that one or another didn't like to be touched. She knew that Rebecca did get off when she got Rowena excited, so Rowena used that to her advantage, making a lot of noise and thoroughly loudly enjoying Rebecca's attentions.

Things between them had been good, even though Rebecca was gone more often than not. She'd been assigned a station on the USS Carl Vinson, a Nimitz class aircraft carrier stationed out of North Island in San Diego, California. Since reporting there she'd been home twice before being deployed to the Bearing Sea and twice more since getting back to the States but was shipping out once again in June. It was her last trip home for what was expected to be a six-month tour of duty.

"Maybe you can come to San Diego for Christmas this year," Rebecca suggested, avoiding the topic they'd been discussing. She didn't understand her sexual appetites and felt very uncomfortable discussing them at any length. She didn't know if it had to do with her Amish upbringing, but she tended to think it had stunted her ability to be extremely open about sexuality.

"Are you sure you're going to be back?"

"We're due back in mid-December."

"Well, I can try," Rowena said.

"You have plenty of time to give your job notice," Rebecca insisted. "And I'll buy your ticket as an early Christmas present."

"But where would I stay?"

"I'm off base now, remember? So you can stay with me in my apartment there."

Rowena had moved up in the department store and was now a manager. She was finally making enough money to afford her own rent. She thought it was convenient that Rebecca had not moved off base into her own place until she'd told Rebecca that she would no longer accept her help with the apartment. Rebecca had argued with her about it, but Rowena had refused.

"Okay, sounds like fun," Rowena said, truthfully very excited to get go back 'home' to California, even if it was just for a visit.

She knew that Rebecca was avoiding talking about the comment she'd made about her being with pillow princesses. It bugged her that Rebecca wouldn't let her reciprocate, it went against her grain, but she knew she couldn't engage Rebecca in a discussion about it, so she just went with the flow.

Chapter 5

"I'd say the psychological effects of losing a parent is fairly devastating to a child," Samantha Briggs said in answer to her child psychology professor's latest question. She'd taken the course to fulfill her science requirement, never realizing that it would get into sensitive areas.

"Do you feel it's worse than the trauma of... say molestation?" the professor posed the question.

"Fortunately, I wouldn't know," Samantha said, "my mothers were always careful to keep me away from men they didn't trust."

"Your mothers..." the professor echoed, clearly momentarily stumped.

"They were lesbians," Samantha provided.

"Were?" the professor queried, his tone edging on sneering.

"One of them died," Samantha said the words, her eyes turning to ice as she did.

Many members of the class looked her way. There were quiet murmurs of surprise and hushed comments of "that sucks" or "how awful." The professor had the temerity to look embarrassed by his own insolent thoughts. He cleared his throat and quickly moved on, posing another question, pointedly of a different nature to someone on the opposite side of the class.

Later, as Samantha sat at a table in the quad, going over her notes for the test in her next class, she felt someone move to stand behind her. Glancing back, she recognized a girl from her psychology class. She wondered if this was the perquisite "I'm sorry about your mother" conversation. It happened a lot whenever she had to tell someone that her mother had died almost two years before. She'd grown to almost resent the conversations, because they never felt honest and real to her.

"You're Samantha Briggs," the young woman stated.

Samantha couldn't help but respond with a fairly sarcastic, "I know."

The young woman drew in a breath, and then moved to sit down on the bench next to Samantha. Samantha had to stop herself from making another sarcastic about the woman inviting herself to sit down. She couldn't, however, stop the grunt of annoyance and the sharp movement of setting her notes aside to look at the newcomer directly. It was obvious the woman had something to say: Sam was hoping that if she gave her all of her attention, she'd say it and then go away.

"It's your mother's fault I lost my family," Desolé Stanton practically spat.

Samantha blinked repeatedly, shocked by not only the tone, but by the words. Her first thought was that this woman's family was killed in a fire that Hunter had worked, but then she looked more closely at the woman sitting next to her. Suddenly understanding dawned, Hunter had told her that Kori's daughter was going to Berkley too. Now here she was accusing Hunter of taking away her family? Seriously?

Samantha allowed a sardonic grin to tug at her lips. Her eyes reflected her disdain for this woman's choice of words.

"You lost your family?" Samantha queried conversationally. "How interesting."

"Your mother ruined my family!" Desolé snapped, surprised at Samantha's attitude. She'd expected the younger woman to at least be apologetic.

Samantha nodded slowly, a look of *okay I'll humor you* on her face.

"Do tell me how."

Nothing in her voice indicated a true invitation, but Desolé took that opportunity anyway.

"She got my mother to divorce my father, he's miserable, I'm miserable. My brother is so stupid, he thinks it's okay, so I'm not talking to him!" Desolé raged.

Samantha's eyes widened with the drama level of the other woman's rant, even as her lips pursed derisively. This woman did like to go on, didn't she?

"I'm sorry, she *got* your mother to divorce your father? She held a gun to your mother's head and forced her to do it?" Samantha asked mildly.

Desolé pressed her lips together in irritation.

"You know what I mean!"

Samantha tilted her head, giving Desolé a sidelong look.

"Do I?"

Desolé huffed out a breath, throwing her hands up in a gesture of futility.

"She's killing my family!"

Samantha's eyes narrowed then, as her lips drew back in a snarl. "Killing them? Seriously!" she snapped, anger now flashing in her eyes. "I'm sorry if your perfect little life got disrupted by divorce, I'm sorry that your daddy is *sad*," the word dripped with sarcasm. "I'm sorry that you and your *adult* brother are having a rough time because Mommy and Daddy are splitting up, because your mother finally chose to do something for her, instead of for you, you simpering brat! But I don't have the time or the desire to sit here and listen to you complain about *my* mother, who watched the woman she loved die in front of her less than two years ago! And I'm not going to listen to you claim that *my* mother is to blame for your stupid little problems when she's finally happy again. And in case you couldn't be bothered to notice so is *your* mother! But I'm guessing you don't notice stuff like that, you only notice that you're not happy, 'cause Mommy and Daddy don't live together anymore! At least they're both *alive*! *My* mother *died*, you mewling little twit, so take your crap and shove it!"

With that, Samantha grabbed her backpack and her notes and stormed off, leaving Desolé to sit staring, open-mouthed after her.

It took Desolé a full hour to replay everything that Samantha Briggs had said to her, and it only took another minute to realize how ridiculous she'd been acting when she'd confronted the younger girl. She couldn't believe how foolish she'd been! It took her another couple of hours to figure out where Samantha lived on campus and for her to make it to Samantha's door in the dormitory. With a shaking hand she knocked on the door. She heard Samantha call out "Come!"

Walking inside, Desolé saw Samantha sitting on her bed. She looked shocked to see Desolé. To gather her thoughts before she spoke, Desolé looked around the room, Samantha's side of the room held artwork, posters, small canvases with paintings of various subjects. One canvas was framed and hung above Samantha's bed, and it was textured with red, brownish and yellow colors.

"That's beautiful…" Desolé breathed as she stared at the painting.

"My mother painted that," Samantha stated simply.

Desolé looked at Samantha drew in a sharp breath, feeling the stab of sorrow at realizing she'd probably just upset the other woman again, even if Samantha was stubbornly gritting her teeth, the emotion in her eyes was hard to miss.

"What do you want?" Samantha's sharp tone, in contrast to the look in her eyes moments before…

"I wanted to apologize," Desolé began.

"Don't bother," Samantha said, "people like you are never really sorry. You just feel bad because my mother died and you were an ass about it."

Desolé was taken back by the cynical words, as well as the anger now flashing in the younger woman's eyes. She found herself getting mad too.

"I'm trying to…" Desolé reasoned.

"To not look bad, because you're afraid of what I'll tell your mother," Samantha told her.

Desolé closed her mouth, swallowing convulsively, having never considered that at all. Her anger sparked then.

"Are you always so cynical?" Desolé queried.

"Only when the situation warrants it."

"I'm trying to say I'm sorry!" Desolé raged.

"Fine! You said it! Now get the fuck out!" Samantha yelled, gesturing to the door.

Suddenly there was a loud bang as a large textbook dropped off the desk to Samantha's right. Desolé jumped at the loud sound, but Samantha winced instantly.

"Sorry Mom," Samantha muttered quietly, her head bowed.

"Huh?" Desolé asked, stunned by the sudden change in Samantha's attitude.

Samantha blew her breath out in exasperation. "My mom gets mad when I cuss."

Desolé raised an eyebrow. "Your mom? Does she have your room bugged or something?"

Samantha snickered at the question, shaking her head. "Not that mom."

Desolé gave Samantha a wary look, wondering if the girl was losing it. "Come again?"

Samantha rolled her eyes, knowing she was about to sound like a nut to the other girl. "My mother's spirit is still around, she keeps an eye on me and my other mom."

"Her spirit…" Desolé repeated, her tone skeptical.

Samantha canted her head. "Kori has met her."

"My mom?" Desolé repeated.

"Yep, and my mom actually hugged her," Sam said, grinning at the shocked look on the other woman's face now.

"No way…" Desolé said, shaking her head. "My mom doesn't believe in that stuff."

"Wanna bet?" Samantha widened her eyes in a challenge.

Desolé didn't answer at first, looking like she really wanted to argue. Just then there was a dance of color in the room and Samantha immediately looked up at the stained glass butterfly that hung from the light fixture between them. The butterfly was turning and the sunlight streaming through window was catching the colors and throwing them throughout the room.

"That's her…" Samantha told Desolé.

"No," Desolé said, shaking her head, "that's from the AC unit."

Samantha glanced at the vent near the light fixture, the small red streamer hanging from it wasn't moving at all.

"Then why's that not moving?" she asked, pointing to the red crepe paper.

Desolé looked up to where Samantha was pointing and couldn't believe what she was seeing. The butterfly was still moving in a slow circle, but there was no movement of the streamer. She gestured to the window then.

"Then there's a breeze…" she began, but then saw that the window was closed. "Holy…shit…" she murmured as she glanced up at the butterfly. "That's really her doing that?"

Samantha nodded, smiling in spite of her previous anger, warmed by the fact that her mother was with her at that moment. It made her realize that her mother didn't want her to fight with this other woman, she was trying to make peace. As that thought occurred, she felt a warmth on her heart, and she knew that her mother was telling her she was right. Reaching up, she touched the spot where she felt the warmth, tears again in her eyes.

"Okay, Mom… I got it," Samantha whispered as a tear fell on her own hand.

"Got what?" Desolé asked, her tone curious now.

Samantha sighed, smiling. "She wants me to stop being mean, and just accept your apology."

"How do you know?" Desolé asked, her tone soft now.

Samantha bit her lower lip.

"I felt it," she said, patting the spot over her heart.

"That is so cool…" Desolé breathed.

In that moment, the argument was over.

***

The fire season ramped up significantly in Southern California when the Santa Ana winds kicked in. Hot gusts from the east were whipping up fires toward the coast and the more populated areas of San Diego. One particular fire started at the east end of the Santa Rosa San Jacinto Mountains. The crew was called out to create a fire break ten miles away. The terrain was rough, and thick with heavy brush.

Dutch's crew and one other were working away, but not making much headway due to the wooded terrain. After a report that the Santa Ana winds were starting to push the fire faster, Dutch decided to man one of the chainsaws herself. She hacked through drought-toughened trunks of bushes that were taller than her. They worked for three hours, not making a lot of progress, but then they could see the smoke from the fire. The team was ordered to shift north and west by ten miles.

The team was climbing onto the bus as Dutch climbed into her work truck. Suddenly she felt a sharp pain in her back and it completely gave out, she crumpled to the ground. Violet and two other inmates who weren't on the bus yet, ran to her aide.

"Captain! Are you okay?" Violet exclaimed, already suspecting it was Dutch's back that had caused the collapse.

The three inmates helped Dutch to a seated position, Dutch did her best to lean against the truck to try and take her weight off her back.

"I'm okay," Dutch said, nodding to the inmates, "thanks."

"It's your back, isn't it?" Violet asked.

"Of course," Dutch said with a roll of her eyes.

"You shouldn't have been wielding that chainsaw," one of the other inmates chided, grinning.

Dutch grinned wryly. "Probably not."

"Cap?" one of the Cal Fire employees queried from the driver's seat of the bus.

"I'm good," Dutch said. "I know, we need to get going. Can you ladies help me up?" She queried lifting up her arms and starting to position herself to stand.

"Cap, I don't think—" Was all Violet had the time to get out, but the captain was on the move. Before she was fully standing though, she winced and grunted in pain and went down again.

"Okay, not so much here..." Dutch said, sounding out of breath.

"We need to get you back to camp," Violet told Dutch, glancing at the bus driver who nodded in agreement.

"Hastings, you drive the cap's truck back, we'll head over to our next spot. Stay in radio contact."

"Yes ma'am," Violet said, gesturing for the other two inmates to help her get Dutch up and into the passenger seat of the truck.

"Radio check," the bus driver's voice came over the radio.

Dutch picked up the mic and said, "Check."

"10-4, headed out, get back safe, cap," the bus driver said, waving as she pulled out of the area and onto the dirt access road.

Dutch lay over on her side on the bench seat of the truck, wincing as she did.

"Don't worry, I'll get you back to camp and get the good stuff in you," Violet said.

"I have Vicodin in here," Dutch said, opening the glove box and taking out a bottle. She popped a pill in her mouth, picking up a bottle of water, out of the case on the passenger floor, opening it and swallowing the pill.

"Well that should start to help," Violet said, starting the truck and putting it into gear.

The access road was bumpy, which had Dutch wincing at each jolt, and Violet saying "Sorry!" every time.

"It's not your fault the road is bumpy, Vi, it's okay," Dutch finally said after the fifth apology.

"I know, but I know you're hurting and I'm trying not to make it worse."

"Well, it's going to suck 'til we get off this access road, that's just a given."

The dirt road was naturally rutted with bumps from rains and wind over the years. It took a full fifteen minutes to get to the proper paved road. Dutch breathed a sigh of relief at the relatively smooth surface. Violet laughed softly at the sound.

They were a half hour into their drive back to the camp when there was a radio call.

"1477?" came the query, siting Dutch's call sign.

"Lapp here," Dutch replied into the mic.

162

"Captain, this is Chief Sandoval, I understand you're heading back to camp."

"Yes, ma'am," Dutch replied.

"I need to detour you. We have some people who should be evacuating near Cottonwood Creek and one of our planes just caught movement as they flew over. Can you go up and see if they've gotten word? They're way back in there."

Dutch nodded, knowing that it was important to make sure people had time to evacuate their property, lest they get caught in the fire.

"Yeah, Chief we can handle it. What's the location?"

"South of 79, off Allmouth, either loop should take you right there. Looks like they have horses and maybe even cattle. Gonna take them time to get them out."

"Got it, we're on it." Dutch said.

"10-4, thanks Dutch," the chief said, smiling at her end.

"So, road trip?" Violet asked her tone overly bright.

Dutch chuckled. "Apparently. Cottonwood is about ten miles down from here, you'll see the exit."

Violet nodded. Following Dutch's directions, she got them to the location in just under a half an hour. As she pulled up to the ranch, she could see that there were at least three horses in the back field, and she hear mooing from somewhere nearby. Looking over at Dutch she could see that she was getting sleepy from the Vicodin she'd taken.

"Want me to handle this?" Violet asked, loathing the idea of the captain having to get out of the truck, possibly hurting herself more.

"Nah," Dutch said, shaking her head and she levered herself up to a seated position, "no offense, but they're probably not even going to like hearing this from me..." Her voice trailed off as she curled her lips in consternation.

"But they definitely won't listen to an inmate in orange, right?" Violet replied, with no accusation or annoyance in her voice.

"Yeah," Dutch said, not sounding pleased by the idea. "I'll be back."

A half an hour later, Dutch still hadn't come back. Violet finally got out of the truck to walk towards the front of the property. She could see Dutch standing talking to the resident, she was holding the railing of the fence, the resident was gesturing and talking, and Violet could hear that the man's voice was raised. Violet stayed back, so as not to interrupt what she hoped was a negotiation to get the man off the property. She could hear the radio in the truck through the open windows but couldn't hear what was being said. She figured it was likely just radio chatter between the other crews and the camp. The winds started whipping up dirt and blowing it all around her, it was a hot wind.

After another five minutes, Dutch finally put her hands up in surrender, and turned to walk back to the truck. Violet could see she was hurting from standing for so long. The radio in the truck was sounding again as the climbed into the seat.

"Captain Lapp, come in!" the voice was calling.

"This is Lapp, go ahead," Dutch said into the mic.

"What's your current location?" the dispatcher asked.

"We're about three miles south of 79 at Cottonwood Creek."

"You need to get out of there," the dispatcher said, with a tinge of panic in her voice.

"What's going on?" Dutch asked, even as she motioned for Violet to start the truck and drive.

"The fire's coming down fast, and it's headed your way. We thought you'd have been back at camp by now."

"This guy doesn't want to leave," Dutch said, glancing over her shoulder at the house they were leaving behind.

"That's on him, you need to get out of there!" the dispatcher barked.

"Got it," Dutch said, glancing to her right and seeing what the dispatcher was talking about, the fire was not far away at all. She estimated two miles tops. "We're not going to make it..." Dutch muttered, feeling a tight knot in her stomach. "We need to find shelter, and we need to find it now."

"There was a shed on the way down to Allmouth, I think it's about a mile up the road!" Violet said, having noticed the outbuilding as she was driving, thinking that it was far too small to be the house they were looking for.

"Hit it!" Dutch said, motioning her forward.

Within a minute they pulled to a stop.

"Grab your gloves, helmet and your pack. Also grab the axe!" Dutch told Violet as they got out of the truck. Dutch did the same.

The outbuilding appeared to be made out of stone, which would hopefully save them from the fire. They had to hike around a quarter of a mile past where they road ended, which was hard to accomplish with Dutch in pain. But within five minutes they were at the shelter. Dutch looked it over, moving slowly but efficiently around the small structure. It was little more than a shed but fortunately, even the roof was terracotta Spanish style tiles.

"This was a good catch," Dutch told Violet, even as she pulled her portable radio out of the backpack she'd grabbed. "Get your helmet and gloves on and see if you can cut back some of this brush, clear us a little bit of space, so it maybe won't come too close. We don't want to be baked like bread," she said, quirking a grin, even though she knew this could be serious. "Camp, come in," she said into the radio, even as Violet set to work on the brush around the small shelter.

"Camp here, go 1477."

"How far is the fire from our location?"

"Checking," dispatch said, using the chip in the phone to pin-point their location. "You've got maybe ten minutes, fifteen tops."

"10-4, we've located some shelter, we'll be hunkering down here."

"10-4, 1477, we'll send help as soon as the fire clears."

"10-4," Dutch said. "Come on, Vi, that's good, let's get inside."

Inside the shelter, Dutch moved to sit in the center.

"Should we deploy our fire shelters?" Violet asked, her voice trembling.

"Yeah, just to be safe." She reached out, touching Violet on the shoulder. "It's going to be okay, Vi," she said as confidently as she could. "You found us a good spot, between this and the fire shelter, we'll be fine, okay?"

166

Violet drew a deep breath in through her nose, tears shining in her eyes, even as she nodded.

"Okay, deploy as you learned, make sure you leave your gloves and helmet on. Take water in with you," Dutch told her.

The fire shelter was a sort of human sized tent made of an outer layer of aluminum foil and an inner layer of silica that would project heat away from the person inside. They were designed to withstand a short-lived grass fire. Each probationary firefighter was taught to deploy the shelter as quickly as possible.

Violet did an admirable job unpacking her shelter and deploying it. Dutch took a little longer, because of her back. Once in her shelter, Dutch continued to give instruction. Knowing that Violet was freaking out and needed to focus on what was important at the moment. The roar and crackling of the fire could be heard not too far from them.

"Remember, keep your face close to the ground. We won't have the fire burn over us with the shelter, hopefully, but we don't want to take any chance. Okay?"

"Okay," Violet replied, her voice muffled by her shelter.

Dutch heard the other woman sniff and she knew that Violet was really worried. Taking the chance, Dutch reached out of her shelter and put her hand into Violet's, touching her hand. To her surprise Violet grabbed her hand, holding it tight.

"Vi…it's going to be okay. Alright? It is. You did great finding this shelter. The fire isn't even going to touch us."

Violet breathed out shakily.

"So…" Dutch said into the silence, "you come here often?"

Violet laughed despite her tears and worry. "Well, I really try to avoid shacks out in the middle of nowhere…"

"Oh sure, I bet you say that to all the boys."

Violet laughed again. "Damn, you caught me!"

"I tell you, those bad girls are the worst…" Dutch sighed.

"Well, you know, good girls go to heaven, bad girls go everywhere!"

"Including random shelters?"

"Including those, yes."

Dutch felt Violet's hand tighten in hers as the fire drew inexorably closer.

"So, heard from Michael lately?" Dutch asked, hoping to distract Violet.

Violet was quiet for a moment, but forced herself to answer, knowing what Dutch was doing and appreciating it intensely.

"Oh yes, I got a letter again the other day, he drew me on a fire truck."

"Aww, was it a good representation?"

"It was pretty good," Violet said, smiling. "I mean, the tires on the front were way smaller than the ones on the back, and the ladder wasn't even connected to the rig, but…"

Dutch chuckled. "Well, you know, maybe it was Picasso-inspired."

"Well, there were no extra boobs on my picture, so…at least he got that right."

Dutch laughed out loud at that, hoping to mask a little bit of the sound of the fire right outside the shelter. Regardless, Violet gasped, clenching at Dutch's hand even harder.

"Vi, it's okay, tell me about the letter from your son, what did he say?"

"He…he…he said that he's excited about second grade in August…"

"Oh yeah, does he like school?"

"He does, it's funny. I never liked school, but he loves it. He's really social."

"Social is good," Dutch commented.

"Yeah, I'm just hoping he doesn't get too social. The first-grade teacher was saying that he was exhibiting signs of ADHD, so I worry."

"So if he has it, you figure out the best way to deal with it."

"I know, I just worry that his father will want to put him on medication, and I really don't want to do that."

"You're his mother, you can refuse, fight him on it. Kids that young shouldn't be medicated if they don't need to be."

"I know, I just hope I can convince Jeff."

"Vi? Do you hear that?" Dutch said.

"What?"

"It passed us."

"It did," Violet said, breathing a loud sigh of relief. "Is it okay to unshelter?"

Dutch put her other hand out of her shelter and felt the temps in the room, it was warm, but not really hot. "Yep, I think we're good."

They both emerged from their shelters, sitting up and smiling at each other. Dutch reached out and hugged Violet.

"You did really good Vi, really good," she said sincerely.

"Thanks to you."

"No, thanks to you knowing your stuff and seeing this shelter. You're getting credit for this one," Dutch said with a grin as they parted. Dutch radioed into to dispatch then.

"Dutch, you two okay?" the dispatcher exclaimed, clearly happy to hear from them. "Are you medium, or extra crispy?"

"Actually, we're good," Dutch said, her eyes crinkling at the corners as she smiled, "thanks to my trusty sidekick here, who found us shelter and cleared it for us. We're five by five."

"10-4, Captain, great to hear! Go Hastings!" The dispatcher crowed. "So you're secure for the moment?"

"Yeah, we're good, but we have no way back. Please, just send someone to get us before the coyotes do." Dutch winked at Violet.

"10-4 Captain, we'll get someone out there in approximately an hour."

"Works for me."

They signed off and Dutch put the radio away.

"I'm going to take a quick look outside to see how we're doing," Violet said, knowing that the captain's back was still hurting by the way she was moving. Violet got up and walked to the opening in the wall, peering out. "All in the black," she said, smiling.

In the black meant that all of the "fuel" for the fire had been burned, and was therefore unable to burn again, thus making is safer for people to be in.

"Just want we want," Dutch said smiling. "Do I want to know how my truck is?"

Violet peered around the corner, finally stepping out of the shelter and walking a few feet. She came back shaking her head. "Probably not."

"Time for an upgrade," Dutch said amicably, as she moved carefully to sit and lean against the wall of the small shelter.

"How are you doing?" Violet asked as she moved to sit across from Dutch on the dirt floor.

"I'm alright, my back still hurts, but this could have been so much worse…" Her voice trailed off as she contemplated the possibilities.

"I know," Violet agreed, nodding, "we were lucky."

"And smart," Dutch added pointedly.

Violet nodded, a shy smile on her lips. "I learned from the best."

"Uh-huh," Dutch replied, rolling her eyes.

"How long have you been a firefighter?"

"About eighteen years. I started when I was in the Navy."

"Wow, really? What made you decide to do that?"

Dutch gave a short snort, shrugging, "I wanted to become Damage Controlman, but you had to do the fireman apprentice first, and I really got into it at that point."

"What's a Damage Controlman?"

"It's basically the emergency response for a ship, fire, EMT, all that kind of stuff. They also take care of the ship with safety issues."

"Wow. Ship? What kind of ship were you on?"

"I was on a Nimitz Class aircraft carrier, called the Carl Vinson."

"And how long were you in the navy?"

"Eight years."

"And stationed…"

"In San Diego. Well, the ship docked here in San Diego, but we were deployed most of that time."

"Anywhere interesting?" Violet asked, hopefully.

Dutch shrugged again. "If you consider either the Indian Ocean, the North Arabian Sea or the Bering Sea interesting, then sure."

"But did you get to visit countries too?"

"Sure. Africa, Malaysia, India. Japan, Russia, and South Korea."

"Wow, that's a lot! I've never been anywhere."

"Well, you should change that."

Violet rolled her eyes. "I wish."

"Anything is possible."

Violet didn't answer, just shrugging.

"What?" Dutch asked.

"Jeff doesn't travel, he gets air sick."

Dutch pressed her lips together, doing her best to keep her opinion to herself. Instead, she asked, "How is that going?"

"What? Jeff?" Violet asked, having mentioned to Dutch once that Jeff had never come to visit her since she was in. Dutch nodded. "Technically I'm still married to him."

"Technically?" Dutch queried.

"Yes, on paper."

"He still hasn't made a move to come visit?"

"No, and I'm okay with that."

"Why?" Dutch asked, curious as to Violet's state of mind.

Violet shrugged, staring at the floor in front of her. "I've heard he's seeing someone."

"And you're okay with that?"

Violet's lips twitched. "I've never really loved him. I mean, not like the books all say love is supposed to be anyway."

Dutch grinned at that. "Well, that I understand."

"Really?" Violet asked surprised. "You don't love Nancy?"

Dutch made a noise in the back of her throat, shaking her head as she did. "Not hardly, I uh," she hedged, touching her forefinger to the side of her nose, "pass time with her."

"Wow," Violet intoned. "I just…wow…"

"Why are you surprised?" Dutch asked, curious now.

Violet shrugged. "She's gorgeous, I just figured…" Her voice trailed off as she realized that she'd assumed Dutch loved the other woman because of that and it sounded hollow now, even in her own head.

"Beauty isn't an equivalent for love, Violet," Dutch said quietly.

"I know, I guess, I just…" She shrugged as her voice trailed off again.

"You just what?" Dutch asked, not wanting to let this go because she really wanted Violet to understand.

Violet pulled a small weed that grew in the dirt of the shelter and picked at it as she shrugged.

"I guess with you being so handsome, and her being…you know…so gorgeous…that you'd just be perfect together."

Dutch grimaced slightly. "Violet, looks are not a replacement for a personality, a heart, a soul, looks are just what you're born with or what you buy."

"Buy?" Violet queried, not imagining that anything on the captain was fake.

Dutch quirked her lips. "Think she was born with that rack?"

"N...no...but..."

"No," Dutch said, for once willing to indulge in a little bit of gossip to prove her point. "She wasn't born with a lot of the things she presents. Regardless that would be okay, if she was a good person. She's not a good person, Vi. I can never picture myself being in love with someone who isn't a good person at their very core."

"Have you ever been in love?" Violet asked, feeling brave from the incident they'd just experienced together. Dutch didn't seem to mind the question at all.

"No, not totally," Dutch said, her smile wistful.

"But almost?" Violet asked.

"Close," Dutch said, "but it wasn't quite right."

Violet wanted to ask who she meant but didn't think she was that brave. Dutch surprised her by telling her anyway.

"Her name is Rowena, she was my first best friend. Well, my first everything really."

"Will you tell me about her?"

"If you want to hear it," Dutch told her.

"Please," Violet said, thrilled that the captain trusted her enough with this kind of information. Most of the officers would never share personal information with inmates. Violet figured that the captain, not being a correctional officer, probably didn't feel like she had to adhere to such rules. Little did she know that Dutch actually trusted her implicitly.

Dutch told Violet the story of her and Rowena, how they'd met, how they'd left for New York together and even why she'd joined the navy.

"Wow, you sent her your paycheck every month?" Violet queried.

Dutch shrugged. "What was I going to do with the money? My needs were simple."

"Still, that's really nice…" Her voice trailed off as she shook her head. She couldn't even get Jeff to keep a job long enough to take care of rent.

"She was my only friend, I wanted to make sure she was okay."

"Man, I could definitely do with friends like you," Violet said, awestruck.

Dutch canted her head slightly. "I thought we were friends."

Violet blinked a couple of times, feeling her heart swell at the simple statement.

"I, well, we are…I mean, I didn't know if…but I'd like to be…I mean…" Violet stammered feeling stupid suddenly.

"We are," Dutch indicated assuredly.

Violet smiled, nodding. "I'm glad."

"Me too."

"So, you didn't love Rowena?"

"I did, but, I guess it's like what people say, I loved her, but I wasn't in love with her."

"Oh," Violet said, feeling almost sad at that statement, "it seems like you two were good together."

"We were, we had a lot of good times, but in the end, we just weren't meant to be together as a couple. She taught me a lot of things and helped me realize who I was meant to be, but it just wasn't a love match." Rebecca remembered well the moment when she realized that she wasn't in love with Rowena.

"Wow, look at you, driving and stuff…" Rowena said, smiling.

Rebecca rolled her eyes. "You have to drive in San Diego, but this isn't even my car."

"Who's car is it?" Rowena asked, admiring the leather upholstery of the classic Mustang.

"One of the guys in my squad," Rebecca said, "he said I had to have a cool car to pick up my 'friend.'"

Rowena canted her head. "Does he know?"

Rebecca shrugged. "He hasn't said anything, I think he just likes to show off."

"Well, it is nice…" The Mustang was classic Candy Apple Red, and was beautifully restored, with shining chrome and beige leather seats. "So, are you dating anyone?" she asked, her tone purposefully casual.

Rebecca shook her head, shrugging again.

"Seriously?" Rowena queried. "No one? Not even a one-night stand kind of thing?"

"What is the point in that?"

"Um, sex!" Rowena exclaimed. Rebecca didn't answer, looking simply unphased by the comment. "Well, I'm seeing someone." Rebecca nodded, her look unchanged. "That doesn't bother you?"

"Why should it?"

"Well, I mean, it might. I mean…we've been kind of a thing."

"A thing?" Rebecca queried, the term sounding strange to her.

"Yeah, you know, kind of like a couple, but kind of not."

Rebecca's lips twitched, like she was trying to reconcile the phrases. "But you are a couple with this other person?"

"Well, yeah, I mean, I guess so." Rowena realized that her current relationship in New York wasn't really defined either. *"I guess I never really ask this kind of stuff. But it's different with you."*

"Why?"

Rowena gave an exasperated sigh. *"I don't know, I guess because you're not like a normal lesbian, bi-sexual, being."*

Rebecca's lips tugged in a slight grin. *"I am undefined."*

Rowena chuckled. *"I guess you kind of are."*

"And we were undefined."

"As a couple, yes, we weren't official, and it was hard to be with you being way the hell over here…and holy shit this place is cool!" Rowena finally looked around her surroundings seeing the ocean to the left of them as they got on the freeway. *"Anyway, so like we never really talked about being exclusive or anything, but with you, it's weird anyway…"*

"Weird," Rebecca repeated.

"Well you know with the Amish thing and all, it isn't like you had relationships prior to us anyway, right?"

"Not sexual relationships, no," Rebecca confirmed unnecessarily.

"Right, so you maybe wouldn't have expected anything, or maybe you thought we were like married, how do I know?"

"You did not know."

"Right. So I wouldn't know if you were going to be all pissed off and hurt that I was dating someone."

"But I am not."

"Right, you say that, but are you being honest?" Rowena asked doggedly.

"I am always honest."

Rowena blew her breath out, shaking her head. "Yeah, I know, I should have known. So in your head, what are we?"

"We are friends."

"That have sex," Rowena added.

"Yes."

"So basically friends with benefits."

Rebecca looked surprised by the phrase, but nodded all the same. "Okay."

It astounded Rowena that her friend was able to so easily accept things as they were. It wasn't something most people could do.

Later that night they'd had dinner and eventually ended up in bed together. Afterward they lay together with Rebecca holding Rowena as she always did.

"So this other person you are seeing would be okay with us doing this?" Rebecca asked, still trying to understand everything.

"Yeah, she's cool, we're kind of in an open relationship kinda thing."

"Open relationship?"

"Yeah, where I do my thing, she does hers."

"So not really a relationship."

Rowena contemplated that question, in truth that was accurate. "I guess, I mean, we hang out and stuff, but we aren't all exclusive."

"And that is okay with you." It wasn't a question.

"Yeah," Rowena said, shrugging, "it isn't like I'm in love or anything, just like us."

"We are not in love," Rebecca said, with a hint of a question in her tone.

Rowena moved out of Rebecca's arms to sit up and look back down at Rebecca. "You, I mean, you aren't, are you?"

Both her tone and her look indicated that she was suddenly worried.

"I love you," Rebecca said simply.

"Right, but you're not in love with me, right?"

"What is the difference?"

Rowena gave a soft laugh, putting her tongue between her teeth trying to figure out how to explain it.

"Well, do you like think of me all the time?"

Rebecca looked mystified by the question, blinking a couple of times, then shook her head.

"Do you feel like you can't live without me?"

"I live without you all the time, we live in different cities," Rebecca said logically.

Rowena laughed, nodding. "True, but does it bug you?"

"I miss you sometimes."

"Right, but that's not love necessarily. Okay, let me ask you one simple thing."

"What?"

"Does the thought of me sleeping with someone else, having sex with someone else," she qualified when she could see that Rebecca was taking her literally on the 'sleeping' part, "bother you?"

Rebecca looked pensive, but finally shook her head.

"If you were in love with me, it would." Rowena said simply.

"Oh," Rebecca said, nodding, looking pleased with that guileless answer.

"So, are you two still friends?" Violet asked, after Dutch related how she figured out she wasn't in love with Rowena.

"Oh yeah, I don't see her very often these days, she's married to another sailor, so she's always stationed here, there, and everywhere."

"She married a sailor?"

"Yep," Dutch nodded, smiling.

"Someone you knew?"

"Yes, she was one of my commanding officers before I left the navy. I introduced them."

"Wow," Violet said, smiling.

"So would you say you're in love with your husband?"

Violet chuckled. "Well, according to Rowena's definition it would seem like I am, I mean it bothers me that he's sleeping with someone else."

"So is that a yes?"

"No," Violet said, shaking her head. "I'm not sad that he's sleeping with someone else. I'm mad that he's doing it while I'm stuck in here, and that he hasn't just filed for a divorce."

"Oh," Dutch said, widening her eyes slightly.

"I'm also mad that he just didn't divorce me before all of this happened. I could have gone back to San Diego proper and done something else with my life. Not been stuck out in the sticks with a job that he moved us here for, and then promptly lost, leaving us essentially stranded."

"Is that what happened?" Dutch asked.

"Yes, he got this job at the golf course, doing landscaping. We moved all the way out to Borrego Springs and got a mobile home so he could work there. I left a decent secretary job and all my family and friends to go with him because of Michael. Then he lost that job and kept losing them."

Dutch pursed her lips, not thinking much of a man that couldn't provide for his family.

"Were there reasons he lost the jobs? I mean, reasons out of his control."

"No, just having an attitude with the boss, showing up late, showing up drunk, sometimes not showing up at all..." Violet sighed.

"Oh. I'm sorry."

Violet shrugged. "It's my fault, I found it necessary to stick with him even when he'd already proved that he wasn't the man I had thought he was."

"How did you meet him?"

"At a bar, I was with some friends, he 'noticed' me."

"Noticed you?" Dutch asked.

"You know, paid attention to me instead of to my skinny, pretty friends," Violet said, grimacing as she saw the captain's lips tighten at her phrase, but it was truly how she'd seen it in those days and still basically did.

"But he wasn't what he seemed?" Dutch asked, seeing that Violet already knew what she'd say about her insulting herself.

"No, I thought he was nice man who wanted a relationship with a woman for more than her looks."

"Not what happened?"

"No, he was living with his parents, and basically latched on to me because my family had money and he figured he'd be able to get some of it if he was with me."

"So what happened?"

"My parents saw him for what he was, and badgered me about it, which of course made me more determined to stay with him.

It was dumb, but then I got pregnant, and all reason went out the window."

"You stayed with him for your son."

"Yes, Michael makes everything worth it, of course then I had to go and be dumb, and now I'm not with him."

"But you will be again, soon," Dutch assured her.

"Six months, that's what I've got left."

Dutch smiled, nodding.

Another half an hour and they were "rescued." Violet was hailed as a hero and Dutch fully supported the title.

A week later, Violet received a Certificate of Achievement for her assistance to a fellow firefighter. Violet's son and mother were there to see her presented, Dutch had invited them personally, it was a very proud moment for Violet. Jeff didn't bother to even offer an excuse for not coming. It said everything to Dutch about the man's character.

Chapter 6

After the incident, Violet was finally made a 'swamper,' so she supervised a unit of camp members. She did an excellent job, even as the fire season stretched into October. Time flew by and before Violet knew it, she was a day from being released. To celebrate the fire teams got together to throw her a going away party. Dutch and the other fire supervisors put money together to buy steaks to grill and food to cook in the camp kitchen. Dutch handled the grill, cooking steaks, burgers, and chicken for the camp's one hundred inmates and twenty-two staff. There were non-alcoholic drinks and sodas and even sparkling cider for toasting. Lastly there were cakes decorated with little fire trucks and toy firemen and women. It was a wonderful evening, and Violet was so grateful to be part of such an incredible group of people. It was odd, but she was feeling a bit sad about leaving.

"You're what?" Dutch asked incredulously.

"I'm a little bit sad," Violet repeated. "You and all the other staff are so great, and so are so many of the girls here…"

"Yeah, but freedom…"

"I know, I'm excited about that too, but a little bit scared."

"Why?"

"I guess I'm so used to things the way they are here…" Violet said, her voice trailing off as she shrugged, not sure she could explain to Dutch.

"But you're not free here," Dutch intoned incredulously

"I am, in a way…I just…" Finally, she shook her head, sure that Dutch wouldn't understand.

"You just what?" Dutch asked, never willing to just let things go.

"I finally fit in here, I'm accepted, I guess you don't understand what that feels like…being an outsider…"

Dutch laughed out loud at that. "You mean the gay Amish girl who joined the man's navy?"

Violet looked back at Dutch with wide eyes, surprised by the abrupt statement, but then she started realizing how stupid her comment had just been. Dutch understood full well what it was like not to be accepted.

***

"What the hell is this?" the sergeant sneered, looking at Rebecca.

"Fireman apprentice Lapp reporting for duty," Rebecca stated, standing at attention. She didn't salute, she knew better than that.

"A fuckin' chick?" the Sergeant queried.

"Yes Sergeant," Rebecca replied.

"What the fuck is wrong with the navy? Sending me fuckin' women? I hear the bridge caught a chick too, what the Hell his happening!"

Rebecca didn't respond, she knew she was going to have to deal with comments like that from many men aboard the ship. It was rare that the navy allowed women on ships, it was the all new navy and the men didn't like it. Regardless, Rebecca intended to earn her place.

Over the next couple of months after they'd put out to sea, she earned plenty. Lots of bruises, cuts, sore muscles, a strained back and a fairly nasty gash to the head when another trainee wasn't paying attention with his hose. Even so, she didn't complain, she didn't cry, she didn't do anything they expected her to do as a "chick." She spent a few evenings on the very back of the ship by herself, nursing her hurt feelings and anger at the men she worked with, but also reminded herself that this was what she'd signed up for. They'd thought she was crazy requesting a Fireman Trainee for A school, but she'd done it, and here she was on an aircraft carrier. Whether they liked it or not.

They'd been at sea for six months and she'd made one friend on the boat, the only other female on it, Mary Adams. They shared a small bunk room, since HQ had required that they have their own space. They'd been given what had previously served as an officer's room but had been converted to bunk space for the two women. They knew it irritated the men on the ship, but it hadn't been something they'd requested. The last thing either of them had wanted was to be different from anyone else, but no matter what, they were being high-lighted regardless. As such, they'd become friends, simply out of necessity.

"How's it going down there?" Mary asked that afternoon when she walked in to see Rebecca laying in her bunk.

"Same old thing, 'you can't lift that, you're a girl!' How's the bridge?"

Mary sighed. "Still talking down to me, like I didn't take and pass the same exams they did. The lil' boss actually asked me to get him coffee today."

185

"Wow, what did you do?"

"I pretended I didn't hear him. I really wanted to get him coffee and dump it right on his head, but I figured that'd get me the brig for sure."

"Yeah, no point in asking for that kind of trouble."

"Well, he didn't ask again, and I saw the captain say something to him, so hopefully he told him that I'm not a servant."

"Hopefully."

The days and weeks stretched. Rebecca spent a lot of time doing drills and learning new skills, taught very grudgingly by most of the trades people on the ship. It was as if they didn't think a woman should know such secrets. Eventually, however, Rebecca started to earn the respect of some of her peers, when they saw how diligent she was in paying attention to everything they said and did. Part of her regimen was to spend as much of her off time as she could studying whatever she'd been learning, be it welding or fire suppression, and also spent a lot of time in the on-board gym. She wanted to make sure she was as strong as she could possibly be, the last thing she ever wanted was for her fellow sailors to think that because she was a woman she wasn't capable of what they were.

Her skills were put to the test one afternoon when an F-18 Hornet with a failing engine attempted to land on the carrier. The pilot did an admirable job of coaxing the aircraft toward the carrier's surface, but the touch-down was rough and the aircraft skittered sideways on the deck. It ended up against the bridge tower, blocking the doors and trapping one of the deck crew between the tilted wing and the bridge door.

"Get him the fuck out of there!" screamed one of the other deck crew, jostling the fire crew as they moved into position to douse the aircraft with retardant. The aim was to keep its tanks from exploding. It was a dire situation.

As men moved around the aircraft there were others dousing the small fires that had started from the leaking tanks that the plane had skidded past and opened up with a sharp wingtip. Rebecca was part of that crew but could hear the yelling about the man trapped.

"I can't get back there!" yelled one of the men on the damage control crew.

"We need to get him out!" yelled another man from the deck crew.

Rebecca heard the commotion and turned to look at the situation. She was small, she knew she could get into spaces many of her colleagues couldn't. And a man's life was on the line. Dropping her hose, she ran toward the bridge. Glancing up as she did, she could see the faces of the bridge crew staring down in varied degrees of concern and downright horror. If the jet's engines exploded, it would likely take out the tower and everyone on the bridge.

At the side of the bridge tower, Rebecca hesitated long enough to assess the danger. Wrenching a hose out of one of her crewmates' hands, she dropped to the ground and belly crawled using one hand—the other clamped over the bucking hose. She got a few bruises from the nozzle but paid no attention to the pain. At the point where she'd made it under the aircraft, she saw the sparks from the fuselage and knew she needed to move quickly. Rolling to her side, she pulled the hose up, holding it in both hands and directing it at the area that was sparking. At the same time, she located the deck crew 'yellow shirt', which meant he handled deck operations with regard to directing aircraft. He'd been the one trying to coax the plane in on the proper angle.

Suddenly a piece of the aircraft snapped and swung down toward her head. Having heard the loud crack, she did her best to roll out of the way—lessening the blow to her head. She shook her head, trying to clear the stars she saw dancing in front of her eyes. Blacking out at this point would mean she'd likely die as well as the crewman. She got back to the task at hand, gritting her teeth as her vision swam.

Once she'd coated the aircraft in fire retardant, she tossed the hose aside. Using a booted foot, she shoved herself forward on the deck and toward the downed man. He was just becoming conscious and aware of where he was.

"Jensen!" Rebecca yelled over the howls of the deck alarms. "Give me your hand!"

Jensen looked around, the dark eyes widening as he recognized the 'little girl' as he'd always sarcastically called her, reaching out her hand to him. He started to panic—was this how he was going to die? With some little girl trying to help him? No way!

"Jensen! Pay attention," she snapped sharply. "Stomme idioot..." She muttered the last in Pennsylvania Dutch calling him a stupid idiot, because she could see he was panicking that she was the one trying to rescue him.

Jensen responded to the tone in her voice and immediately shot out his hand. She grabbed it and clasped it tight. Using muscles she'd developed studiously in the on-board gym, she began backing out of the area, even as she noted the pilot was pulled out from the other side of the cockpit of the plane. She dragged Jensen—who did his best to help, but had at the very least two broken legs—out from behind the aircraft, to the cheers of many of the deck crew.

Suddenly she was pulled out along with Jensen. She made the mistake of trying to stand but blacked out shortly thereafter.

She woke in the sick bay, where she was told that she had a very hard head. That was something she'd known her whole life. They sent her back to her bunk with an ice pack and some pain killers and told her to rest.

It was dark when Mary got back to their room. She looked around as she entered and saw Rebecca laying on her back asleep. So as not to disturb her roommate, Mary was very quiet as she got ready for bed. The day's events kept running around in her head however.

She'd been terrified when she'd seen the jet crash, but it was much worse when someone commented that with the aircraft against the tower, they couldn't get out, and that if the jet exploded... The Captain had cut the other man off at that point, but Mary could see by everyone's reaction that it would be very bad. They had all stood staring down at the plane, watching the damage control team work to keep the jet from exploding and get the pilot out. They hadn't been able to see what had been happening under the jet, and that her own bunkmate and friend had been the one to save the day. She'd heard about it afterwards though as they did their best to assess the damage and get underway again.

It had been a very long day, but she'd been eager to check on her friend. She'd gone to the sick bay to see her, but had been told she'd been sent to her bunk. That had surprised Mary, but she'd made her way to their room quickly, only to find Rebecca asleep.

After laying in her bunk for a couple of hours, and not being able to sleep at all, Mary heard Rebecca turn over and grunt in what sounded like pain.

"Are you okay?" Mary asked from her bunk above Rebecca.

"Yes, just brushed the bump on my head."

Mary leaned over, craning her neck so she could look down at her shipmate. "Are you okay, though, like really?"

"They said I have a hard head," Rebecca replied smiling.

Mary looked circumspect, then started to ask something, but stopped. Rebecca waited, not sure what Mary was thinking.

"Would it be...I mean..." Mary finally stammered. "Could I come down there?" she asked finally.

Rebecca's eyes widened slightly, but she nodded all the same. Mary climbed down from her bunk, and moved to sit on the bunk next to where Rebecca's arm. Mary shook her head, doing her best to hold back tears.

"I haven't been able to sleep. I just keep thinking about what could have happened, and seeing that plane hit the deck, the sound of metal on metal...It was so scary." Her voice shook even as she wringed her hands in her lap.

Rebecca sat up and put her arm around Mary's shoulders. "I know it's scary, but it didn't blow up, it was okay. You're okay."

Mary leaned in to her, her whole body shaking now. Rebecca gathered her in her arms, holding her, knowing that there was nothing she could say to make it better at this point. She imagined even the men on board that had witnessed the crash were having a hard time getting the images and worries out of their heads.

Rebecca was ruminating on the day's events herself as she sat holding her bunkmate. She was quite shocked when she felt Mary's lips touch her softly. Rebecca immediately pulled her head back, looking down at the other woman.

"I'm, oh...I'm sorry..." Mary stammered. "I thought you were..."

"I am, but I didn't think you were..."

"I'm not...I just...well, I guess maybe I am...I don't know." Mary touched her fingers to her own lips. "It just seemed, right...I mean, you kind of saved my life today."

Rebecca considered that statement, then shrugged. "I did my job."

"You risked your life."

"Which is part of my job."

"It is not!" Mary exclaimed.

Rebecca didn't answer at first, not wanting to upset her friend more. "I understand that what my job entails could be dangerous," she clarified.

Mary sighed. "Either way, if you hadn't done what you did, I'd probably be dead right now. Everyone is saying that you saved the whole bridge." Rebecca looked disconcerted by this information. "You're a hero."

"I am not," Rebecca protested.

"You are," Mary replied, her eyes looked back into Rebecca's. "Thank you," she whispered and then her lips connected with Rebecca's again, still tentative, but this time she didn't move away.

Rebecca tightened her arm around Mary slightly, and kissed Mary back. Mary sighed against her lips, relaxing into Rebecca's embrace. This encouraged Rebecca to kiss her deeper, which had Mary's hands grasping at her shirt. They kissed for a few minutes, and Mary's soft moans and sighs gave Rebecca the leave to do more. Rebecca's hands became more sure, as they slid up Mary's sides, her thumbs stroking along Mary's side, near her breasts hidden under a baggy tshirt.

Mary couldn't believe her body's reaction to the other woman's lips on hers, she wasn't one to question something when it felt good. She knew she'd locked the door to their room, and since they were far *removed from the other sailors on the ship, she knew they wouldn't be heard.*

The truth was, she'd had kind of a crush on the other woman since day one. No, she wasn't a lesbian, but she figured she was likely at least bi-sexual and she wanted to try it out. Rebecca Lapp was a very sexy package with her short mullet style hair and her lean, well-muscled body. Mary had decided that her bunkmate was a lesbian, because of the fact that she wore no makeup, didn't act girlie at all, and she'd also heard her talking to her 'friend' Rowena on the phone a few times. Some of the things she'd said to Rowena, sounded like the girl was her girlfriend. So Rebecca had become a source of interest to Mary, but she'd never acted on it, until now. When Rebecca's hand moved to slide under her T-shirt however, she pulled away immediately. She caught Rebecca's confused look.

"I'm sorry," Mary said, shaking her head, tears in her eyes suddenly, "I just...it's not you..."

"Can you tell me what it is?" Rebecca asked gently.

Mary pressed her lips together. This always happened, getting intimate with anyone was always a risk for her, she knew that, she wasn't sure why she always put herself in this kind of situation, it was always doomed now.

Rebecca waited patiently, her thumb stroking Mary's wrist soothingly.

Mary smiled sadly. "It really isn't you, I've had issues with intimacy over the last few years."

Rebecca nodded understandingly, but still waited for the rest of the story.

Mary reached up, putting her hand to her chest, her look pained. "I had breast cancer diagnosed when I was only fifteen. They removed a tumor...It left me scarred and misshapen..."

Again Rebecca nodded, leaning in to kiss Mary softly on the lips, it was a condolence, an apology and an 'I'm sorry' all rolled into one very sweet gentle touching of the lips. When Rebecca's lips left hers, they moved to just next to her lips, still soft, still sweet. The moved a little further over, and then again. Eventually Rebecca's lips made their way to her neck, and continued down, while extremely gentle hands touched Mary's waist.

Mary felt tears sting her eyes, as she realized what Rebecca was doing. She wasn't surprised when she felt Rebecca's fingertips on her skin at her waist, under her shirt. The material of her T-shirt was shifted slightly upward as gentle caresses moved ever so slowly upward. By the time Rebecca's hands and lips met, Mary's breasts were exposed. Rebecca's lips touched gently on the scar on the left breast, and continued to kiss until the entire area had been covered.

Rebecca made very slow, deliberate love to her, and Mary found herself thinking that maybe being a lesbian wouldn't be such a bad thing with someone like this. After her resounding orgasm, Mary moved to lay on Rebecca's side. Glancing up, she noted that Rebecca's finger rubbed her temple.

"Oh, God, did I hurt you? I mean, your head...?" Mary was aghast that she hadn't even though about that.

"No, I'm fine," Rebecca assured.

"Oh, well, should I..." Mary started to say, gesturing to Rebecca's body, unsure of how to put it. She wasn't sure she even knew how to give another woman an orgasm.

"No, you're fine," Rebecca replied with a soft smile.

"Well, that doesn't seem fair."

Rebecca chuckled, pulling Mary closer for a moment, appreciating that she cared, but perfectly fine without reciprocation. Mary was surprised to feel the need to snuggle up to the other woman. It was odd to her that she didn't feel at all uncomfortable after what had just happened between them. In her mind it would be strange to her, if she really wasn't at least bi-sexual. They were both quiet for a long few minutes. Then Mary lifted her head and looked up at Rebecca.

"Thank you for the way you handled, this..." she said, gesturing to her breast.

"A woman's body is amazing no matter what, it deserves to be loved."

Mary smiled, this woman was definitely not like all the men that had treated her like she wasn't really a woman because of having misshapen breasts. A few had had the temerity to suggest she get a boob job to "fix it."

"What would you think about me getting a boob job to make them right again?" Mary questioned.

Rebecca looked back at her for a long moment. "Is that what you want to do?"

Mary shrugged, looking down. "Some men have suggested I do it."

Rebecca quirked her lips. "I'd say that if you wanted to do it for you, then by all means, but if you're doing it to fit someone else's idea of what is beautiful, then it isn't a good idea."

Mary nodded. "Sometimes I feel like saying to people, 'it's my body, you have no say.'"

"I think that's a wise thing to say," Rebecca said, smiling.

Mary smiled too, nodding. It felt good to talk to someone about things like this. They were both odd women out in a big military machine, but they could at least be there for each other.

***

Violet was released the following day. Her mother and son came to pick her up. She was hugged and cheered on by many of her fellow firefighters. Dutch stood at the door as she left, and surprised her with a hug.

"You'll do great out there," Dutch told her, "stay in touch."

"I will, thank you for everything," Violet replied, feeling tears stinging the backs of her eyelids.

"It was all you," Dutch told her, giving her an extra squeeze.

"All me, right," Violet snickered, smiling even as they parted.

As her mother drove away from the camp, Violet did her best not to cry, but she wasn't completely successful.

Six hours later, she felt like nothing in her previous life had changed. She was at home, with Michael, who'd happily gone off to play in his room in the trailer. Jeff was at "work," which her mother had told her was basically hard labour. Violet noted that he hadn't even bothered to be home when his wife had gotten home after three years...

Looking in the refrigetator Violet noticed there was nothing healthy whatsoever to eat. She sat down to make a list of things to get at the grocery store, marveling at the surreal feeling of being back. Then it occurred to her to check their bank account. She saw that they had a whopping $20 to their name. Violet sighed, shaking her head. She knew she had money she could tap into, and was willing to do that to feed herself and her son.

She had made a small amount of money over her time at the camp. It wasn't much, they were paid $2 a day that they fought fires. Because the fire season had been fairly lengthy, she'd made money late into October. She'd saved that money the entire time. When she'd left the fire camp she'd saved up a total of $1,200, added to that was the $200 "gate money" she was given by the Department of Corrections. It was her intention to save that money for a "rainy day," but feeding her son was more important.

Finishing her grocery list, she called to Michael and they went shopping. She bought fresh vegetables and enough meat to feed her and Michael for at least two weeks. She planned on starting to apply for jobs right away and hoped she could get something quickly. In the end she managed to keep the money spent under $50. It was amazing to her how far her money went when she didn't buy a lot of junk food. She was very proud of herself, she hadn't bought anything that wasn't healthy.

That evening she was cooking a meal for her and Michael, since she hadn't heard from Jeff to know when he was coming home. She was humming to herself as she cooked, when the back door of the trailer opened and Jeff stepped through. His brown eyes seemed to assess her, like he was trying to decide if he was happy to see her or not.

"So you made it home," he commented, his tone matter of fact.

She wanted to say "no thanks to you", but only nodded, continuing to chew on the carrot she'd just put in her mouth.

Jeff walked over to look into the pans on the stove. "What's that shit?" he asked snidely.

"Mine and Michael's dinner," she replied blithely. "I didn't know when you'd be home."

"Pfft," Jeff snorted, "I wouldn't eat that horseshit anyway. I'll grab something at the bar." He gave her a narrowed look. "What the hell did you use to pay for this anyway?"

Violet remained calm, and lied her ass off. "My mom gave me some money."

"Good! Did you get beer?" he asked even as he opened the refrigerator. "What the fuck!" he snapped, looking at Violet.

She glanced over her shoulder at him and shrugged. "I didn't have enough to buy beer. I guess you'll need to pick some up on your way back from the bar." She could see his eyes narrow. He was looking at the items in the refrigerator, he opened the freezer and made a disgusted sound.

"What the fuck is with fish and chicken?"

"They're for dinners."

"I don't eat that shit!" Violet didn't say anything she just continued to cook dinner. "What the fuck am I supposed to eat in my own fucking house?"

"Trailer," Violet muttered, unable to stop herself.

"What did you say?" Jeff asked, his voice taking on a menacing tone.

"I was just saying it's a trailer, not a house."

Jeff stared at her open mouthed.

"And now this trailer's not good enough for you?" he asked, his face taking on a nasty look.

"It's fine, Jeff." Violet sighed. "There wasn't enough money to buy anything extra. This is what we could afford." She gestured to the food in the pans and the fridge. Then she gave him a pointed look. "What are you planning to use to buy dinner and drinks at the bar?"

Jeff looked immediately contrite, but shrugged. "I made money today."

"Are you going to put any that in the bank for rent? Or bills?"

"Hey I fucking slaved in the dirt for this shit," Jeff snapped, "and now I'm entitled to a night out, and I'm gonna go, what are you gonna do? Try and stop me?"

Violet looked back at the man that was her husband, so many things ran through her mind. She wanted to point out that it was apparent he hadn't kept up with much while she'd been away, and that just because he'd worked for one day, that somehow gave him the right to go out and drink it all away? She wanted to remind him that she'd busted her butt fighting fires while he'd been drinking beer at home, and this was the thanks she got? Oh, and by the way, it's nice to see how much you missed me... So many things she wanted to say, but she knew that nothing she'd say would make any difference to Jeff. Finally she shrugged, shaking her head and turning back to dinner, not wanting to burn anything.

Jeff smirked at her back and then left the room to go take a shower. He had a date tonight, and the last fucking thing he was doing was hanging around with this cow. She was a fucking criminal, did she really think she was too good to live in a trailer? Idiot!

After dinner, Violet settled Michael with a video and went for a walk. She did some jogging and made a point of remembering to keep her heart rate up. The last thing she wanted was to gain weight again.

Later that evening she was feeling a bit sad and lonely. She missed her workouts with the captain, and chit chatting with her afterwards. They didn't always talk about anything important, but it was always nice to have someone to talk to that wasn't judgemental.

Going into the bedroom Violet looked for her laptop, but couldn't find it. Finally she located a newer laptop that apparently Jeff had gotten himself. She turned it on, hoping that it wasn't password protected. Relief was immediate when she saw that it wasn't. Violet guessed that Jeff probably hadn't figured he needed to protect it since no one was around to check on him.

She took the laptop out to the living room and sat on the couch, checking her email account. She was thrilled to see emails from her friends at the camp. They all asked her how her first day "out" had gone. She answered all the emails, but was sad not to see an email from the captain. She knew she was being silly, that the captain had better things to do than write to an ex-inmate. Sighing she closed down the laptop and put it back where she'd found it.

Later she and Michael watched a movie together. Michael was into the Marvel series at that point, so they watched *Thor*. Violet found herself tearing up on the very slight romantic parts of the movie. Feeling completely silly, she wiped away her tears. She was just emotional, she told herself.

That night, she was in bed trying to sleep when she heard Jeff stumble into the room. He bumped into the bed, then bumped into the closet door trying to get it open. He didn't bother to be quiet and Violet knew he was drunk, she could smell another woman's perfume as well. Pretending to be asleep, she made a point of not moving, laying on her side. Finally Jeff climbed into bed behind her, she was quite shocked when she felt his hand slide up her back. *Was he crazy? Or just really drunk?* She didn't respond, hoping that would end his attempt at affection or whatever it was. *Not that lucky,* she thought a moment later when his hand was replaced by the hard-on pressed aginst her butt. Suddenly she felt a little bit sick. The last thing she wanted was to have sex with this man, especially knowing that he'd likely had his dick in someone else earlier that evening and hadn't showered.

She still pretended to be asleep, and he pressed harder, his hand fumbling with her underwear to move it aside. *Seriously!? He was going to just stick it in whether I'm awake or not?* That thought made her move. She turned over suddenly, coming face to face with him.

"What are you doing?" she snapped at him.

"I...I..." he stammered shocked, then he started to sneer, "I'm gonna fuck my wife that's been in prison for fucking forever."

"Oh, wow..." Violet murmured. "So very romantic..."

"What the fuck are you saying?" Jeff snapped.

"I'm saying, no, not happening, no, get over on your side of the bed," Violet said, surprising herself with her nerve.

"You're telling me no?" Jeff asked dumbly.

"I'm telling you no," Violet assured.

"This is bullshit..." Jeff muttered, even as he shrunk back to his side of the bed, much to Violet's relief.

"Oh, it smells like you got some tonight, so I wouldn't complain too much if I were you."

"What're you talking about?" Jeff replied, already looking guilty.

"Please don't treat me like I'm stupid," Violet said, her tone emphatic. "I know all about the other women, so just keep using them, and stay away from me."

Jeff's eyes widened, he didn't know where this new Violet had come from, and he wasn't sure he liked it at all. Finally he turned over to put his back to her, making annoyed grunting sounds. He'd figured he was going to tap that tonight, *two cows no waiting,* was how he saw it. The last thing he'd expected was for Violet to say no. She'd never said no before. What the hell had happened in prison?

***

"Man you got some big ones!" Matt exclaimed when he reached up to grab her breasts eagerly.

Violet did her best not cringe away from him. Angela had told her that Matt was all into her and that she should just let him take her virginty 'for God's sake!'. Since everyone was doing it, Violet felt like she should be doing it too. They were in her bedroom, her parents were gone for the night. He'd come over to "watch a movie," but had immediately made it known that he wanted to have sex. His hand had made its way to her breasts over and over during the movie, finally she'd given up and taken him up to her room, determined to get this over with. She had fantasies that the guy was actually interested in her.

He'd finally managed to get her out of her clothes, of course she'd had to help him, while trying to hide her embarassment that she'd been wearing Spanx to hold in her fat rolls. He'd snapped the waistband, chuckling at what he thought was a funny action. It had hurt, but of course she couldn't say that. She knew that in his mind it was okay to tease fat girls about being fat and trying to hide it. While she'd struggled out of the Spanx, he'd made his play for her breasts, squeezing them like he was testing cantelopes, hurting her again.

"Maybe this isn't a good idea..." she said softly, as she set aside the garment.

"Aw, come on, I finally got ya outta all that shit," he said gesturing to her pile of clothes. "I gotta get something outta it."

Violet pressed her lips together, trying to suppress the hurt she was feeling. Finally she nodded, and moved to lay down on the bed. Matt hastily removed his clothes; Violet was both relieved and a little revolted by the fact that he was chunky too. Before she knew what was happening he was scrambling up on top of her. She did her best not to shove him away, but his weight was crushing.

When, after some shifting, grunting and cussing he shoved himself inside her, she ground her teeth together at the sharp pain. He pumped a few times, and then gave a loud grunt, shoving his mercifully short penis in as far as it would go and then he was done. He climbed off her looking very pleased with himself.

Violet got off the bed and went into her bathroom closing the door and locking it. She got into the shower and did her very best to wash the whole experience away. She stayed in the shower until the water became cold. Climbing out, she dried herself and did her best not to think about what had just happend.

"Just write it off as finally losing my virginity," she told herself.

After a full hour in the bathroom, Violet peeked out to note with both relief and some hurt that Matt was gone. She wondered if he left the minute she went into the bathroom. She went to bed that night *feeling sick and was suddenly seized with the thought that Matt hadn't used a condom. What if she got pregnant?*

She lived in utter terror for the next two weeks until she got her period. By that time, Matt had told everyone that she was a "lousy lay" and referred to her as a "dead whale" to all his friends. Just one more "fat girl experience" was how Violet thought of it.

***

The next two months were really difficult for Violet. She applied everywhere she could think of within walking distance, since she didn't have a vehicle. Jeff refused to let her use his truck, with the excuse that he might need it—like that happened much! She applied at three different RV parks, and a few camping parks which were within two miles of the mobile home park where they lived. She'd even been brave enough to apply at the closest fire station, a county station, where her reception had been less than warm.

"What are we gonna do with a fat chick?" she'd overheard one of the men say as she stood at the counter, having asked for an application.

"Maybe we can use her to smother the fire," another firefighter had snickered.

The three men had burst into laughter. Violet had turned and walked out with tears in her eyes. It was a terrible day.

It was another month before she finally landed a job with the Desert Ironwood Resort—a motel that featured older rooms and a pool in the middle of the desert, alongside a small general store. Violet worked in the store. She hated it, but it was bringing in enough money for her to buy food for her and Michael and start saving some money to eventually get out.

Jeff was only getting worse as time wore on. One evening, when he came home from a rare day of work digging ditches for a local RV park, he stopped to look at Violet. She was tired from a long day at the store, and wasn't in the mood for his crap so she didn't bother to look at him.

"How many fires did you fight today?" Jeff asked, his tone nasty.

"How much money did you make today?" Violet countered.

Jeff curled his lips in annoyance. "You think you're such hot shit? You couldn't get a job as a firefighter, still too fucking fat huh? Maybe those people at the camp were just desperate."

Violet didn't answer, she knew that nothing she could say would change Jeff's attitude. The man was a jerk, that was all there was to it. She couldn't figure out what she'd ever seen in him in the first place.

Finally, she sighed. "Don't you have a shower to take and some floozy to go boff?"

She could see that Jeff wanted to say something else, but he couldn't seem to formulate it, so he just laughed nastily and walked by her on his way shower.

Later that night, Violet pulled out Jeff's laptop again, turning it on and checking her emails. She was thrilled to see one from R.Lapp@calfire.ca.gov. She opened saw that the captain was checking on her asking her how she was doing. She wrote back immediately.

Things here are lousy; I had a rough time finding a job, no one wants to hire an ex-con. I finally got a job in a store that's hot all day, but at least I'm making some money so I can take care of me and Michael. It's crazy, but I miss the girls at the camp, and I miss you too, Captain! How are you doing? Thanks for your email, it brightened my day!

Sending the email, she felt better that at least the Captain hadn't forgotten about her.

A few days later she recieved an email back from the Captain saying that she was back with her unit in El Cajon, and that her time had been up at the fire camp. She also asked Violet how she was doing keeping up with her fitness. Violet was very happy to be able to report that she was walking the mile to work each day, as well as doing her nightly walk of eight to ten miles and lifting some weights that one of the people in their trailer park had been selling.

It's not quite the level you had me at, but I'm doing really good with eating and continuing to exercise every day, she wrote, pleased that she didn't have to make up excuses for getting off track.

The next time she was able to check emails was a week later. Jeff was once again not working, so he was home all the time and on his laptop. Violet avoided him as much as she could. On the seventh night of his week-long stay in, she came home from work having picked up some groceries. As usual he rooted around in the bags and complained about there being nothing good.

"Feel free to pick up more work so you can buy what you like," Violet told him, her tone no-nonsense. Jeff's lips twitched like he wanted to say something, Violet waited.

"Maybe I should go out and steal people's credit cards so I can buy whatever I want," Jeff muttered angrily.

Violet stared at him open-mouthed for a long few moments, finally closing it to give him a sarcastic grin.

"Well, since what I bought with those stolen credit cards was a few more months in this luxury trailer, food on the table, and the bills paid for while you whored around with every trollup in this town, I think you should be thanking me."

It was Jeff's turn to stare at her, his mouth agape. "You're blaming me?"

"Nevermind, I don't know why I even bother," Violet said, shaking her head.

He walked off muttering under his breath, she heard terms like "stupid cow," but ignored him. He left the house a little while later.

When she opened her email she saw that the captain had contacted her again. This time the email contained a link to the State Cal Fire website and it was for taking the test for the Firefighter 1 classification with the agency. Dutch had written that the exam was open currently and that she should take the test. She clicked on the link and excitedly signed up to take the test. Fortunately, all she had to do was answer questions pertaining to her experience and that experience was weighed 100%. She passed the test with a 90% and was told she was in rank 2 for the list. She forwarded the information she received to Dutch.

Three days later she was sitting at the counter in the store she worked for. A man had just walked up to buy beer and she was handing him his change when her cell phone rang. She waited until she thanked the man and he left the store before she picked up the phone. She assumed it was going to be yet another collection call for the truck Jeff had bought while she was in prison. He hadn't been making payments on it for the last three months. She refused to use her meager pay to pay for the outlandishly expensive motor. She still wasn't even sure how he'd qualified for it in the first place.

"Yes?" she sighed into the phone.

"Good morning," came a familiar voice.

"Captain?" Violet queried in disbelief.

There was a warm chuckled on the other end of the line. "Technically I'm a Chief, but we'll go with that for now."

"You got a promotion?"

"No, I was referred to as the Fire Captain at the camp, but my official title is Batallion Chief," Dutched explain patiently, "but more importantly congratulations on the test."

Violet smiled warmly, even as her admiration for the other woman doubled. "I was pretty pleased with it."

"You should be," Dutch assured her. "So how's it going otherwise?"

Violet hesitated, not wanting to simply dump all of her baggage on her former boss.

"I mean with your home life, Vi," Dutch put in.

Violet sighed deeply. "It's terrible," she said, still unsure of how much to say. "I just feel like I'm stuck and I don't really have a way to change things at this point."

At her end, Dutch narrowed her eyes, nodding as she did. "How often do you visit your parents?"

Violet thought it was an odd question, but answered regardless, "I'm hoping to take Michael to see them next week."

"They're here in San Diego, aren't they?"

"Yes, in Alpine."

"Well that's not too far from us here in El Cajon, would you have time for lunch when you're here?"

"Of course!" Violet exclaimed, excited at the chance to see the Captain again. "That would be great!"

"Perfect. Just text or email me and let me know when you'll be in town and I'll make time, okay?"

"So it's okay to save this as your phone number?"

"Yes, this is my work cell phone, so please do."

"Great! I'll let you know as soon as I get a solid plan."

"Okay. You take care until then."

"I will, thank you, Cap... I mean..."

Dutch laughed. "Talk soon, Violet."

They hung up then. Violet found that she smiled a lot the rest of the day.

A week later, Violet was at her parents home. She smelled the familiar scents of fresh flowers and the mixture of lemon and hardwood floors. Her parents' home was a $1.2 million dollar show piece. A five thousand-plus square foot property that was appointed with the best of everything, including a home theater room and a billiards room. Her mother had a lovely sun porch where she met with her friends over tea and scones to discuss the latest books and scandals. Violet had never fit in with their perfect world, so she'd stayed in the background, avoiding as many gatherings as she could.

She'd convinced her mother to keep an eye on Michael for a few hours while she went and had lunch with Dutch. There was a huge pool in the back yard so she knew it wouldn't take a lot to keep Michael happy. Her mother had actually liked Dutch, so she'd been more amenable to watching Michael. Borrowing one of her parents car, an older-model Mercedes, Violet made the twenty-five minute drive down to the El Cajon fire station.

At the counter, she asked for Captain Lapp.

"You mean Chief Lapp?" the girl at the front desk queried.

"Yes, sorry," Violet said, shaking her head, as she rolled her eyes at herself.

"You're Ms. Hastings?" the younger woman queried then, surprising Violet.

"Ye-yes." Violet uttered, stammering in her shock.

The girl stood up, and walked over to the door at the side of the counter.

"Come on in, Chief's expecting you," she said with a warm smile.

She was led to an office not too far from the counter. The girl knocked once and opened the door. "Chief, Ms. Hastings is here."

"Thanks Mandy," Dutch said, smiling warmly at the girl, then stood to walk over to Violet, hugging her. "It's good to see you."

Violet allowed herself to enjoy the embrace, smelling Dutch's usual mixture of light cologne and smoke. As she stepped back she smiled. "You smell the same."

Dutch laughed softly. "Not in a bad way, I hope."

"Oh! No, no, ma'am, just, like cologne and smoke."

Dutch chuckled, stepping back over to her desk to pick up her phone and reaching over to pick up her jacket, it was getting windy out and it had a chill to it.

"You ready to go?" she asked Violet.

Violet was busy looking around Dutch's office. Much like her office had been at the camp, it was very simple, with a sturdy wooden desk and chairs in front of it, and a simple black office chair behind it. Still there were no real decorations, except for the Cal Fire emblem on a canvas sign on the wall behind the desk. Dutch was not much for decorating.

"We've got some fancy choices here," Dutch said, grinning as she drove away from the office. "Denny's or Applebee's?"

Violet chuckled. "Well, Applebee's has good salads, so let's go with them."

Dutch smiled, nodding.

After ordering a very modest Thai Shrimp Salad, only 410 calories, Violet could see the approving smile on the other woman's face. Dutch ordered a Grilled Chicken Ceasar salad and handed the waitress the menu.

"You're doing really well," Dutch told Violet. "You look like you really have kept up with your fitness."

"I have, thanks to you," Violet said, smiling. "I've lost another fifteen pounds. It's not happening fast, but you always said it shouldn't."

"True, but I also always told you that the number on the scale isn't important. It's how you feel and how strong you've become."

Violet pressed her lips together, smiling as she nodded, "I know, you're right, but for me it's easier to measure in pounds lost."

"But muscle weighs more than fat, so it may not be a true reflection of your journey."

Violet laughed happily. "I've missed you Captain...er...I mean...What do I call you now?"

Dutch grinned at her slip, shrugging. "We're no longer inmate and Fire Captain, so I'm thinking you could probably call me by my name."

"Yeah, but which one?" Violet asked.

"Whichever you're comfortable with."

"Well...what are my options?"

Dutch looked back at her, blinking a couple of times, "Well, there's Dutch..."

"Or?"

"You don't like Dutch," she surmised.

Violet curled her lips in consternation, not wanting to offend her former boss. "I just...I don't think it is really all you are...And it almost seems racist..."

Dutch burst into laughter, "Racist?"

"Well, you're Pennsylvania Dutch, right?"

"It's not that simple, but sure, let's say that. Okay...Well, my close friends call me Becca."

"But..." Violet stammered.

"Violet," Dutch said, putting her hand over Violet's on the table. "I would consider you a close friend."

"Really?"

"Under the circumstances we were in, I certainly told you more about myself than I told anyone else at the camp."

"Oh, wow, okay...Well, then I'd like to choose option B," Violet said, smiling widely.

Dutch smiled, her eyes crinkling at the corners. She was glad that Violet was finally getting more comfortable around her. The younger woman was far too timid.

They made small talk until their lunch came then ate in companionable silence. As they were finishing, Dutch leaned back in her chair.

"So how's the job, getting any better?"

Violet shrugged. "Not really, the work is really boring and I end up sitting a lot during the day, so it's not helping me physically at this point. I miss fire fighting, at least then I felt like I was doing something productive."

Dutch nodded sagely. "And the situation with Jeff?"

Violet's lips tugged in an unhappy grimace. "I don't think there's much left there. I'm just worried he'd fight me for custody of Michael, and he might win, because technically he makes a better living than me even if he doesn't work for long periods of time."

"What does he do?"

"He's a landscaper."

Dutch nodded, narrowing her eyes slightly. "So if you could become a firefighter again, would that help?"

"Of course," Violet said with emphasis, but then she shrugged, "but I don't think that's going to happen, not where I'm at in the middle of nowhere."

"What if you were here in San Diego?"

Violet shook her head sadly. "I couldn't afford to live here."

"What about your parents?"

Violet smiled wryly this time, "While I love my parents, I think my mother would drive me insane inside of a week. She's a bit...um...judgemental."

Dutch nodded, her look considering, "So what if you could find a place for say $600 a month?"

"In San Diego?" Violet replied incredulously. "Am I renting a box under a bridge?"

Dutch chuckled, always finding Violet's personality fun. "Well, what if you came to work for me, right back down that street, and rented two rooms in the house I'm currently renovating?"

Violet looked back at Dutch, dumbfounded. Her mouth hung open and she blinked a couple of times. When she closed her mouth she turned her head slightly, giving Dutch a sidelong look, her eyes narrowed.

"Is this like some kind of candid camera thing?"

"What kind of what?" Dutch asked, confused by the question.

"Um, like a joke."

"Not that I know of," Dutch said, looking slightly less mystified. "I have an opening for a couple of firefighters and since you passed the test, I'd like to offer you a job."

"No way!" Violet exclaimed, startling the waitress that was bringing them the check. Dutch held out her hand, grinning at the waitress. "I'm sorry," Violet said then, noting that Dutch seemed to be paying for her lunch. "Cap, I, er, I mean Becca, I can pay..."

"No," Dutch said, shaking her head even as she handed the waitress cash. "So do you want the job?"

"I, um, well..." Violet said, trying to adjust to everything that had just been said and quantifying all of it in terms of what it would mean for her and Michael. Finally she folded her hands on the table in front of her, giving Dutch a direct look. "I would absolutely love to work for you again."

"So that's a yes?"

"Yes, that's a yes." Violet said smiling as she bit her lip, unable to believe her good fortune.

Chapter 7

"Come on in, your mom should be home soon," Hunter told Kori's son at the front door to their house. "I'm out back here barbequing if you want to join me. Beers are in the fridge."

"Thanks." Hunter Stanton smiled as he followed his host inside. "This is a nice place," he commented as he took a beer out of the refrigerator and twisted off the top.

Hunter grinned, nodding. "We like it."

Out in the yard, Hunter stepped back over to the Traeger she and Kori had bought as a housewarming present to themselves.

"So where is Mom?"

"She got caught up in a last-minute meeting with the Governor."

Kori's son almost choked on his beer. "Holy shit, she's meeting with Midnight Chevalier herself?"

Hunter chuckled. "You do know that your mom is the head of Cal Fire, right? And California is on fire, pretty much constantly at this point. Midnight wants constant updates on how things are going."

The younger man, blinked a couple of times, looking like he was trying to assimilate what Hunter had just said, then shrugged. "I guess I didn't really see it that way."

Before Hunter could answer, the doorbell rang again.

"Can you grab that? I need to check on the tri-tip."

"Sure." Walking to the door, he opened it to his sister. "Hey sis."

"Hi," Desolé stepped inside, hugging her brother and looking around the foyer of the home as she did. "Wow, this is...a lot."

"A lot?" her brother repeated. "What's that mean?"

Desolé took in the antique looking hall tree and bench, "Well, that looks a bit expensive, don't you think?"

"And?" Stanton queried incredulously.

"And how much is Mom having to spend to furnish this house? I mean seriously," Desolé whispered harshly.

"That actually belongs to me," Hunter commented from the sliding door, "it's been in my family for about a century now." With that she walked to the refrigerator and took out another beer, walking back outside without another word.

"That was bitchy!" Stanton hissed at his sister. "Why did you even come if you're just going to be a snot the whole night?"

"I—" Desolé began, her face flaming in embarrassment. "I didn't know she was standing there."

"Doesn't matter, you were being a bitch."

Desolé pressed her lips together, realizing she'd assumed her brother would be on her side in this. "You like her?"

He shrugged, "She seems nice, and she obviously makes mom happy. What's not to like?"

"Dad's miserable."

"Dad's always been miserable."

"What does *that* mean?"

"It means that he always loved Mom way more than she loved him, and that's always made him kind of sad. Haven't you ever seen it? Or weren't you paying any attention?" His tone was even, but his words cut all the same.

"Don't be an asshole," Desolé snapped.

"Then stop being so freaking judgmental and realize we don't know anything about how mom really feels, and it's not our business anyway."

"She's our mom, it's our business."

"Says you." With that, Stanton turned and walked away from her back out into the yard.

Desolé stood rooted in place for a long few moments, not sure what to do. That's when the doorbell rang again. Without thinking she turned to open the door and stood facing Samantha. They'd seen each other a few times since the incident in Sam's dorm room, they'd smiled and nodded to each other, but hadn't really communicated a great deal.

"Hey," Samantha said, walking into the house.

"Hi." Desolé nodded as she stepped back.

"Where's my mom?"

"In the back there." Desolé gestured toward the slider.

"Okay, come on." Sam led the way to the toward the backyard, stopping to grab a soda out of the refrigerator, offering Desolé one.

"Thanks." Desolé took the offered drink and fiddled with the tab on the can as they walked out into the backyard.

"It's looking good, Mom!" Samantha commented as she glanced around the yard. Hunter had been working on a retaining wall and had since added some plants. Samantha walked over to

217

the pot that held Heather's tree, reaching out to touch the trunk. "Hi Mom."

Hunter noticed the perplexed look on both Stanton and Desolé's faces, "Heather, Samantha's mom, is buried there."

"I've heard of this…" Desolé said softly. "They're burial tree pods," she told her brother, "people are put into a pod that becomes a tree."

"Whoa," Stanton commented, his eyes widening slightly.

"It's a very environmentally conscious way to be buried," Desolé insisted.

"Well, Heather was all hippy all the time." Hunter grinned, her eyes on the pot, she immediately felt a slight push. "It's true!" She laughed, looking in the direction the push had come from.

"Huh?" Stanton queried, looking at Hunter like she was maybe losing her mind.

"Mom didn't like that." Samantha smiled as she walked back over to the three.

"She always said she was bohemian," Hunter said, looking at her daughter. "I kept telling her that was just code for hippy." This time the push was hard enough to move her slightly.

Stanton immediately looked uneasy. "What just happened?"

Hunter and Samantha exchanged a look, leave it to Heather to introduce herself right away.

"So, my mom is still kind of with us," Samantha placated.

"With how?" Stanton asked.

"In spirit," Desolé informed her brother.

"Wait, how do you know about this?" he asked.

"Samantha introduced me to her last month."

"Say what?" he queried, paling slightly, maybe they were all losing it.

"Heather has a tendency to keep an eye on us," Hunter explained, "but in spirt form."

"So you believe in ghosts?" the young man asked, looking like he was reevaluating Hunter altogether.

"I didn't used to." Hunter shook her head. "But Heather has made me a believer." At that moment Hunter's phone rang, making them all jump slightly. Laughing, she took the call, walking inside.

Stanton regarded Samantha and Desolé critically. "And you both believe this stuff?"

Samantha shrugged. "My mom has made herself very clear, she's still here, watching over me and my other mom. Your mom has met her too."

Hunter Stanton looked utterly stunned. "Wait, what?"

"Yep." Samantha nodded. "Back home in Fort Bragg, your mom was visiting our house. She talked to my mom, and my mom responded."

He started shaking his head, his face screwed up in disdain now, "What the fuck are you people smoking here?" To his shock, he suddenly felt a push as his back. Convinced his sister had done it, he turned to look behind him, realizing suddenly that Desolé was five full feet away from him. "Who did that!"

Samantha chuckled, even Desolé grinned. "I told you," Samantha reminded him, "and my mom doesn't like people to cuss, so…" Her voice trailed off as she gave him a pointed smirk.

"Seriously, what the fu—" he started to say, but immediately felt what had to be a hand on his back again. "Okay, okay, sorry,

I won't cuss!" At that, he felt the pressure lighten, and suddenly felt a slight pressure on his cheek, like a hand had been placed there. "Wow…" he murmured, his look wonderous now.

"Uh…" Hunter began as she walked back out of the house, her look skipping from Kori's son to Samantha. "I'm guessing your mother made her presence known?"

Samantha giggled. "She pushed him for cussing."

"Oh yeah." Hunter nodded. "She really hates that."

"Honestly," Desolé said, smiling wistfully, looking at her brother "I'm feeling a little jealous here. What's it feel like?"

Before he could answer, Desolé felt a warmth like a hand on her shoulder. "Oh…" she breathed softly, her eyes lighting up with joy.

Hunter and Samantha exchanged a look of understanding. Heather was making her wishes known, she wanted them to be a family, and was willing to do what it took to make that happen.

When Kori finally made it home, Stanton and Desolé couldn't help but be impressed with the way Hunter had a glass of wine poured for her by the time she put down her brief case and jacket. The two kissed hello, and it was obvious it was something they did all the time. Kori's children observed the way Hunter took care of Kori and treated her with both respect and kindness. Hunter and Kori finished each other's sentences and talked passionately about their plans for Cal Fire, and for their future. Hunter also talked to both Stanton's about their plans for the future. It turned out to be a nice night for all of them.

A few days later, Hunter lay sleeping on her back. Her arm was over her face, and it was obvious she'd basically kicked off her boots and lain down. Kori, who'd just gotten home from a late night in the office, smiled. Hunter had been down in Southern California for a couple of days, meeting with the teams and the battalion chiefs in the area. She'd even seen some action, getting the opportunity to fly a tanker to help battle a grass fire.

Walking over to the bed, Kori leaned down and kissed Hunter's lips softly. Hunter woke immediately.

"Hey there," Hunter murmured.

"Hey." Kori smiled. "When did you get home?"

Hunter glanced at the clock, it was eight thirty. "About an hour ago. How are things here?"

"Oh, the usual chaos during fire season…" Kori said, rolling her eyes. "We had a pilot go down," she said then, her tone turning serious.

"Shit, what happened?" Hunter asked, moving to sit up.

"Aircraft malfunction, pilot had to ditch in Lake Berryessa."

"Holy f—hell," Hunter muttered, quickly adjusting her adjective as she saw the light flicker, knowing Heather still didn't like her to cuss and made it known. Kori noted the change in language direction and chuckled, knowing why Hunter had changed what she was going to say. "So what plane? What crew?"

"One of the DC-6s, apparently two of the four props failed, and the other two were stalling out… It was Dax Ray's crew."

"Damn…is she okay?"

"Yeah, she and her crew got out just fine, a bit banged up, and Dax is gonna be on light duty for a while, but they're alive."

Hunter shook her head, blowing her breath out as she leaned back against the headboard. "We got a few aircrafts down in So

Cal that are on their last legs too. We gotta get on this evaluation, babe."

Kori sat down on the bed, looking over at her partner. "I know. We just need to free you up, which isn't going to happen during the main fire season, and we need to get on finding someone to handle the fixed wing evaluation. We need to start spending Midnight's money or she might change her mind."

Midnight Chevalier, the governor for the State of California, was very proactive about her people having what they needed to do their jobs. She'd already given the green light to start replacing planes, but Kori and Hunter wanted to do it right, not just blow a ton of money because they could. Hunter was nodding, her mind already turning over the possibilities.

"You think maybe Gun would know someone?" she asked, referring to their friend at OES who used to be a gunner in an Apache helicopter in the Army.

Kori shrugged. "It's worth the ask."

The two exchanged a warm look, they loved to be able to work together this way, looking for ways to improve their shared passion for firefighting.

"Then let's get on it tomorrow," Hunter said.

"Yes," Kori said, moving to kiss Hunter, "but tonight..."

"Oh..." Hunter murmured as they lay back on the bed, kissing. "Yes, let's handle this first."

***

A month later, Violet was surprised when Dutch offered to come down and help her move what items she was taking out of the trailer. It was mostly Michael's bedroom things and a few boxes of items of hers. The bed, however, was a captain's bed and required taking apart before it could be moved. Unfortunately, Violet was hopeless about tools.

She had filed for divorce to a very incredulous Jeff. She was seeking full custody of Michael, and to her surprise Jeff wasn't fighting her on that. She knew that he probably believed she would fail and fall flat on her face, but she had no intention of that happening. She hadn't planned on requesting child support, knowing Jeff would never pay anyway, but her father, a prestigious lawyer in San Diego insisted that she at the very least ask for it.

"You never know," he told her.

So she had, and that was the part Jeff was fighting. It was ridiculous.

Jeff had been impossible over the last month, complaining constantly about anything and everything. He continually accused her of trying to steal this or that, usually some old piece of junk or random nick knack that suddenly held precious value to him. Violet did her best to ignore him. Unfortunately, ignoring him made him lash out more often at Michael for the smallest infraction. Spilling Kool-Aid on the already stained and ruined carpet became a major issue; leaving his toys on the living room floor that was usually littered with discarded fast-food wrappers or beer bottles became major offense. Violet finally lost her temper when Jeff spent an hour badgering Michael about his room, and then screamed at him to "hurry the fuck up!"

"Jeff, leave him alone!" Violet stormed, looking at her son, who was near tears. "It's okay honey, go out and play with your friends, you've done enough in your room for today."

She waited for Michael to leave the trailer and then wheeled on her not-soon-enough-to-be-ex-husband.

"Are you serious with the clean your room crap?" she queried like he was insane.

"He needs to learn to clean up after himself," Jeff sniveled, his tone exhibiting offense that she'd even ask.

Violet pointedly surveyed the living room and kitchen, which she'd ceased to clean, other than whatever mess she and Michael made, and it wasn't pretty.

"Have you looked around?"

"What's that supposed to mean?"

Violet looked back at Jeff, then shook her head slowly. "You really can't be as stupid as you act, if you were you'd forget to breathe!"

With that she walked out of the room, into their bedroom and slammed the door. She heard Jeff slam out of the trailer a few minutes later. She sat down on the edge of the bed and sighed.

Because of all the tumult, when the morning of her and Michael's move dawned Violet was nervous. She was hoping that Jeff would make himself scarce—naturally he didn't do as she wished. Regardless she was happy when she heard a truck drive up. Glancing outside she saw Dutch's silver Ram 2500 truck. She was surprised, however, to see another woman get out of the truck with Dutch. She was a beautiful black woman with long braids, interspersed with bright blues and purples. Violet walked outside to greet them.

"Vi, this is Azalea Hamilton, she's new too, not to Cal Fire, but new to our station."

"I ain't new," Azalea replied sassily, a smile on her face. "I'm a whole month up in here in So Cal!" She laughed even as she said the last. She had a great laugh, and Violet liked her immediately.

"Well, it's great to meet you," Violet said, smiling brightly. "Azalea is an interesting name."

"My mother's a reformed hippie, I blame her," Azalea said with a charming grin. "You can call me Az."

"Okay," Violet said, nodding. "So are you on the crew too, or…"

"Nope, I'm a boss, like Dutch here. I run another crew—a better one," Azalea answered, winking at Dutch as she did, a mischievous smile at her lips.

"Yeah, yeah," Dutch said, rolling her eyes. "So, let's get to it." Dutch gestured to the trailer.

Suddenly, Violet was struck with a sense of shame that Dutch was going to see where she lived, but she knew that she was headed for something better. As the three entered the trailer, Violet quickly noted that there were no looks, or widened eyes between the other two women, they merely waited for her to tell them what to take. Jeff had finally made himself scarce, to Violet's relief. She led Dutch and Az to Michael's tiny room, showing the captain's bed that needed to be dismantled. There were a few comedic moments where the pros and cons of power tools were debated.

"There's more control with manual tools," Dutch reasoned calmly.

"It's all about control with you Dutch-boi!" Az replied as she shook her head. "Power tools get the job done!"

"As do manuals, and they don't require charging," Dutch answered, her look amused.

"Blah, blah, blah," Az replied, laughing even as she rolled her eyes dramatically. "You use your clunky, old non-cool tools over there and I'll use my power tools and we'll see who gets the job done faster. Vi-Vi, you be the judge!"

Violet laughed at the change to her name. Knowing that it was more than likely that the reason Dutch preferred manual tools to electric had to do with her Amish background, she kept her mouth shut. In the end, it turned out to be a tie.

"How is that possible?" Az queried to no one in particular.

Michael ran into the room at that point and looked crestfallen. He half-heartedly smiled at Dutch, saying, "Hi ma'am."

"Hi there Michael, this is my friend Az."

"Hello," Michael said dutifully.

"Michael, what's wrong?" Violet asked, worried that Jeff had been badgering the child again.

Michael dragged the toe of a ratty tennis shoe back and forth on the carpet, his head down.

"I wanted to help take my bed apart."

Dutch and Az looked at each other, amused.

"Well, we can just put it back together and we'll watch you take it apart," Az said, grinning.

"Really?" Michael asked excitedly immediately looking up at Violet to get her okay.

"No, absolutely not," Violet said, her tone all mother. "These two are helping us out of the goodness of their hearts, we're not going to create more work for them."

"Wait!" Dutch exclaimed. "Looks like there's still a screw left. Michael, I'm exhausted, can you take care of this one?"

"Sure!" Michael cried as he practically tripped over his own feet in his excitement.

"Easy!" Dutch said, reaching out to steady the boy, even as she handed him the screwdriver.

"He should use mine," Az put in, holding up her power drill.

"Let's let him learn on something he can't bore through his finger with first, okay?" Dutch replied.

Violet watched as Dutch showed her son how to remove a screw, doing her best to keep the tears she felt burning in her throat from showing in her eyes. She caught Az's pointed look and quick grin. It warmed Violet's heart so much to see Dutch take her time with Michael to show him things, just as she had at the fire camp months before. It was such a stark contrast to the way Jeff treated his own son, it hurt her heart a bit.

"Okay so just remember: lefty loosey, righty tighty," Dutch told Michael.

"Got it!" Michael said smiling brightly. "Look Mom! I did it!"

"You did," Violet said smiling warmly at her son. Her eyes connected with Dutch's over Michael's head, and she inclined her head to her new boss. It was obvious from Dutch's pursed lips and the humor sparkling in her eyes that she'd purposely put the screw back in so Michael could remove it. It was a very sweet gesture. One of many that day.

In the end, the removal of all of Violet's items took a mere two hours. It took more than a little coaxing to get Michael to hug Jeff who'd finally reappeared, conveniently when everything was done. Finally, Michael gave Jeff a grudging half hug, most of his body turned away from his father, and then ran back to Violet. Dutch regarded Jeff for a long moment, then turned and opened the crew cab door for Violet, waiting patiently. Violet nodded her head and took Michael's hand to help him up into the truck, telling him to scoot over so she could get in too. Within a minute the four were on their way back to San Diego.

It was a two-hour drive, but they stopped in Julian to grab some lunch. They pulled up at the Miner's Diner and Soda Fountain, and Michael was thrilled at the old time feel to the place. Dutch shared his enthusiasm, and even though Violet knew that Dutch didn't normally drink things like soda, she challenged Michael to seeing how many flavor combinations he'd try. It was a fun lunch and Dutch insisted on paying for it, even over Violet's protest.

"You two are helping me move," Violet explained. "I should at least feed you lunch."

"Nope," Az said, shaking her head.

"Nope," Dutch repeated.

Violet sighed, shaking her head. These gallant women were going to be the death of her. Inwardly, however, she felt her heart ache a little again, there never seemed to be an end to the nice things Dutch did for her.

After another hour's drive they turned onto the road to the old schoolhouse. It was an old Craftsman style. It was very obviously in need of repair and work, with chipped and faded pain, and some cracked and broken moldings, but it was still a beautiful, old house.

"Oh my gosh! This is amazing!" Violet exclaimed as she climbed out of the truck. "When was this built?"

"Late 1800s," Dutch said, smiling warmly. "She's going to take some work, but she'll be back to her original beauty again in no time."

"And you're doing this all yourself?" Violet asked as she started to pull smaller items out of the back of the truck.

"Yep, floors, drywall, tile, some electrical, although I leave the big stuff to the professionals."

"Wow you know how to do all that?"

Dutch smiled, nodding. "I learned over the years."

"I guess they didn't teach the girls that kind of stuff, huh?" Violet asked, referring to the Amish.

"Nope."

The three of them, with help from a very excited Michael, finished unloading the truck. Az and Dutch put together Michael's bed and got Violet set up in the room she was staying in. Michael was thrilled to have the attic room with its angled ceiling.

Later, Dutch walked Az out to her car. At her car door, Az turned around, giving Dutch a sidelong look.

"So what's going on with the probie?" she asked Dutch directly.

Dutch looked back at her surprised by the question. "Uh, she needed a place to stay…I have room."

"Uh-huh…" Az said, closing one eye, suspicion written on her face, "and what else?"

"We're friends," Dutch said, knowing what Az was getting at, "she works for me."

"Yeah, right, like that's an issue!" She held up her hand then, "Wait, does she swing our way?"

Dutch chuckled. "Just thought to ask that?"

"Hey, it don't matter to me, lots of women think they're straight, then they wake up." That statement was accompanied by a wink.

"I see," Dutch said, amused.

"So you don't have any designs on her?"

"I do not."

"Cool, then it's okay if I ask her out?"

Dutch blinked a couple of times, surprised by both the question and her internal reaction to that. Suppressing the desire to say "no" that came immediately to her mind, she nodded mutely, staunchly refusing to look at her reaction to closely.

That night the three of them had dinner. Violet cooked, having been thrilled to discover all manner of meat, vegetables and sundry items available in Dutch's well-stocked kitchen.

"Violet this is really good," Dutch told her after a few bites. "Thank you for cooking, it's usually the last thing on my mind."

Violet smiled brightly, she was used to being bitched at by Jeff for making a healthy meal or "crap" as he called it.

"I thought I'd try something different since you have so many wonderful vegetables."

"Yeah, there's a farmer's market down the way a bit every weekend. I try to get down there as often as I can."

"Well, I'm more than happy to do this when we're home at night, I love to cook."

Dutch smiled warmly. "Wow, I won't know what to do with myself. Half the time I end up throwing vegetables out because I never get around to using them. I volunteer to do the grilling and whatever prep you need help with." She reached over, touching

Michael on the shoulder and smiling. "I'm sure Michael's happy to help too, aren't you?"

Michael lit up at the option. "Sure!"

Again, Violet smiled. She could see her son coming out of his shell around Dutch and she really appreciated it. Later, as they washed the dishes and Michael puttered around his new room unpacking things, Violet smiled up at Dutch.

"Thank you so much for being kind to him," she said, glancing up to indicate Michael.

Dutch looked surprised. "He's a good kid, why wouldn't I be kind to him?"

"Jeff wasn't always," Violet said sadly. "Actually he either ignored him or yelled at him about stupid stuff." Her eyes glazed with tears as she shook her head. "In all my years I'll never know what my time in prison and him being stuck with Jeff did to him."

"Kids are really resilient, Violet, I think he'll be just fine. He knows you love him, and that's what's important."

Violet nodded, trying to get her emotions under control. The guilt of having left her son for three years was overwhelming at times. That night she went to bed, feeling safe and happy for the first time in a long time. Dutch had everything to do with that.

The next day Violet began her formal Cal Fire training classes. Dutch let her use her truck and drove the Cal Fire one into work every day, knowing that Violet couldn't afford a car of her own just yet. That night Violet got home late, having gotten lost a couple of times. She climbed out of the truck to hear Michael's excited squeal of delight. Walking inside, she saw Dutch standing behind Michael, who was using a piece of sandpaper on the banister. She stood watching, not wanting to spoil the moment.

"Like this?" Michael asked, glancing up at Dutch.

Dutch nodded, smiling. "Just make sure you go with the grain of the wood. Do you know what that means?"

Michael shook his head, looking worried about Dutch's reaction to that.

"Okay," Dutch said patiently, "touch this here." She put Michael's hand to the banister. "See how the lines run down? You just follow those lines, okay?"

"Okay, but is it okay to touch it?" Michael asked, looking worried.

Behind them Violet grimaced, she knew Michael's question stemmed from years of being yelled at by Jeff not to touch things.

Dutch smiled widely. "You absolutely need to touch so you can feel if it's getting smooth or not." Again, she took Michael's finger and ran it along the banister. "See? Is it smooth?"

"Not right here," Michael said, looking very serious.

"That's when you put that sandpaper to work. You want to check it every so often, so you don't over sand it."

"Okay." Michael nodded, looking thrilled to be getting to do this work.

Dutch happened to glance back then, seeing the glaze of tears in Violet's eyes. She asked her about it later when Michael had gone to bed. They were sitting in the living room with the TV on, but not paying any attention to what was on.

"Why did that upset you earlier? When you came home," Dutch asked.

Violet smiled, shaking her head. "I'm sorry, I know you're seeing way too much of that with me."

Dutch leaned forward, putting her hand over Violet's hands, her look direct, "You never have to apologize for crying, Violet. I just want to understand."

Violet took a deep breath, expelling it slowly as she nodded. "Well, the thing is that Jeff never let Michael do things like sanding that banister. He was never patient with him, and he was always yelling at Michael to leave things alone and telling him not to touch his "shit." It was just so nice to see you showing him how to sand and telling him it was not only okay to touch, but also telling him why. It just makes my heart so happy that you do that kind of thing with him. I know, it's silly." She said the last words looking down at her hands, doing her best not to cry again.

"It's not silly," Dutch said, "you love your son and you want him treated with love and respect, that's not too much to ask or expect, Vi."

Violet pressed her lips together. It was crazy that her boss got what Michael's own father never seemed to understand.

"You'd make an amazing parent, you know?" Violet told Dutch.

Dutch gave a soft snort. "I don't know about that, I really don't see that kind of thing in my future."

"Because you're still dating women like Nancy," Violet teased.

Dutch laughed at that, nodding. "Yeah, that's probably part of it."

"Well maybe you need to settle down with a good woman instead."

Dutch rolled her eyes, "Yeah, yeah," she said dismissively.

"What about Az? You two get along, and she seems way more together than most."

Dutch guffawed at that one. "No, no, not her. Besides, she's interested in you."

"What?" Violet asked, dumbfounded.

"Yep."

"Why?" Violet asked, shocked.

Dutch gave her a sour look. "Why not? You're beautiful, smart, funny, and a very determined woman. Why wouldn't she be interested in you?"

"I, well, I…" Violet stammered, knowing she couldn't say what she was thinking because she didn't want to make Dutch think she was fishing for compliments. "I guess, I just didn't really think she would be."

Dutch nodded, quirking her lips in a sardonic smile. "Well, I guess you were wrong."

Violet blinked a couple of times but nodded slowly. She had a hard time believing someone as dynamic as Azalea Hamilton was even remotely interested in her.

Over the next couple of weeks, Violet spent a lot of time in training classes where she was being taught to work on a crew. Dutch had wanted her to get her formal training out of the way before she was put on the crew to learn on the job. Violet applied herself to the classes with a passion that surprised her instructors. They found her enthusiasm without ego very refreshing. Before long she was at the top of the class. It disgruntled some of the men, but they were grudging admirers of her ability to apply what they'd learned in class. Violet was beyond thrilled with everything she was learning.

In the meantime, Azalea had texted her to ask if she'd be interested in going out sometime. Violet had stared down at the text in amazement for a full minute before finally responding, saying "sure." She didn't want to assume it was a date.

On her last day of class, Violet received a text from Azalea asking if she was free that evening. Violet responded that she was. Azalea said she'd pick her up at Dutch's at seven. Dutch had already told Violet that she was happy to watch Michael for her, so Violet just had to decide what to wear. In the end she chose to dress simply, having no idea what Azalea was planning on. She wore jeans and sapphire blue shirt that looked very nice on her. She was understated on her makeup and didn't wear a lot of jewelry.

Azalea arrived at Dutch's door. She wore faded jeans, black cowboy boots a black long-sleeved shirt, and a do-rag on her head that looked like the American flag. Her braids included red and blue colors this time. Violet wondered if the other woman dyed them to match whatever she was wearing at the time. Azalea gallantly took Violet's hand, kissing her knuckles and grinning rakishly as she did.

"You ready?' Azalea asked.

"Yep," Violet said, waving to Michael and mouthing "thank you" to Dutch. The two were engaged in a fierce game of checkers.

Azalea led Violet out to a red convertible.

"Wow, what kind of car is this?" Violet asked, smiling as Azalea opened the passenger door for her.

"It's a Fiat Spider," Azalea announced proudly as she got into the driver's seat. "Just got her a couple of weeks ago."

"It's really nice," Violet replied, admiring the black interior and inhaling the new car smell. "I just love that smell!"

"Yeah," Azalea agreed, her eyes dancing with glee, "me too."

As they drove down the hill from the house, Azalea glanced over at Violet. "You look really nice tonight," she said, reaching over to touch Violet's hand that rested on the center console.

Violet smiled softly. "Thank you."

Azalea noted the demure response, she knew from Dutch that Violet had fairly lousy self-esteem. To smooth over the awkward silence, she reached over and turned the radio up a little as Halsey's 'Bad at Love' played.

"I thought we'd start off with dinner, is that okay?" Azalea queried.

"Sure." Violet nodded.

"Any specific cravings?"

Violet shook her head. "Wherever you'd like."

"Cool, there's a place called the Greek Sombrero down here in Jamul."

"Sounds interesting."

At the restaurant they ordered their food, a wonderful mix of Greek and Mexican, and ordered a couple of drinks. Sitting back, Azalea gave Violet an assessing look.

"So, tell me what I need to know about Violet Hastings," she said, grinning warmly.

"Uh…"

Azalea chuckled, seeing that she'd stumped the girl. It happened a lot when she asked that question.

"Let's start with the easy stuff, how do you know Dutch?"

Violet's eyes widened, and Az realized she'd backed into another difficult topic, but that only intrigued her.

"Well, she was the captain at the fire camp where I was an inmate," Violet stated calmly.

Az blinked a couple of times, shock showing on her face, she opened her mouth to answer, but no words came out. She hadn't really expected a shocking answer to that question.

Closing her mouth slowly, she tilted her head, "So you were an inmate…How? I mean…what did you do?"

"Well," Violet began, gripping her glass of chardonnay a little tighter, "I used stolen credit card information to pay my bills."

Az nodded slowly, waiting for the rest of the explanation. When none was forthcoming she responded, "Why?"

Violet pressed her lips together, having known that these kinds of questions would forever come up. She also knew that she'd need to start answering them with honesty and integrity if people weren't always going to see her as a criminal. *No time like the present to start,* she thought to herself.

"I was trying to support myself and my son when my husband was out of work, I got desperate and stupid. It was the wrong thing to do and I paid for it."

Az looked a little taken back by the answer, but then pursed her lips as she canted her head again.

"Fair enough," she said. A smile played at the edges of her mouth. "So you were a firefighter at the camp?"

"Well, no, I was a nursing assistant, but Cap, I mean, Dutch, helped me become one."

Again, Az looked surprised, but grinned. "She's really taken you under her wing, huh?"

Violet smiled bashfully. "Yeah, she's really incredible like that, I owe her so much."

"Well, I can bet ya that you wouldn't have made it if you hadn't done the work. Dutch doesn't seem like a sucker for a pretty face." Az gave her a wink as she said the last.

Violet couldn't stop the shocked look on her face, then she bit her lip, as she blushed. She couldn't believe that someone like this woman was actually calling her pretty!

"What's that look?" Az asked quizzically.

"What look?"

Az looked back at Violet, her eyes narrowing slightly in assessment. "You don't believe you're pretty," she stated simply.

Violet's mouth contorted into a self-effacing grimace, even as she shook her head. "I was always just the 'fat girl' growing up, I guess I've never really given that up."

Az nodded wisely, her look somber. "What we believe ourselves is what others will see, you know."

"You think so?"

"I think that letting yourself live in the past, and letting other people define your own self-worth is a dangerous thing."

Violet smiled softly. "You sound like Dutch."

"Probably why she and I get along so well," Az agreed. She canted her head then. "So why don't you believe people when they tell you that you're beautiful?"

Violet was taken back by the question; it took her a few moments to even formulate a reply. Finally she shrugged. "I feel like people are just being nice."

Az looked like she was evaluating that answer and nodded. "Okay, but why would people want to be nice to you? I mean, to your way of thinking they're lying to you, so why would someone go that far?"

Again, Violet had to think about that and come up with a response. "I guess I don't know."

"If I want to be nice to you, I can do things like open a door for you or smile at you," Az said, leaning back in her chair. "I certainly don't have to go so far as to ask you out, right?"

Violet pressed her lips together immediately, but she didn't hide her skeptical look fast enough.

"Seriously?" Az asked incredulously. "What did you tell yourself when I messaged you?"

There was a long pause as Violet debated her answer, finally she sighed. "That it wasn't really a date."

Az gave her a deadpan look, her hazel eyes sparkled mischievously a moment later as she leaned over the table and kissed Violet square on the lips.

It was a long, slow, sensuous kiss that left Violet speechless as Azalea sat back down in her chair, her look pointed.

"Think it's not a date now?"

Violet pressed her lips into a smile as laughter bubbled up in her throat. She burst out laughing, shaking her head. "I believe you, really, I do. I promise."

Azalea laughed too, knowing that she'd shocked the other woman, but having felt that it was imperative to jolt Violet out of her state of self-doubt. Their dinners arrived a few minutes later and talk turned to other topics. It was a comfortable dinner and Violet found that Az was definitely a free spirit with her own way of seeing things.

"My mom was a hippie who kinda squatted on my dad's property in Napa at one point," Az explained, "and they've been together since."

"A hippie, huh?" Violet asked smiling. "It makes sense. You seem very eclectic."

"You mean weird," Az teased.

"I do not!"

Az laughed at the aghast look on Violet's face. "Breathe sister, I'm just kidding."

After dinner Az drove them over to Hillcrest and they went to a club called Gossip Grill. Sitting out on the patio they had a couple of drinks and Violet could see that Az had a lot of friends there. Many of them came by to say hi to her, intrigued by the fact she'd brought a date.

Violet found that many of the butch lesbians were eyeing her with interest. At one point, Az reached over, taking Violet's hand in hers, giving one woman a narrowed look.

"She's with me, go on about your business…" There was a hint of humor in her voice, but her look was serious.

"Do you know her?' Violet asked.

"Yeah, she's always on the prowl," Az said, "but if she wants to ask you out, she's gonna just have to wait her turn."

Violet widened her eyes and chuckled. "Yeah right."

Az just shook her head, the woman didn't take compliments at all, did she?

"Gurrrrl!" came a voice from behind them then, and Az started laughing immediately as she turned around.

"I didn't know you were coming out tonight!" Az said as she stood up and hugged the very tall woman who'd just walked in.

"Oh you know me, when the mood takes me, I put on my best dress and out I come!"

"Well, Dooley, this is Violet. Violet this is my friend Dula Julia." Az said, gesturing to the woman.

"Nice to meet you." Violet stood extending her hand and peered up at the woman.

"Oh I like this one…" Dula said, winking at Az.

"Back off!" Az exclaimed, laughing.

"You know she ain't my type! I like 'em long and lean, and I don't mean body style!" Dula answered with a wink, then she sauntered off on heels that had to be six inches high.

"She seems like a character," Violet observed.

"The drags always are."

"Drags?"

"She's a drag queen, honey," Az said with a slight smile.

"Oh," Violet said, dumbly. "I, I didn't…I mean."

"It's okay, you haven't been in the life long."

"So did she, I mean, he… he meant men as his type?"

"She," Az emphasized, "prefers female pronouns, and she is into women who strap up." Violet's bewildered look had Az explaining. "Uses a strap on… dildo…"

"Oh!" was Violet's shocked exclamation, as she blinked rapidly.

Az gave her a crooked grin. "I'm guessing you've never experienced that either?"

"Uh, well, um, no," came the stammered reply.

Az just chuckled. "Stick with me honey, I'll teach you some stuff."

Violet took a long swig of her drink and did her best to steady her nerves. This was a whole other world!

241

Later, on the drive home, Az looked over at Violet. "So are you sure you're into women?"

"I, what do you mean?"

Shrugging Az drew in a breath. "Well you are still married to a man, right?"

"For now, I mean the divorce papers have been signed and everything, it's not like—"

Az's hand on her stopped her, "Violet, relax! I just meant in terms of reality. Are you divorcing him because you're into women, or...?"

"No, not because of that, I'm divorcing him because I'm not in love with him, but yes I like women, I just don't have a lot of experience with them."

"But some?"

"Well, yes, mostly bad though."

"Bad how?"

"Well, prison..." Violet said, not wanting to recount her experiences.

"Oh!" It was Az's turn to be surprised. "Nuff said. But if it was bad, how do you know that you actually like women?"

Violet pressed her lips together, looking embarrassed, blushing attractively.

"Aww come on! You gotta tell now!"

Violet shook her head, trying to think of what else she could say to distract Az, but it was too late.

"Tell!" Az shouted, laughter in her voice. When Violet still wouldn't talk, Az narrowed her eyes suspiciously. "You have a crush on someone..."

Violet's foot started tapping as she pressed her lips together again, looking anywhere but at Azalea.

"Oh my Dog it's Dutch isn't it?" Az deduced.

"Oh your 'dog'?" Violet queried, trying for distraction.

"Don't believe in God, so I use Dog instead. It's Dutch, isn't it?" she then repeated.

Violet gasped audibly. "What makes you say that!" she practically shouted.

Az tilted her head. "Well that reaction for starters. And you've known her for a long time now. And she is hot in that butchie sort of way…"

Violet simply sighed, knowing that she couldn't lie, but still not willing to admit anything.

"So how come you haven't done anything about that?" Az asked.

Violet snickered in response, then she gave Az a sober look. "She's been so great to me, I wouldn't want to screw that up."

"How would telling her you're into her screw things up?"

"Um, she's not into me," Violet said, her tone indicating that there was no question in her mind about that. "I don't want to make her uncomfortable, or to think that she should never have helped me out."

Azalea looked back at Violet and just shook her head. The woman was astounding when it came to evasion tactics.

"You don't believe in God?" Violet asked then.

Azalea warred with the idea of letting the conversation about Dutch go, but decided she'd pushed enough for the moment. "Nope, never have."

"Wow," Violet replied wide eyed, "I guess I never thought about not believing in God."

"Well, yeah, that's how they like you," Az replied grinning.

"They?"

"Churches, Bible bangers…"

"Oh," Violet nodded, "them."

"The big them, the over-reaching them, the all-knowing-but-not-knowing them," Azalea stated, obviously rather passionate about the topic.

The rest of the evening passed with Violet being consistently surprised by things Azalea said. When Azalea stopped in front of the schoolhouse later that evening, Violet's head was still spinning a bit with all she'd learned about the colorful character that was Azalea. Without a word, Az leaned over and kissed Violet on the lips. It was a nice tender kiss, but not overtly sexual. Violet was relieved, she had no idea what she'd do with a major sexual advance at this point in their friendship. Azalea made it easy.

"This was fun," Az said, her eyes sparkling happily, "we should definitely do it again sometime, okay?"

Violet nodded, feeling herself blushing as she reached for the door handle to get out. Going inside, she thought about the evening as she did her best to be quiet. She opened Michael's door to peek in at him and was surprised and slightly alarmed to see he wasn't in his bed. Immediately, she walked to her room just down the hall, thinking that her son might have gone into her room to sleep, he wasn't there either. Now she was worried. She hesitated for a moment at Dutch's door, but finally knocked lightly. She heard Dutch tell her to come in.

Opening the bedroom door cautiously, Violet looked in, her eyes adjusting to the dim light from the bedside lamp. She could see Dutch sitting up reading a book that now lay face-down on her lap. Michael was tucked into the other side of the large bed, snoring away.

"That's where he is," Violet said softly, relief evident on her face.

Dutch smiled softly. "He 'got lonely' or so he said."

"I'm so sorry, Dutch, I just…" Violet began as she moved to remove her child from her boss's bed.

"Vi, it is fine," Dutch said, "let him sleep." Then her eyes twinkled in the dim light. "Did you have a good time?"

Violet did her best not to wring her hands at the thought of her son bothering Dutch with his neediness and did her best to focus on the question Dutch had asked her.

"I…it was fun, yes."

Dutch canted her head slightly. "But?"

Violet widened her eyes, not realizing she'd given herself away. Regardless she did her best to recover. "No, 'but.' It was fun, Azalea is a very colorful character, she's the life of the party."

Dutch nodded slowly, her look indicating that she wasn't fooled by Violet's dodge. "But you're not going to see her again?"

Violet's eyes widened slightly, surprised by Dutch's question, then shrugged. "I'm not sure. I mean, I really like her and all, but I just don't know how this is all supposed to work."

"Work? What do you mean by that?"

Violet chewed on her lower lip, not sure what she should or shouldn't say to her boss.

245

Dutch nodded, sensing Violet's turmoil. She moved carefully to get out of bed, making sure she didn't disturb the sleeping child, and gestured toward the open bedroom door. Violet walked out into the hallway. Dutch led the way down to the kitchen, there she made them both tea and sat the cups on the table sitting down and waited for Violet to do the same. When they were seated, Violet held her cup in both hands, still not sure what to say.

"What do you mean by you don't know how this works?" Dutch asked again.

"I mean these kinds of relationships."

"These kinds of relationships...versus what?" Dutch asked.

"Well, normal ones..." Violet said off handedly, then inhaled sharply, realizing she may have insulted Dutch. Dutch didn't look insulted however, she simply nodded.

"That is the problem," Dutch said then, "you assume there is a difference." There was no annoyance in Dutch's tone. Violet had learned over the years to recognize the signs of people being angry or aggravated with her, she was relieved not to hear either in the other woman's voice.

"Well, isn't there?" Violet asked.

"Why?" Dutch asked.

"Well, usually there's a girl and a guy..."

"And the assumption in a 'normal' relationship is what? That the man takes the lead?"

"Yes," Violet answered.

"But isn't it true that the man doesn't always take the lead? For instance, Jeff was not the provider in your marriage, was he?"

Violet shrugged. "He tried to be."

"But he wasn't," Dutch said. "So you took matters into your own hands, correct?"

"And wound up in jail for it."

"True, but the fact remains that you took the lead."

Violet sipped her tea and pondered what Dutch was saying.

"So you're saying that either women in a relationship can take the lead?"

"I am saying that it is about the personality, not about the sex of the people in the relationship."

Violet thought about what Dutch was saying and wanted to ask questions, but hesitated, she knew she might be stepping over a line she shouldn't.

"What is it you want to ask?" Dutch queried, seeing the hesitation clearly on Violet's face.

"I'm not sure it's any of my business," Violet began, "but are you usually more dominant in your relationships?"

Dutch's look didn't even flicker, it was obvious to Violet that the question didn't bother her at all.

"Sometimes, but not always." Dutch shrugged. "Again, it depends on who I am in a relationship with."

"Like your relationship with Rowena?"

"Exactly, Rowena was much more dominant in our relationship than me, but when I needed to, I took charge."

"Like when you joined the navy?"

"Precisely."

Violet contemplated her situation, nodding as she did her best to let go of stereotypes she had lived with all of her life. The man was in charge, the man provided, the man made all the moves, it was a man's world. But not in this world, not with women, not with lesbians. Her natural thought had been that the more butch women assumed the roles of the "boy" in the relationship.

"So nobody is the boy…" Violet muttered, partially to herself.

Dutch chuckled. "No boys is kind of the point," she said with a wink.

Violet laughed softly, nodding as she did, "Thank you, that makes much more sense to me now. I really hadn't thought of it that way before."

"You have grown up in world where men make all of the rules, we do not have those rules."

"You grew up in that world too, though."

"Yes, but I came to terms with my adjusted reality a long time ago. You are just starting out."

Violet nodded, smiling. "Just a babe in the world."

"Indeed."

A couple days later Azalea and Dutch were talking and Dutch happened to relay the conversation she'd had with Violet. Azalea was not surprised by the conversation, but also secretly pleased that Dutch had actually taken the time and the step of explaining things to Violet. To Azalea's way of thinking, however, Violet had a lot to learn about interacting with all manners of lesbians. As such, she decided she needed to be the one to help the new possible lesbian out.

"Okay, so, watch what goes on at the bar…" Azalea nodded toward the bar area at Gossip Grill. She and Violet were sitting across from the bar, stationed at one of the tables where they could observe the people around them. "That really hot femme in black is sitting there like a cool customer, right?"

Violet scanned the bar, to locate the woman Azalea was talking about. Her eyes caught on the beautiful honey blonde with black leather pants, high heeled boots and a purple low-cut sweater. Indeed, the woman looked like she was brimming with confidence.

"And now here comes that cute little butchie we were watching earlier. This boi just doesn't give up!" Azalea enthused, as she watched the younger woman, with the short, cropped hair, jeans, combat boots and a tank top sidle up to the blonde. They'd watched the butch girl chat up no less than five women in the last hour. "Will she, or won't she?" Azalea murmured as the young butch leaned in to talk to the blonde. The blonde leaned away as the butch leaned in.

"Doh! Not this time, brutha!" Azalea all but crowed.

"I don't get it," Violet said, even as the butch girl continued to talk to the blonde.

"Blondie's not in."

"How do you know?"

"See how she's leaning back ever so slightly? No matter what that little butchie says, she doesn't change her position." Azalea nodded toward the couple. "Oh, but wait…" she murmured then. "Now here comes a contender."

Violet looked around the area and saw another woman approaching the bar, this woman was femme, with long dark hair, makeup, heels the works and she had her eye on the blonde. As Violet watched, the dark-haired woman approached the couple and smoothly moved between the young butch and the blonde, smiling down at the blonde as she leaned in to kiss her lips.

"Doh!" Azalea exclaimed, "They're a couple! Bad move, butchie!" As they watched the blonde held up her left hand indicating her ring finger. The young butch woman had the grace to bow out, smiling and nodding at the couple.

"Wow, you're good at this!" Violet enthused, shaking her head.

"You just gotta know what to watch for."

Violet nodded her head, happy to have made a friend of Azalea, the woman was more than happy to help her with her confidence and understanding the world of lesbians. There were so many nuances and unspoken rules.

"Hey, can you go grab me another beer?" Azalea said, shaking her empty beer bottle.

"Of course," Violet said, moving to stand up.

Walking over to the bar, Violet smiled at the butch woman she and Azalea had been observing.

"Hello," the butch woman said, smiling, her blue eyes twinkling.

'Hi," Violet replied, moving to stand at the bar. She immediately felt the woman slide up next to her and pressed her lips together. This was something she was used to, she waited for the negative comment about her weight, or something equally rude. It happened to her a lot, not recently but it was what she had come to expect from people.

"Can I get that for you?" the woman asked.

"I…" Violet stammered, thinking she must be missing the punchline. "Get what?" she asked, her stomach clenching as she wondered what would be said next. She turned her head to look over at the woman and was shocked to see her smiling warmly.

"Your drink, I'd like to buy you a drink."

"I…oh…well…" Violet stammered again, not sure how to react.

"Unless…" the butch woman said, glancing over her shoulder, "that smokey number you're with is…I mean, aw damn, I didn't do this again did I?" Her voice was self-effacing, her look read disgust, and Violet felt heart sick that this woman had suddenly lost all of her confidence.

"No…no…" Violet pronounced, smiling, even as she felt her heart ache a bit for the other woman. "Az and I are just friends. I…I'm just not used to handsome strangers wanting to buy me a drink," she said with a wink.

The smile that lit the other woman's face made Violet's heart soar. Had she really just said exactly the right thing? Had she also just flirted with another woman? Oh my God! It was a moment in her life she'd never expected to have. And it felt amazing!

"Well, then I guess I'll just buy you both a drink," the woman said. "I'm Duke."

"Hi, Duke, I'm Violet," she replied, with an outstretched hand. Duke took it, kissing the back of it as she bowed slightly. Violet was charmed.

She, Duke and Azalea spent the rest of the evening hanging out and having a great time. She even danced a few times, it was a great night. Violet was still smiling when she walked into the house that night. She was surprised to see her roommate sitting on the couch.

"You look like you had fun," Dutch said, smiling as she set aside the book she'd been reading.

"I did!" Violet enthused, "I actually got flirted with!"

Dutch blinked a couple of times. "Why do you say actually?"

Violet sat down on the couch next to Dutch. "It doesn't happen to me," she said candidly.

"I find that difficult to believe."

"Oh, you can believe it." Violet smiled.

Dutch shook her head. "So tell me about the flirt."

"Oh, her name is Duke, she's very cute in a butch sort of way."

Dutch nodded, "Are you going to see her again?"

"Uh," Violet hesitated, not having thought that far in advance, "I...well, I don't know. She did ask for my number."

Dutch nodded. "It sounds like she wants to see you."

"Yeah...go figure," Violet said, her tone wondrous.

Dutch curled her lips as she shook her head. "Will you never have confidence in yourself?" She sighed.

Violet considered the question. "I'm sorry, I know you don't understand this, but it's really hard. When you've been fat your whole life, and people have always treated you like you don't matter because of it, you start feeling that way. It's hard to let that go."

Dutch looked thoughtful, shaking her head, "You are right, I do not understand, but you need to start giving yourself some credit for all your hard work. You also need to let people surprise you."

Violet looked back at Dutch, she seemed to contemplate the idea

"Let people surprise me...." she said, as if tasting the phrase. Dutch always had a way of putting things that made her stop and think. "I think I could try."

"Good."

Chapter 8

After all of her training, and testing, Violet finally became part of Dutch's crew. She worked as a cutter, much as she had with the Corrections Camp. It felt good to be back doing what she felt had saved her. She found that they quite frequently worked with other fire crews, including Azalea's. At one point they were up in the forest doing drills with other fire agencies. The drill was to work with local and other Cal Fire crews and aerial support to help the teams learn to work together to fight fires. It involved setting up proper fire lines, moving the hoses into place, planning clear cutting and coordinating with the aerial support to spot flare ups and directional shifts of the fire.

It was educational, but also fun to interact with other crews. Violet was surprised to be very included in every aspect of the drill. Dutch called out instructions to her crew, directing them to areas where the fire was 'flaring up' and indicating where they needed to shift. The urgency of the commands, as well as how quickly every crew member responded, gave Violet a real feel for the new crew and how they operated.

To her surprise, she received a lot of good feedback from other fire crew members on her performance. She was told that her technical knowledge was great, but also that she knew her job and did it well. It felt really good. She was still grinning about yet another compliment, as she made her way back to the bus the San Diego unit had come up on, when Azalea caught up to her.

"Look you getting all the attention..." Az said, giving her a wink.

Violet laughed. "They said I know what I'm doing."

"Uh-huh, that and you look hot doing it!" Azalea laughed.

Violet stopped dead in her tracks, looking shocked. "They didn't say that."

"Not with their mouths." Az grinned lasciviously.

Violet thought back to the men that had been saying things like "You really got that down!" and "Damn girl, you cleared all that?" or "Look at you go!" They hadn't been in any way inappropriate, had they been being sarcastic?

Azalea could read the surprise and subsequently insecurity on Violet's face, and she put her hand on Violet's arm to stop those thoughts.

"Vi, stop it! They were being nice, and I'm sure they were being truthful about what they thought of your mad skills, but you apparently didn't see the guys checking you out all day."

Violet shook her head, giving Azalea a look to tell her that she thought she was losing her mind. "No one thinks that."

"Thinks what?" Dutch asked as she caught up to the two other women.

"Vi thinks that those guys from Tahoe don't think she's hot," Azalea put in.

Dutch's eyebrows shot up as her eyes widened. "Then I'd say Violet isn't paying very close attention."

"Right?" Azalea agreed, throwing her hands up in dismay.

Violet looked from Dutch to Azalea and shook her head, thinking both women had lost their minds.

"Why is that so hard for you to believe?" Dutch asked as they walked toward the bus.

"Because no one looks at me like that." Violet shrugged.

"You don't think anyone looks at you that way," Azalea marveled, then she gestured back toward the men heading toward their buses. "*They* were looking at you that way, Vi! Wake up!"

Violet winced at Azalea's outburst. Azalea huffed out a breath of annoyance and walked ahead to the bus. In her head, Violet knew that Azalea was trying to be nice, and that she was really trying to help. It just wasn't always that easy for her to believe anyone would see her in any way attractive. There'd been too many years of comments like "Call SeaWorld, Shamu escaped" or "Mooo!" out a car window as they passed her on the street. It wasn't something she could just forget about.

Dutch watched the emotions play across Violet's face and felt bad for her. From the many conversations they'd had, Dutch knew that Violet wasn't ever going to recognize compliments when she received them. On the bus home a few minutes later, Dutch joined Violet in one of the last seats at the back.

"She means well," Dutch indicated nodding toward Azalea who was chatting with another firefighter in front. "She's spent her whole life knowing who she was and what she had to offer. It comes easy to her."

Violet drew in a deep breath, blowing out as she nodded her head, "And she wants me to be like her."

"No," Dutch corrected, "she wants you to see how beautiful you really are, inside and out."

Violet was flummoxed by these women. "Why does she want to help me?" Violet asked ingenuously.

Dutch gave a confused laugh. "Because she cares about you, we both do."

"But why?" Violet's bewildered tone made Dutch's heart ache.

"Why wouldn't we care? You are sincere, you try your best at everything you do, you're trying to make a good life for you and your son, and most of all you're a very sweet, kind person. I'm not sure why you can't believe people would care for you."

Violet shrugged, shaking her head. "Other than the people that are required to, like my parents and my son, no one ever really has for long."

"That just makes others blind and stupid," Dutch dismissed in open disgust. "I'd rather not be lumped in with those people."

Violet looked back at Dutch for a long moment, wonderment clear on her face, then her face lit up with a bright smile. "You're right, I should appreciate that you and Azalea care for me, and I should stop being such a brat about it."

"Dat klopt!" Dutch said, smiling as she translated, "That's right."

A month later they were in the midst of fire season. Azalea and Dutch's crews had been called out for a fire in east San Diego near the Pine Creek Wilderness area within the Cleveland National Forest. It was a densely forested area, and the fire was gaining speed, moving east to west due to Santa Ana winds coming in from the desert. The teams met up at the base camp set high on a ridge above and to the east of the fire. The logistician, Sam

Walker, was laying out her maps as the teams gathered around her.

"Okay, the fire actually already jumped the line we had set up, so now we're scrambling to set new ones. Az, I want you to take your team to anchor point alpha, here," Sam said, pointing to an area a mile south of Corte Madera Road. "Dutch, I want you to start cutting your line at anchor point bravo, here." This time Sam pointed to an area a mile east of the area where Corte Madera Road curved south.

"Let's head out!" Dutch called to her team, even as Azalea got her team moving back toward their rigs.

Withing minutes the teams were in place, with the trucks parked along the access roads. Grabbing their equipment Dutch's crew, including Violet, moved to designated spots to begin cutting the fire line.

"With these winds, let's make it a good twenty feet!" Dutch called to her crew. She heard the order repeated down the line as the crew split to the farthest point to begin cutting down brush and clearing it.

Violet worked with the chainsaw, cutting at the thick brush and stepping to the side as the others cleared. She moved along the area they were clearing. She could see the fire down the slope, the hot wind out of the east was pushing the fire, and she knew this could be bad if the fire continued. It was fast moving and headed towards homes and towns. Pushing on, she and her colleagues pushed south, while the other group pushed north toward where Azalea's team was working, cutting a line to hopefully contain the fire.

Dutch had just ordered her team back to the trucks. They would head back to the base camp to insure they were out of the path of the fire, and then wait to receive updated orders. She was taking one last jog down the line to insure it was clear, moving near the trees caught her eye, and she stopped. There was a crashing sound, and suddenly she could hear hoof beats.

"Son of a…" she muttered as she tried to formulate a plan to move, a huge buck came plunging out of the forest and headed straight for Dutch. Doing her best to move out of the way, the deer veered suddenly and slammed into her at full speed.

"Anyone got the chief?" Was the call on the radio ten minutes after they'd all made it back to the trucks.

In one of the crew trucks, Violet listened intently for the reply, she was alarmed when none came.

"She was walking the line," Violet told one of the other crew members, who radioed it in. "Let's go!"

The crew got out of the truck, as she saw others doing the same. They quickly spread out, and before long a radio call came back. "Found her, she's out cold!"

Back at base camp, smelling salts were shoved under Dutch's nose, which had her starting awake immediately and wincing a moment later.

"Heilige Hel…" Dutch muttered as she touched her head gingerly.

"Take it easy, Chief," the medic attending her cautioned. "You took a pretty good clobbering. Do you remember what happened?"

Dutch blew her breath out slowly, to combat the pain in her throbbing skull, she could see Violet and Azalea standing nearby looking worried, she felt her vision swim a bit as she got dizzy.

"I...There was a buck...Enorme...huge," she translated her own words, "he came charging out of the woods, I tried to dodge, I failed. He won."

The medic chuckled at the description. "I'm thinking you have at least a mild concussion, I'm guessing the deer hit you on your left side, since you have yourself a nasty bruise on that side of your face. Then it seems that you probably hit your head on hard ground when you fell. I'd like to run some tests to get an idea how severe the concussion is. Are you feeling dizzy?" The medic had observed that Dutch was blinking slowly, and wavering a bit, even in a seated position on the gurney.

Dutch looked back at the medic for a few long moments, before answering, "Yes."

"Any nausea?"

"Some." Dutch nodded and was immediately sorry she had as she winced again as pain shot through her head.

"Head hurts too, I see." The medic grinned. "I'm gonna send you down for a doctor's assessment, and probably a CAT Scan."

Three hours later, Dutch was sitting in a hospital bed at Sharp Grossmont Hospital. Her left cheek and eye were black and blue and every angry looking. Violet, who'd finally made it down to the hospital got permission to see her.

"Are you okay?" Violet asked immediately, taking in the bruises on Dutch's face, even as she reached for Dutch's hand.

Dutch took Violet's hand, even as she nodded carefully. They'd given her something mild for the pain. "They are still waiting for the results of the scan."

"How are you feeling though?" Violet worried.

Dutch sighed. "I feel like someone used my head for a soccer ball."

"Ouch." Violet winced. "I have to admit, I freaked out a little bit when they found you lying on the ground out there."

Dutch squeezed Violet's hand gently. "I am sorry."

Violet shook her head. "You don't have to be sorry, I just want you to be okay."

A couple of hours later they finally stated that Dutch had a concussion, and that while they were releasing her from the hospital, she'd need someone to monitor her at home.

"I've got that covered," Violet told the doctor. "What about pain management?"

The doctor looked at Dutch, seeing the furrowed brow of someone in pain, "I'd recommend ice, and some NSAIDs, like Aleve or Motrin."

Violet didn't look convinced that any of that would help, but nodded all the same.

When Violet and Azalea got Dutch home, they helped her to her room.

"Was there anyone you wanted me to call?" Violet asked, suddenly realizing that perhaps Nancy, Dutch's absent girlfriend, would want to be there.

Dutch shook her head carefully as she started to reach down to untie her boots.

"I got it," Violet said, kneeling down to deal with the shoes.

"So where's Nancy these days?" Azalea asked pointedly.

"We are not seeing each other anymore," Dutch answered simply.

Violet glanced at Azalea, who gave her a *See!* look. Violet just shook her head, knowing that Azalea was pushing.

"Okay, I want you to get some rest," Violet said, shooing Azalea out of the room, lest she start more trouble. "Do you need anything? Water? Ice pack?"

"I am okay," Dutch indicated as she eased into bed, "thank you, Violet."

"I'll be back to check on you in an hour or two," Violet replied as she closed the door partially.

Back in the living room, Azalea turned to her. "See? She's not even seeing that Nancy ho-bag anymore, you need to go for it!"

"I'm not 'going for it'! She's hurt, and I'm going to take care of her. That's it."

Azalea gave her an annoyed look. "You know..." she began.

"Yes, I know." Violet rolled her eyes, then went into the kitchen to figure out what to make for dinner. Michael would be home from school soon, and she wanted to have some plan for him. She wondered if she should ask her parents to take him for a few days, so Dutch could rest.

Azalea had followed her into the kitchen and stood leaning against the counter as Violet started taking inventory of what she had for dinner. Glancing at the other woman, Violet could see that Azalea wasn't done with this conversation.

"Are you staying for dinner?" Violet asked over her shoulder.

"I'll stay for dinner, and I'll be back to check on both of you a few times over the next few days." Azalea's voice was matter-of-fact, and Violet knew that Azalea was planning an all-out assault on her soon.

There had been many conversations over the last couple of months. Conversations about how Violet should just go for Dutch, and that clearly Dutch cared about her, but just was too respectful to make any moves. Over and over again, Violet had told Azalea that she thought she was crazy.

"She feels like she's gotta watch out for me, that's all," Violet had indicated one night when they were once again discussing it. They'd gone out to Gossip Grille again, and Azalea had been Hell-bent on getting Violet to agree with her.

"Oh for fuck's sake!" Azalea threw her hands up. "You keep telling yourself that."

Violet crossed her arms in front of her chest, refusing to defend her position yet again. As far as she was concerned 'Bec,' as she'd begun to call Dutch, was a good friend, and someone she admired. Sure, she thought she was gorgeous and would love things to be different, but they'd been living in the same house for months at this point and nothing had happened, so it was obvious Dutch didn't want anything to happen.

"How many women in here have bought you drinks?" Azalea changed tactics.

"What? I don't know, a few. They're friends with you, so they're nice to me."

"Oh yeah, that's it," Azalea deadpanned as she rolled her eyes.

"Do you see any of them around?" Violet gestured to the space around them. "No, you don't."

Azalea smacked her forehead, and shook her head, like she was trying to fathom Violet's thinking.

"Lemme lay this out for ya…" She gestured in a circle around them. "See, they make the first move and then you," she said, jabbing her finger in Violet's direction, "follow up if you're interested."

Violet blinked a couple of times, but then started to shake her head.

"Don't!" Azalea had nearly exploded. "I've been doing this a lot longer than you, and that's how it works. But here's the thing…If you're not interested, you purposefully aren't getting it."

Violet didn't respond, simply sipping her drink, and Azalea could see that she was going to avoid the topic again. Huffing her breath out, Azalea shook her head and gave up at that point.

Back in the kitchen in Jamul, Azalea was staring at Violet as she moved around the kitchen, pulling out pasta and meat from the freezer. The subject of Azalea's current annoyance avoided her eyes.

"You're hopeless, you know that?" Azalea sighed finally.

"I do, yes." Violet nodded.

Azalea couldn't help but chuckle at Violet's simple response. Just then Michael came through the back door.

"You're home…" Michael said, looking shocked. "I thought there was a fire."

"Bec got hurt, so we're back early, but the fire is contained too," Violet informed him as she kissed him on the forehead.

"What! Bec's hurt?" Michael exclaimed.

"She's going to be okay," Violet assured, "but her head hurts right now, so we're gonna be super quiet okay?"

"Did she get burned?" Michael asked, his eyes wide with fear.

"No," Violet was quick to tell him, not wanting his mind to go down that path, "she got hurt a…different way," Violet stammered as she tried to figure out an easy way to tell her son what happened.

Michael looked quizzical, but it was evident that he wasn't sure he believed his mother.

"She got beat up by Bambi's dad," Azalea told Michael.

Violet guffawed at the description, even as Michael's look shifted between the two of them.

"It's true," Violet told Michael, still somewhat chuckling at Azalea's sense of humor, "she got knocked down by a big male deer."

"How?" Michael's eyes were wide with complete innocence.

"The deer was trying to get away from the fire. Dutch was in the wrong place at the wrong time," Azalea told him.

Michael grimaced. "Ouch."

"Yep." Violet nodded.

"So, deer one, Dutch nothing, huh?" Michael stated slyly, which had both Violet and Azalea laughing.

Walking into Dutch's room, Violet was loathe to wake her, but the doctor had said it was important that Violet check on her every hour or two to ensure that she would wake easily. Dutch lay on her right side, in the center of her full-sized bed, her left arm extended to the side. Violet could see that even in her sleep, Dutch was grimacing. Kneeling down, Violet touched Dutch on the forehead, careful to avoid the bruises on her cheek.

"Bec," she whispered softly, not wanting to startle Dutch, but Dutch didn't respond. "Bec," Violet repeated, a little bit louder this time, also giving her shoulder a bit of a push. Finally, Dutch stirred.

"Mm?" Dutch murmured as she opened her eyes slowly.

"How are you feeling?" Violet searched Dutch's face, even as she asked the question. "You look like you're still hurting."

Dutch curled her lips in a grimace and nodded slightly. "Yes, I am."

"Okay, do you want to try ice, or medicine?" Violet knew the answer even before Dutch said it.

"Ice, please." Her voice was barely audible.

"I'll be right back."

Down in the kitchen, Michael was sitting at the counter doing his math homework.

"Is she awake?" he asked eagerly.

"She is, but she's hurting right now, babe, I want her to be out of pain before you go check on her. Okay?"

Michael bit the inside of his cheek, contemplating the idea of Dutch being in pain. He looked up to Dutch, she was always so nice to him and she was teaching him stuff all the time. Seeing her in pain didn't sound like something he wanted to experience. Finally, he nodded his head and went back to doing his homework. Violet was relieved it had been that easy. Part of her knew that he needed to see for himself that Dutch was okay, but she was also cautious about him being too rambunctious and causing Dutch more pain.

Back in Dutch's room, Violet handed Dutch the ice pack with a towel.

"See if this helps," Violet said softly. "Just be careful not to leave it on too long, the doctor said about twenty minutes. Do

265

you want me to come back in twenty to take it away?" Violet asked, seeing that Dutch was already looking like she was falling asleep again. Dutch nodded.

After a few tries with the ice pack, Dutch finally opted for Advil. Violet had just gotten back to the kitchen to help Michael with the rest of his homework when she heard heavy footfalls, and then the sound of horrible retching. Hastening to the bathroom, Violet saw Dutch move to sit down on the floor next to the toilet, even as she reached up to flush the toilet. Violet grabbed a washrag and rinsed it with cold water, handing to Dutch, who took it with a shaking hand.

"I guess not so much on the meds, huh?" Violet asked solicitously.

Dutch frowned, shaking her head slowly, even as she moved to get up. Violet moved to her side, helping her. "Do you want to try the ice again? Or I can call the doctor…"

"Let us try ice again," Dutch told her.

Three hours later things were getting desperate. Dutch was in severe pain, and ice packs weren't working. Violet had been on the internet trying to find any information she could get. She'd called the doctor's office, but they took a message for the doctor. Walking back into the room, Violet had a bottle of water and more pills for Dutch to try.

"Az went and got these, they are Advil liquid-caps. They're supposed to dissolve fast…" Her voice trailed off as Dutch started waving her hand, making a distinctly nauseated face. "Let's try it," Violet urged, "we have to get you out of pain, the only other option is a trip to the Emergency Room. Since there was a twenty car pile-up on 8 East about an hour ago, who knows how long we'd wait."

Dutch blew her breath out through her nose. "I do not want to throw up again."

"I have a plan for that." Violet assured her.

"What plan?" Dutch asked suspiciously, even as she moved to sit up slightly so she could take the pills.

Violet handed her the pills and the bottle of water. Once Dutch had taken the pills and washed them down, Violet put the bottle on the nightstand. Sitting down next to Dutch on the bed, she reached out and took her arm. She slid her thumb down from Dutch's palm to her wrist, positioning her thumb between the two large tendons there, then gently pressed down. Looking down at Dutch, she asked, "How's your stomach feeling?"

Dutch looked like she was taking an internal gauge, then looked bemused. "Not too bad," she stated in wonder. "How did you do that?"

"Acupressure." Violet shrugged. "I found it on the internet. If I can keep you from throwing up the meds long enough for them to work, hopefully they'll make you feel better."

Dutch blinked a few times, then smiled, nodding her head. "Very smart."

"Sometimes," Violet mused.

"Often times," was Dutch's rejoinder.

"You just lay there and rest, and let's hope this works."

Violet continued to apply the pressure point, moving her thumb every other minute as the instructions had said, so as not to restrict the blood flow for too long. Before long Dutch was asleep. Violet continued to do the acupressure, just in case, since she wasn't able to ask Dutch how she was feeling.

Violet started awake when she felt someone stir next to her. It took her a long moment to figure out where she was. She was still sitting in Dutch's bed, leaning against the headboard. Looking down, she saw that Dutch was watching her.

"How are you?" she asked her patient.

"Headache is better," Dutch told her, "I think it might not explode after all."

"Well, that's a relief. Brains are so hard to get out of the sheets." Violet winked at her. "Did you want to try and eat something now that your stomach is settled?"

Dutch nodded.

Violet went downstairs and heated up some chicken broth and brought up some bread to eat with it, she didn't want to chance upsetting Dutch's stomach any further. Bringing it back, she helped Dutch sit up and put pillows behind her so she could sit comfortably.

Dutch proceeded to eat a little bit of the broth, a couple of crackers and drank the entire bottle of water Violet had brought for her. Violet sat on the side of the bed, watching to make sure Dutch didn't need anything.

"Thank you for this." Dutch nodded toward the bowl.

"You're welcome, I have to take care of the boss," Violet joked.

Dutch reached out, taking Violet's hand. "You always take good care of me." Dutch's voice was sincere.

"And I always will, as long as you let me." Violet's smile was warm, she meant every word.

Dutch squeezed her hand. "I am not used to this," she intimated, "I usually do the taking care."

With a downcast look, Violet shrugged. "I'm used to having to do everything." She raised her eyes to smile softly. "But I have to say, it's really nice to take care of someone that deserves and appreciates it."

Dutch shocked her by kissing her hand sweetly. "We can take care of each other."

Violet felt a sharp pang in her heart, she knew that Dutch meant as friends, but she also knew she wanted it to be more than that.

"I'd like that. Now, let me help you settle back down so you can rest some more." Her voice took on an officious tone, as she shifted pillows and helped Dutch ease back down on the bed. "Do you want any more Advil? It's been six hours."

Dutch took in a deep self-assessing breath, blowing that breath out she shook her head.

"Okay. Let me go take this stuff downstairs. Do you want anything?" Violet asked.

"I am good, thank you." Dutch smiled.

"Okay." Violet nodded, then headed back down to the kitchen, once there she deposited the bowl in the sink, and walked into the family room, where Michael and Az were engaged in a battle on a video game.

"Az, I need a favor..." Violet said to the other woman.

Dutch was out for a week, convalescing. The day she walked back in the office she glowered at the stack of messages, mail and paperwork on her desk. It took her an entire day to get through half

269

of it. She'd just picked up another stack when she noticed the transfer request. It caught her eye because there weren't many requests this time of year. Sitting back down at her desk, she picked up the sheet and read the name, her eyes widened.

Picking up her phone, she pressed the intercom for her assistant. "Jan, please get Violet Hastings in here as soon as possible."

Violet walked into Dutch's office a half an hour later. "You wanted to see me?"

"Have a seat," Dutch told her, gesturing to the chair Violet stood in front of. Violet sat down, she was nervous, and Dutch could see it by the way she fidgeted. "So, what's the meaning of this?" Dutch asked, holding up the transfer request.

Violet took a deep breath, blowing it out slowly. Reaching behind her, she closed Dutch's door. "I wanted to talk to you about that, but I figured it wouldn't be till we were home."

Dutch looked back at her for a long moment, blinking a couple of times. "Let's talk about it now," she said, her look unreadable.

Violet pressed her lips together, trying to gather her thoughts. Finally, she looked back at Dutch. "Well, the way I see it, I can't work for you anymore."

Dutch's mouth opened in shock, then she shook her head, as if unable to believe what she'd just heard.

"Why not?" she finally asked, her voice relaying her surprise.

Violet held her breath for a long moment, debating her next words, then she sighed, "Because I really, really want to date you."

"Oh." It was a single word, uttered with such incredulity that it was almost laughable. Dutch's mouth worked, like she was trying to form words, but nothing was coming out. After a long minute, she stated, "I think we should definitely talk about that part when we get home."

Violet winced comically. "See? That's what I was saying."

"I know!" Dutch exclaimed, followed by a chuckle and a smile. "Get back to work!" she ordered then, still looking jovial.

"Yes, ma'am!" Violet replied, saluting sharply as she got up.

As it turned out, they didn't have time to talk that evening, because both units were called out to a fire in East San Diego. The fire was a fast spreading and wild, that ate up thousands of acres of land. One day turned into a week, and then two weeks. Fire crews from all over the United States came to help fight the ever-growing fire.

Dutch and Violet were lucky to grab a few hours of sleep wherever they could, and in whatever clearing was safe, there was definitely no time to discuss dating. They'd agreed to talk about the prospect of dating once the summer was over and fire season would hopefully start to die down.

When the weather finally started to cool, it was mid-September. It seemed that Fall was just around the corner. It was early on a Friday morning, Dutch had to work that day, but Azalea's team was off, so Violet would be home that day. Even so, Violet got up and made Dutch coffee and breakfast.

"What is this?" Dutch asked, smiling as she walked into the kitchen, seeing the table set with food.

"Breakfast." Violet smiled brightly. "I thought we might have a chance to talk…" She let her voice trail off, so Dutch would hopefully know what she wanted to talk about.

Dutch nodded her head slowly, a slight grin on her lips. "Indeed."

Violet handed Dutch a cup of coffee, black, like she always drank it. Then she sat down at the table with Dutch and clasped her hands together in front of her. She was doing her best not to be nervous, but she had no idea if Dutch was even amenable to going out with her. Their relationship hadn't changed since she'd made her admission about wanting to date Dutch, and Violet wasn't sure if that meant Dutch didn't want anything to change, of if indeed she was waiting until they could talk. Now the time had come and Violet needed to know.

"So…" she began hesitantly, "about dating…"

Dutch took a sip of her coffee, nodding as she did. "Yes," she said simply.

"So, the reason I want to date you, I mean, I know that you're against dating someone you supervise, and I totally get that, but—"

Dutch held up her hand to stop Violet's rambling. "I said yes."

"To…" Violet stammered.

"To dating you," Dutch supplied.

"I…oh…well…wow." Violet faltered, having been sure she'd need to convince Dutch to give it a try. Dutch took a bite of the eggs Violet had made her and looked back at Violet as she chewed. "Okay then." Violet finally nodded.

"When?" Dutch asked.

"Um, tonight?" Violet queried, afraid she'd lose her chance if too much time passed.

"Tonight it is." Dutch nodded, "I should be home by around five."

"Great!" Violet enthused, smiling as her mind already started racing with plans.

That day in the office, Dutch found herself wondering what Violet would want to do. She had plenty memories of nights on the town with Nancy and they weren't happy ones. Dutch knew that Violet was different, although she had been out to dinner and the bar with Azalea a number of times…Dutch wasn't sure what Violet had in mind, but she started mentally preparing herself for dinner and going out to a club afterwards. Glancing out her window, she could see clouds gathering, it seemed like rain was headed their way. Frowning, Dutch pictured the soggy evening ahead. Shrugging, she figured things would go the way they were meant to go and there was nothing she could do to change it. She continued with her work, gathering data for end of year reports.

As she drove home that evening, the rain had started, but it was still light. The weather forecasters were calling for the rain to become harder in the next few hours. Dutch didn't relish the idea of going out in the rain but knew she couldn't disappoint Violet. She resigned herself to going home and taking a shower and getting ready.

Driving up to the old schoolhouse, Dutch smiled. The porch light was already on, and the lights in the front room were welcoming. She had to admit that she enjoyed having someone to come home to; her house felt more like a home to her with Violet and Michael in it. It struck her that she really hadn't thought about it that way before. Prior to them moving it, the house had seemed cold and dark, it had been her goal to bring back the house's former glory and make it a lovely home for someone. She'd never really imagined that it would perhaps become a home for her.

Climbing out of the truck, she quickly made her way up the front steps and onto the porch. Her boots were instantly muddy, so she sat on the bench on the porch to take them off. As she stood again, the front door opened and Violet opened the door, smiling at her.

"Hi!" Violet smiled brightly.

"Hello." Dutch returned the smile, as she walked into the house.

"It's getting a little nasty out there," Violet said, seeing the dark clouds and the trees blowing in the wind that was coming up.

Dutch nodded, hanging her jacket up in the hall closet. "It's supposed to rain even more tonight."

Violet smiled softly, her eyes sparkling with mystery. "Well, then I guess it's a good thing we're not going out in it."

"We're not?" Dutch tilted her head, surprised by this information. "You've changed your mind?"

Violet laughed, a warm happy sound that made Dutch smile again.

"I thought we'd have a nice dinner, and maybe watch a movie here." The relief that flooded Dutch's veins was so painfully obvious to Violet that she shook her head. "You didn't think I'd drag you out in that"—she gestured to the wet, windy world outside the door—"did you?"

Dutch pressed her lips together, her look contrite.

"Well, I'm not that mean," Violet told her, sensing that someone like Nancy would have done just that. "Now, why don't you go take a nice long shower. Dinner has about another half hour to forty-five minutes to go. So take your time. I made a pot roast."

Dutch could not keep the smile off her face, even as her stomach reminded her that she hadn't eaten lunch that day.

"That sounds wonderful!"

A half an hour later, Dutch walked into the kitchen, dressed in khakis and a black polo shirt. Her hair was freshly washed, and she smelled of sandalwood, which smelled like heaven to Violet. She was struck once again by how very handsome Dutch was and it amazed her no end that Dutch was such a wonderful person on top of her incredible good looks. In Violet's experience, that wasn't how it usually worked. The best looking people usually made her feel the worst about herself.

Violet had continued to work out, to keep up her strength and stamina, and she'd definitely become more toned, but she still had curves and was by no means skinny. What she had gained was some self-confidence. Thanks to constant support and compliments from not just Dutch and Azalea, but from others in her unit, mostly men, but it still felt good. The raise in self-esteem had given her enough courage to take the chance of asking Dutch to date her. The fact that Dutch had agreed just made the feeling that much sweeter.

Dutch noticed that Violet had put on different blouse, it was a flattering olive-green color—very feminine and accentuating to her shape, without being too revealing. She'd also touched up her light, natural looking makeup and run a brush through her chestnut brown hair. To Dutch, Violet looked beautiful, without a lot of makeup or artifice. Violet was naturally stunning, her kindness and warmth shined through her milk chocolate brown eyes.

"You look lovely," Dutch told Violet, taking her hand and kissing her fingers.

Violet nearly swooned at the gallant gesture, she smiled up at Dutch, "Thank you, you look so handsome." Her voice held awe.

"Bedankt," Dutch said.

Violet turned her head slightly. "Thank you in Dutch?"

"Very good," Dutch chuckled, as she inclined her head. "Dinner smells great."

"Well, have a seat and we can eat," Violet told her.

A few minutes later, Dutch was once again very impressed with Violet's cooking ability. She'd not only made a pot roast with carrots, onions and celery, but mashed potatoes, fresh bread, and a homemade apple pie for dessert. During the meal they discussed a variety of topics, including life in the Amish world.

"It sounds like it was a much simpler way to live," Violet said, her look serene.

"It definitely was," Dutch agreed, "but I wasn't able to be my true self there."

Violet nodded, wincing slightly. "So you've never seen any of your family again?" she asked gently.

Dutch shook her head.

"That must be really hard."

"I am shunned, I can never return, that is the decision I made," Dutch shrugged.

Violet reached out, putting her hand over Dutch's on the table. "That doesn't make it any easier though, does it."

Dutch looked down at their hands together, turning her hand over to interlace her fingers with Violet's, then she looked back up at her.

"It was never easy," she admitted, but then she squeezed Violet's hand gently, "but I could never have something like this, if I had stayed."

Violet felt a warm feeling in her heart at those words. She smiled demurely, not sure what she could say to such a declaration.

"Let me clear the dishes, and then we can figure out what movie we want to watch." Violet said as she stood from the table.

Dutch stood too, moving to help.

"You go relax, I've got this," Violet told her.

Dutch shook her head. "You cooked, I need to do my share."

They cleared the table together and then settled down in the den to pick a movie to watch. Dutch had one TV in the house, and it was in her den, located just below the kitchen in the split-level main room of the old schoolhouse. She'd admitted that she rarely watched it, however. Violet had a small movie collection that she'd brought with her, otherwise Michael used it to play video games when he was allowed time.

They'd just begun to watch a romantic comedy, sitting side by side on the large sectional in the room, both with their feet up on the large ottoman, when the rain outside seem to be pounding on the roof. Dutch picked up the remote, pausing the movie, as she tilted her head up to listen to the rain. Violet sat up, listening to the rain too, they looked at each other.

"I love the sound of the rain," Dutch said.

"Me too." Violet smiled softly.

Dutch held out her arm, motioning for Violet to come closer. It was the most natural movement, and Violet found the idea of laying in Dutch's arms listening to the rain was the best possible way to finish their first date. She moved back, leaning against Dutch, feeling Dutch's arm encircle her shoulders. Violet snuggled against Dutch's warmth, inhaling the scent of smoke and sandalwood that always emanated from the woman.

"This was a great idea," Dutch stated, her smile wistful.

"I'm glad you like it," Violet said, reaching her hand out to caress Dutch's hand that rested on her lap. She found that she wasn't nervous or self-conscious at that moment and it astounded her. Her fingers traced patterns on the back of Dutch's hand, as they listened to the rain.

It was a full half hour before the rain finally slowed. Dutch glanced down at Violet.

"Did you want to watch the rest of the movie?" she asked, as Violet moved to sit up, but Dutch saw another thought cross Violet's face, even though she tried to hide it quickly.

"I..." Violet began, but couldn't say what she really wanted.

"What?" Dutch encouraged.

"I wanted to...but I don't know, how..." Violet huffed out her breath in frustration as she suddenly felt embarrassed.

"How to what?"

Violet pressed her lips together as she grimaced. "To kiss you."

Dutch smiled, her eyes crinkling at the corners. "How about you let me handle that part?" she said, and before Violet could even respond Dutch leaned in, her lips moving over Violet's in a way that made her feel like she'd never truly been kissed before.

Dutch's mouth on hers was warm, sweet and so sensual, Violet could not believe this was the same woman she'd been friends with all this time. She couldn't help the soft moan that escaped her lips as Dutch's arms encircled her, pulling her closer and deepening the kiss. When Dutch's mouth finally left hers, Violet felt almost weak. She stared up at Dutch, her look dazed.

"Wow," she said simply.

Dutch chuckled warmly. Moving to stand, she picked up the remote and turned off the TV, then put her hand out to Violet, who took it as she stood as well. Dutch led her upstairs.

In the bedroom, Dutch leaned in to capture Violet's lips again. Violet felt her whole body tremble at the feeling of Dutch's kiss, it was both strong and warm. Dutch moved to sit down on the side of the bed, and Violet followed, their lips never parting. Violet let her hands roam over Dutch's arms, feeling the strength she'd so often witnessed and reveling in it. She could feel Dutch's hands on her back, holding her close, but not overly tight. When Dutch's hand moved to slide through her hair to the back of her head, Violet shuddered, thinking of all the times she'd seen an actor do that in a movie and wishing someone would do that to her. Her body was alive with sensations, and she ached in a way she never had before. Was this what true sexual excitement felt like? No wonder people would do anything for that feeling!

When she felt Dutch's hand on her skin, at her back, Violet marveled at the warmth. Dutch's hand stroked her skin reverently, and it was an amazing feeling. Dutch took her time, not moving too quickly, and Violet knew that she was giving her the time to be comfortable with what they were doing. At that thought, Violet felt a tug at her heart, knowing this amazing person was so considerate of her lack of experience that she was take her time like this.

Before long, however, Violet found that her body was demanding more, and that feeling had her being a little bolder. She wanted to touch Dutch's skin, to nuzzle that wonderful scent and feel Dutch's skin under her lips. Reaching up, she unbuttoned Dutch's shirt, sliding her hands inside to touch her shoulders. When she heard Dutch's soft moan in response, she felt her entire body start to pulse with need. In her need to feel Dutch against her, she reached up and pulled off her blouse, pushing the sides of Dutch's shirt aside. Dutch obliged by taking off her shirt, laying it aside and gathering Violet in her arms, pressing their bodies together.

They kissed for what seemed like hours, and before long had shed all of their clothing. Dutch had just stood to shed her pants and boxer briefs, with Violet looking on from the bed and admiring Dutch's chiseled muscles, abs and overall lean form. She had a sudden flash of what her body must look like by comparison. Embarrassment fell like a lead curtain over her and she was suddenly ashamed of her body again. She immediately moved to grab covers to hide herself.

Dutch could see the change in Violet immediately and knew by the way she grabbed the quilt from the bottom of the bed to pull up over her that it was because she was suddenly shy. With patience born of years of practice, Dutch knelt next to the bed, her eyes looking into Violet's. She reached out, touching Violet's face, a look of appreciation in them.

"You have such beautiful eyes..." Dutch said, her voice holding a note of awe, as she trailed her hand over Violet's cheek, "and skin so smooth." She moved her hand to trace lightly down Violet's neck and along her shoulder. Leaning in, she nuzzled Violet where her ear and neck met, her lips trailing a kiss down her neck. "And you smell so good." As her lips continued to move down to the tip of Violet's shoulder, Dutch ever so gently slipped the quilt down, moving her lips down as she did. "I never dreamed a woman could be so warm, so soft and so inviting…" She went on, her lips moving down Violet's breasts, making Violet's breath coming in soft gasps.

Dutch moved to continue her exploration of Violet's body, taking the time to touch and taste every part, while continuing to whisper loving, sweet words. She made it all the way down to Violet's toes, and then worked her way back up Violet's now trembling body.

By the time Dutch had made her way to her thighs, Violet couldn't think straight, let alone be shy or embarrassed. Her body was aching for Dutch to take anything she wanted. She could feel Dutch's warm breath on her, and the aching between her legs waited with anticipation to feel those strong lips on her. Dutch, however, moved to kiss her way back up to Violet's lips, settling her body over Violet's, and between her legs. Leaning down, she took possession of Violet's lips again in a strong passionate kiss, pressing her body against Violet's, pressing her heat against the wet and heat of Violet's body.

Violet was sure she would explode from the feeling of Dutch's lean strong body against hers, as Dutch began moving, sliding her body back and forth against Violet's as her lips coaxed more and more passion from Violet's lips. The heat was building, like a spring that was being wound tighter and tighter. Dutch's body moved in a way that contacted Violet's hardened nipples and aching pussy with just enough friction to have Violet pulling at Dutch, wanting more contact.

"Please, please…" Violet found herself panting. "Oh my God…" she moaned as Dutch's body slid over hers one more time and suddenly she was exploding, and an orgasm rocked through her—the likes of which she'd never experienced. To her surprise, she heard Dutch give a shout of excitement as her body rocked against hers.

When their orgasms ended, Dutch moved slightly to lay on her side, keeping her body partially covering Violet's, as they both did their best to catch their breath.

"Wow…" Violet repeated her earlier comment, her voice still slightly breathless.

Dutch grinned. "You can definitely say that again." She reached over, touching Violet on the cheek so Violet would look at her. "That was amazing."

"For you?" Violet croaked out the question in her surprise.

Dutch laughed, it was a wonderful, warm, sound that made Violet feel so happy in that moment. "Yes for me." Dutch put her lips to Violet's shoulder again, kissing her skin. "You have always been different for me."

"I have?" Violet couldn't believe what she was hearing.

"You've made me want to draw out the best in you. And in doing it, I think it drew out the best in me as well."

Violet blinked a few times, unable to believe what she was hearing. "You've always been so kind to me, I never understood why."

Dutch shook her head as she grinned. "Because you are kind, because you take so much into yourself to do great things."

Violet shook her head. "I don't understand that."

"Well, that, right there," Dutch said. "You admit when you don't understand something. You approach things so much differently than some would in your place." When she saw that Violet wasn't getting what she was saying, Dutch leaned up on her elbow, looking down at Violet. "You could have stayed where you were when I met you. You could have played the victim when you were put in jail for trying to help your family. A lot of people would have, but you didn't. And you looked for ways to better yourself, you didn't just sit around waiting for someone to help you. You helped you."

"You helped me, do that," Violet said.

"No, I gave you an opportunity," Dutch said, "what you did with it, was completely up to you. And you did incredibly at it, and even saved my life, remember?"

Violet smiled, it felt so good to hear this, not just to hear it, but to hear it from someone she respected so much. It was an incredible feeling. With those thoughts swirling around inside her, she turned over to face Dutch. She reached out, touching Dutch's cheek.

"But you gave me that chance, and you showed me what true kindness looks like." Her voice was thick with emotion, tears of gratitude shown in her eyes, "You gave me the confidence in myself to push for what I wanted. You talk about me saving your life, but you really saved mine first, but seeing something in me that I didn't even know was there."

"Violet it was always there," Dutch told her, "you pushed through so much in your life. Even when it seemed like everything was against you, you continued to try to better yourself. You wanted a better life for yourself and for Michael. I simply gave you a chance to prove to yourself and them that you could do this work."

"But you didn't have to."

"No, I didn't have to, but I'm so glad I did."

"Why?" It was the question that Violet never seemed to have a full answer for, why had she gotten so lucky?

Dutch smiled softly, moving her finger to touch Violet's chest where her heart was located. "Because I discovered someone who was funny, and sweet, generous and kind, someone who would take what she was offered without asking for more, but gave back everything she had to succeed. Even here." Dutch gestured to the house around them. "You've made this more of a home than I have ever managed."

"But you welcomed us here," Violet said, "you didn't have to do that, so I wanted to make it as nice for you as I could."

"And you have," Dutch agreed, "you have no idea how nice it is to have someone give back."

Violet thought back to what Azalea had told her about Dutch's relationship with Nancy—that she was a "pillow princess" only receiving of pleasure, never giving it back. She guessed that was the case in more than one way.

"You've given us so much," Violet told her, "you've not just let us into your home, but you've shown Michael love and affection he's never had from anyone but me. You've become a kind of father figure to him, and that's something I love so much about you."

"Love?" Dutch asked, to Violet's surprise Dutch's tone actually sounded wistful.

Violet smiled, her eyes reflecting everything she felt at that moment. "Of course I love you."

Dutch reached up between them, touching her own heart in a way that was both heartbreaking and moving at the same time.

"I never knew how that would feel." Her tone was awestruck.

"How what would feel?" Violet asked, unsure of what Dutch meant.

"Having someone feel the exact way I feel, the hope was always there, stille ember."

Violet tilted her head, knowing Dutch had slipped into her native language.

Dutch smiled softly. "A quiet ember." She gathered Violet in her arms against, leaning in to kiss her softly. "See if you can guess this one: ik hou van jou."

Violet wrinkled up her nose in confusion, then shook her head slowly.

"I love you," Dutch translated.

"Oh," Violet stammered. "Well then okay!" she enthused, feeling the shock run through her system. "I love you," she replied, knowing that she'd finally found a home for her heart, and what a home it was with her wonderful firefighter. Her very own quiet ember.

Acknowledgements

Thank you Sharon Bettega for your insight and friendship! Thank you to Sarah Markel for your advice on fire scenes!

About the Author

Sherryl D Hancock is from California is the bestselling author of the lesbian romance *WeHo* series. Her books regularly touch on important topical issues such as mental health, the Don't Ask, Don't Tell policy and abuse.

You can find more on the author and her books at: sherrylhancock.com and vulpine-press.com

Also by Sherryl D. Hancock:

The lesfic **WeHo** series follows a group of women from Los Angeles as they navigate the ups and downs of love, life, work, and everything in between.

www.vulpine-press.com/we-ho

The **MidKnight Blue** series. Dive into the world of Midnight Chevalier and as we follow her transformation from gang leader to cop from the very beginning.

www.vulpine-press.com/midknight-blue-series

The **Wild Irish Silence** series. Escape into the world of BJ Sparks and discover how he went from the small-town boy to the world-famous rock star.

www.vulpine-press.com/wild-irish-silence-series